Praise for *Cr*

Grace Hawthorne's third novel, *Crossing the Moss Line*, is an entertaining read from beginning to end. Hawthorne invites her well-drawn characters to the table, and then serves up a uniquely Southern tale spiced with drama, authentic dialogue, and just the right amount of slightly wicked humor. I laughed out loud at the last line. Readers will not regret the time spent with *Crossing the Moss Line.*

Morgan James

Author of the Promise McNeal mystery series and

the Southern novel,

Sing Me An Old Song

"She's done it again. Starting with the award-winning *Shorter's Way*, then *Waterproof Justice* and now *Crossing the Moss Line*, Grace Hawthorne has proved she is truly a storyteller's storyteller. On top of that, I learned some Georgia history I wasn't aware of before. Great fun."

Janice Butt

Founder of Women's Imaginative Guild of Storytellers (WIGS)

"In *Crossing the Moss Line*, Grace Hawthorne's descriptions are so vivid you see, hear and even smell what's going on. Needless to say, her characters are equally on target. You recognize folks you know or have known. Grace's books will appeal to all readers, not just to those of us who were born and raised 'down here.'"

Ron Kemp

Owner of Anatron, Inc., Analytical Electronics

To Jackie —
Keep writing.
Grace Hawthorne

Crossing the Moss Line

Grace Hawthorne

To Freeman

Acknowledgements

First and foremost, thanks to my Beta Readers: Jan Allen, Judy Burge, Fontaine Draper, Pat Lindholm, Cynthia Pearson, Barbara Pennington, Dawn Strickland and Sharon Stulting. Working with these insightful, intelligent women is the best writing decision I ever made.

E. Richard Clark is a well-known artist whose watercolor works have won many honors. As a self-taught painter growing up in the South, he provided me with invaluable insights into the mind of Bird, as a young artist.

Leonard Oddo, who spent many years as an FDIC review examiner, helped me sort out banking regulations in the 1940s.

Martha Church, a lawyer and neighbor, added a note of authenticity when I was creating the New York law firm of Jacob and Rubin, LLP.

Murray Friedman, a fellow member of the Southern Order of Storytellers in Atlanta, was and is my source for all things Jewish.

Kathleen Mainland provided me with a steady supply of recycled paper. (Yes, I read both computer and hard copy.) Over the course of this book, we saved at least one forest.

Jim Freeman is my husband, my friend and my nemesis. I read every chapter to him as soon as I finish it and he always laughs in the right places. Then he reads the revisions—and there are many—and scrutinizes the manuscript to insure that the timeline is consistent from start to finish. The fact that this book makes sense, it is due in large part to his diligence.

Also by Grace Hawthorne

Shorter's Way

Waterproof Justice

CHAPTER ONE

"We'll take the whole lot, the whole shipload."

The broker studied the two young men standing in front of him and shook his head. "Foolishness, total foolishness," he thought to himself. "The whole boatload?" But then, who was he to turn down money...and a lot of it too. Cash on the barrelhead, up front. That's the way he liked doing business.

The 300-ton Windward rode at anchor in the small harbor at Bunce Island. The trading site was in the Sierra Leone River about 20 miles upriver from Freetown. It was a small island in the country's largest natural harbor, which made it an ideal base for the large ocean-going ships of European traders.

Due to the conditions aboard and the length of the voyage, he knew the buyers would lose at least ten percent of the cargo in the crossing and that was probably on the low side. However, once the papers were signed and he had his money, he'd be on his way. Not his responsibility any more.

Caleb Harding and Patrick Donegan exchanged worried glances and tried to maintain an air of confidence. They knew they were on shaky ground; they just hoped it wasn't too obvious. Normally they would have dealt with a business agent in Savannah, but to save some money, they decided to handle the transaction themselves.

They pooled every cent they had, negotiated what they thought was a good price at $500 a head, and set very specific guidelines about exactly what they wanted. They also promised the captain a bonus if he delivered the cargo in good condition. If everything turned out as they hoped, they were on their way to owning the richest rice plantation in Georgia. If not... well, one way or the other, it was too late to turn back now. They followed the agent into his office to conclude their business.

The crew aboard the Windward paid no attention to them. They had enough to do with loading supplies and getting the ship ready for the long voyage ahead. In addition to spare sails, ropes, nails, pitch, tar, coal and oil, they loaded food supplies including ship's biscuits.

Jonesy, the new cabin boy, was as curious as he was green. "Here you go, try one of these," a craggy old sailor said and tossed him what looked like a cookie. Jonesy tried to take a bite and nearly broke all his teeth.

"Ahh come on, what's this?" he asked.

"Hardtack, me boy. Sealed up tight, it'll last for months at sea and there'll come a time you'll be glad to get it. Best soak it in your tea to soften it up a bit before you try to eat it, but don't forget to bang it on the table a couple of times first."

"Why would I do that?"

"To knock out the beetles and the weevils and any other nasty little beasties who've made a home for themselves in your biscuit." Jonesy looked a little sick and the crew laughed.

The seamen continued to load on the salt pork, dried fish and various grains. Finally Jonesy stopped and looked toward the hold. "How do you stand the noise?"

"Just ignore it. It'll quiet down. The first week or two's the worst. After that, things get quiet, sometimes too quiet."

14

Jonesy tried, but he didn't think he would ever be able to ignore the cries and wails coming from the hold. They made the hair on the back of his neck stand up. No language that he could understand, just mournful, eerie sounds.

"That's the way it started way back there in 1802," Granny Johnson said. "They signed some papers, handed over some money and our people became the property of Caleb Harding and Patrick Donegan. *Buchra,* that's what we Geechee people called the plantation owners. I get the misery in my head just thinking about it even today. Don't you know that was a bad time. People from lots of tribes all crammed in together, strangers, starting a journey of thousands of miles, what we call The Middle Passage.

"Those slave traders didn't just take anybody, you know. They wanted us because we know about growin' rice and cultivatin' long-fiber cotton. Mr. Harding and Mr. Donegan ordered us like you'd order a table or a jacket from Sears and Roebuck. And we didn't come cheap, no siree. They paid a pretty penny for each and every one on that boat. That's why they didn't never sell a single one of us. We was too valuable.

"Strange they were willin' to pay good money for us, even see to it that we was fed and watered on the way over, but they took our names away. Far as I know, not one single African name survived. You'd think they coulda left us that much of Africa, but they didn't. Once we got settled here on Ibo Island, our family took the name Harding. That's how it worked back then.

"That boat load of about a hundred souls was the start of the Geechee people. What those plantation owners didn't count on was that we are a proud people and we know how to rise up over our circumstances." Granny laid aside the sweetgrass coil basket she was weaving long enough to relight her pipe.

15

"You children heard that old sayin', 'Good comes from bad' and that's been true time and time again. Because they brought us directly here to Ibo, we didn't never mix with nobody. Didn't nobody interfere with us and we stayed true to ourselves. We didn't never lose our African ways.

"Y'all better pay attention now to what I'm tellin' you. Our language, our religion, our customs, our food, our stories, our whole way of lookin' at life, all that's rooted back in our homeland, back in Africa. Folks like me who've lived a long time, we know how important it is for you young folks to know your history. I'm gonna keep makin' sure you know who you are and where you came from."

Taking advantage of the summer weather, the voyage across the Atlantic to the Caribbean and up the east coast was relatively calm. The ship stopped at various ports to pick up fresh supplies and water. Periodically the captives were brought out of the dark, filthy hold up on deck for a little fresh air and exercise. The sailors searched the lower decks and anyone who had died was unceremoniously thrown overboard. Eventually the noise did quiet down.

"Yeah, it was just noise to them men on that *bateau*, gibberish. Like the Tower of Babel in the Bible. Lots of different tribes everybody speakin' their own tongue. At first the people couldn't understand one another. But what those sailors took as defeat and silence was really the beginnin' of a new language. Gullah Geechee. Like a good gumbo, a little of this, a pinch of that. We took African, Indian, Spanish, English, Carib, mixed it up and made it our own."

Finally the Windward reached Georgia, but the trials of the captives weren't over. To prevent the spread of disease in Savannah, city officials built a nine-story quarantine facility, or "pest house," on the west side of Tybee Island. Men and women like those aboard the Windward who had been brought directly from West Africa were quarantined while they waited for a physician to inspect them and determine if they had any infectious diseases. If they were sick, they were confined to the hospital until they were cured.

Only after they were pronounced clean were Harding and Donegan allowed to transport their possessions to their final destination, Ibo Island. History said the island had gotten its name from a tribe of captives from southeastern Nigeria who jumped overboard and drowned themselves rather than become slaves.

Almost all of the Windward's original cargo survived the Middle Passage. After the oppressive, dark of the ship's hold, just setting their feet on solid, dry land and lookin' into an endless blue sky was an improvement. In their first moments on Ibo Island, they were greeted with hot, humid, buggy air...just like West Africa. In their first weeks, they came to recognize tidal streams and marshes, the fish in the rivers and the sea. It wasn't home, but it was somehow familiar so they took what comfort they could from that.

The one thing they didn't recognize was a strange, gray hair-like plant hanging from the trees. It didn't have thorns. It didn't have fruit or flowers. It was just there, softly blowing in the breeze. Spanish moss takes nothing from its hosts: the live oaks, cypress, sweet gum and crepe myrtles. It lives on rain, fog, sun and dust. In many ways it defines the area in which it grows and to some extent, it defines the people as well.

As soon as the cargo was released from Tybee Island, Harding and Donegan wasted no time in putting the slaves to work. Covered with mosquitoes and sand flies, they stood knee-deep in water, to clear 500 acres of swamp. They cut the cypress trees, hacked out the thick undergrowth, leveled the ground, dug irrigation ditches, constructed dikes, planted and tended the rice...all by hand. Simultaneously and undetected they also began to create the Geechee culture.

"Through the Middle Passage and all those slavery days, we survived. After the Civil War, we survived. When slavery was over, we survived. After the First World War, we survived. After the Great Depression, we survived. Now it's the spring of 1942, there's another war going on and we're still survivin'. One hundred and forty years and we're still here and holdin' on to our African ways."

Granny took a long pull on her pipe. "That's not too bad, if you ask me. The Christians got the Father, Son and Holy Ghost. Well, we Geechee got God, the rootman to conjure up spells, the numbers man to help us win a little money once in a while and the spirits of all our dead ancestors who don't never go away. That's what we got and that's plenty good enough."

Like every child on Ibo Island, Bird and his sister Robin Hamlin had heard these stories all their lives. It was their entertainment and their history. In the evenings, people came together, the children made themselves comfortable in the low hanging branches of the oak trees and listened to the "old folks" tell stories. Sometimes they were Middle Passage stories, sometimes creation stories or trickster stories about how the people tricked the master.

Robin put down the sweetgrass bottom she'd been weaving. Later on Granny would "feed the basket," build it up and add a handle and a top. "Come on, Bird, we gotta get home." Bird gathered up what he had been working on and followed his older sister down the sandy road. The trees reached out and touched branches high above the ground, making a cool green tunnel. Robin was never sure whether the wind made the moss sway or whether the moss made the breezes blow.

"Wait," Bird said and turned back to Granny's. Robin paid him little mind since he was always running off some place. She walked on another couple of yards just to put some distance between her and the road that went back to the old Donegan place. No need to take chances. She didn't want to get caught by a boo hag or a haint that might be hanging around there.

It was common knowledge that anyone who wandered into a haint's territory—which could be anywhere—without some protection from the root doctor could find themselves in serious trouble. Of course, there are some warning signs to let you know when a haint was close. First, the air would get hotter than usual and very, very damp and it would smell like something rotten.

Haints were scary, but they also had some weaknesses. They didn't like indigo blue. In the old days, indigo was an important crop on Ibo, second only to rice. After the leaves fermented and the liquid was drawn off several times, the overseers gave the bottom of the pot to the slaves.

Granny told how they'd take that thick, dark residue and paint their doors and window frames. The smell alone was enough to keep haints away. Geechee people still painted their doors and windows blue.

Salt was a good repellent too, but you couldn't just run around pouring salt on anybody you thought was suspicious. Best just to avoid the haints all together. Still she didn't want to get too far ahead, because she knew Bird would show up sooner or later.

When Bird got to Granny's, he jerked open the screen door leading to the wide front porch. Granny looked up from her work. "You forget somethin', child?"

"Yes'em." Shyly he took a piece of paper out of his pocket, smoothed it out and handed it to her.

She studied the pencil drawing. "Well look at that. That's me, ain't it? Sho is, looks just like me, pipe and all. I can most

19

nearly smell the smoke. Bird, you got 'the gift,' no doubt about it."

The boy smiled. It wasn't the first time someone had told him that. He kissed Granny on the cheek and ran out, slamming the door behind him. From the yard, he waved goodbye and then ran to catch up with Robin, his bare feet making small dust devils along the road.

"What'chu give Granny?"

"Nothin'. Just a thing I drew."

Robin believed somebody must have given her brother some powerful good root—what some of the old folks called mojo—because he could draw anything he saw. He'd been doing it since before he started school. Their mamma said he could draw before he could talk, which explained a lot. He still didn't talk much. Instead he carried a beat-up old school notebook wherever he went. When something caught his attention, he'd sit down and draw.

Geechee people had gotten used to seeing him hanging around, and he sat so quiet and so still, they hardly noticed him anymore. Then when they least expected it, he'd hand them a drawing. Almost every house on Ibo Island had at least one of Bird's sketches tacked up on a wall. His drawing mojo was enough to make him famous on their little island.

CHAPTER TWO

Bird did like to draw a lot more than he liked to talk. In fact, he didn't understand why everybody made such a fuss about something so easy. At first he thought everyone could draw just like everyone could see. It took him a while to figure out not everyone saw things the same way.

Robin saw everything all at once. The sky, the river, the boat, the people, the nets, the marsh grass, flowers, everything. Bird saw things one at a time. A cloud, the ripples on the water, the color of a boat, hands casting a net, marsh grass bending in the wind, the tracks raccoons made that looked like tiny hand prints, blue-purple beach morning glories and sea oats. Most people talked about what they saw. Bird drew it.

One of his favorite spots was on the edge of the marsh behind their house. And his favorite time of year was spring when the big, high tides came. Then the whole marsh turned white with water. It was like the marsh grass was growing out of a field of milky white glass.

At low tide, it all turned green. Bird liked to get up close enough to see the little clams that grew in the mud, or the outline of a creek running through the marsh. All that was hidden at high tide. And the best part was it happened twice a day, every day.

Bird was patient. He knew if he sat still enough the birds would come. White egrets and ibis and blue herons and a million seagulls. And down in the grass were the funny little marsh hens that raised a ruckus loud enough to be heard all the way up to the house.

His other favorite place was the big, flat beach facing the open ocean, although looking out over all that water scared him. It had no stopping place, it was too big. The ocean only felt friendly at the edge where he could walk in the foam and get his feet wet.

Like most people on Ibo, Bird didn't know how to swim. The rivers and the ocean were for work, not for play. At least that was true for humans. It was the dolphins that seemed to have all the fun. Bird had his fun on land, after his chores were done, of course.

Geechee culture taught that each person was expected to contribute something to the community; to excel at something. Bird worried about that a good deal. Robin was the smartest girl in school. She could already weave sweetgrass baskets and she was learning to be a healer like their mother. His dad could fix anything that was broken and build beautiful things out of wood.

Granny was the best weaver on Ibo. People bought her baskets to store things around the house. She also made sweetgrass hats for the local girls to wear on Sunday. But her real talent was creating new designs and making fancy baskets to sell to tourists along Highway 17.

Because there was no doctor on Ibo, Bird's mother, Ammee, was the person local folks came to when they were sick. She didn't do root or cast spells. Her remedies came from the plants that grew wild on the island or things women usually had on hand. People counted on her, so Ammee had cures for almost everything. Honey with sea lavender oil for burns. Honey and lemon for sore throats. Chamomile tea and honey to calm colicky babies.

Spider webs were an ancient way to stop bleeding. Lard or butter smeared on a bruise kept it from turning blue. Green cockleburs made into a poultice cleared up skin ailments and warm Coca Cola settled an upset stomach.

Earaches were cured by heating a thick slice of onion in a little oil, wrapping it in a rag and laying it on the affected ear. For a cold or a cough, Ammee recommended a tent over a pot of hot water with sprigs of thyme.

Moonshine was also used for medicinal purposes. Even with the current wartime rationing of sugar, Ammee managed to make the best shine in the county. A potion of shine and hot peppers drunk as fast as possible cured a fever...as long as the patient didn't say "thank you."

Bird tried, but so far he hadn't found anything useful he was good at. One hot May afternoon near the end of the school year, he was trying hard to stay awake when Miss Lucy Chalmers, his teacher, started telling stories. She had lived in New York City for a while and she talked about Harlem a lot. It was a sure-fire way to get sleepy children to pay attention.

She told them what it was like to be at the Apollo Theatre on talent-show nights. The audience got to choose the winners and if they didn't like somebody, a man with a broom came and swept them off the stage. The whole class laughed at that.

Once she had their attention, she went on to talk about the Harlem Renaissance. She read them a poem by Langston Hughes and told them the story of *Porgy and Bess*, an opera about Gullah street venders in Charleston. Then she talked about painters and mentioned an artist named Palmer Hayden.

At the word "artist," Bird raised his hand and started asking questions.

"What kind of pictures did he draw? Is he still alive? Where does he live? Did you ever meet him?"

It was so unusual for Bird to speak up, the whole class stopped to listen. Miss Chalmers had just planned to talk about the Harlem Renaissance, not specifically Palmer Hayden, but she didn't want to discourage Bird's curiosity. "Well, let's see," she said checking her notes. "Palmer Hayden grew up in the south, in Virginia."

"Just like me," Bird thought.

"He was born in 1890, so how old would that make him now?"

Robin's hand shot up. "He'd be 52."

"That's right. To answer your question, Bird, I never met him, but as far as I know, he's still living in Harlem. It says here he started drawing when he was a small child."

"Just like me."

"He studied in New York City and he drew pictures of people in the city, but he also drew pictures of people he knew who lived along the rivers and the coast."

"Just like me."

"He became very famous and lots of people bought his paintings."

Bird rushed home from school to tell his mamma and dad the news. There was a man who made money selling his pictures. That planted an idea in Bird's mind.

The next Saturday morning just about daybreak, "day clean" Granny called it, Bird asked her if he could go along to help set up her sweetgrass basket stand along Highway 17. He brought some of his drawings and Granny helped him display them. When a customer stopped to look at Granny's baskets, she pointed out Bird's sketches.

"Those are pretty good, son. How much do you want for that one?" Bird kept his head down and didn't answer.

"Does he talk?" the man asked.

"Yessir, he's just shy." No need to try to explain that Geechee children were taught it was rude and disrespectful to look a grownup in the eye without permission. Granny sold two baskets and negotiated the grand sum of 25 cents—two dimes and a nickel—for Bird's drawing. Bird had finally found something he could do to be useful. He was anxious to get home and give the money to his mother.

Ammee congratulated him and took the two dimes which went into a coffee tin hidden in the bottom of the rice can under the sink. Slyly she added two pennies to the nickel and handed that back to Bird. "Your dad says a man should always have a little talkin' money in his pocket. So you keep this." Bird ran out the door jingling the coins.

When Ammee and Jacob were first married, she insisted that part of his salary and any money she made be put back for emergencies. Like most of the families on Ibo, they lived off the land and were self-sufficient. But in the world on the mainland, the only thing that counted was cash money. Ammee had heard stories of folks losing their land because they couldn't repay loans or pay their taxes. She was determined that was never going to happen to her family.

After he sold his first sketch, whenever he wasn't in school, Bird went to the mainland with Granny to sell his pictures. Granny still did all the talking, but he was proud to be able to add his money to the coins in the coffee tin. He might not be making a lot of money like Palmer Hayden, or helping the Geechee community exactly, but he *was* helping his family and he liked the sound of talkin' money in his pocket. He started looking for new things to draw and that caused him to see Ibo Island a little differently.

Life on the island had a softness to it, like the moss. Time moved slow and easy. Bird spent hours drawing and listening to the sounds of the island. The pine trees were so tall you had to really listen to hear them whisper in the wind. The palmetto plants squatted on the ground and rattled in the slightest breeze. Bird liked the live oaks best. He always thought of them as ancient old men with long mossy arms, just sitting silently watching what went on in the world.

Water made sounds too. Along the rivers, the marsh grass hummed a low song and fish jumping added a high note from time to time. His dad's net made a swishing sound as he cast it over the water. The ocean had a big sound, steady and deep and strong.

Best of all, Bird loved the way the island could play tricks on him. When the fog rolled in, everything disappeared just like magic. The best time to go down to the dock was early in the morning when the ferry and the little fishing boats came in. The whole world was silent except for the noise the big fog-drops made hitting the dry palmetto plants. The island would cover itself in a blanket of gray mist and challenge Bird to find specific shapes. He would listen and strain his eyes to see through the heavy fog. And the island would always surprise him. A boat would appear, but never in the place he expected it to be.

Ibo was one of the smaller barrier islands off the coast of Georgia. It was about ten miles long and three miles across. Children were free to roam without fear of getting lost. They were taught to respect the waters. They provided food and income but they could swallow curious children who wandered too near. Life moved only as fast as a person could walk, or ride in Mr. Cathy's ox cart, or pole a boat on the rivers or inlets.

It was a tight community of about 70 people spread out among ten families. Everything they needed was within walking distance, the church, the school and the little store Bird's dad built. Because there were so few kids on the island, the one-room school only covered grades one through six. After that, kids took the morning ferry to the mainland and then rode a bus the rest of the way to the big school.

Bird had just turned 12 and was about to finish the sixth grade. Summer vacation hadn't even started yet, and he was already worrying about next September. He was not looking forward to it, in fact, he was dreading the whole idea. With the exception of going with Granny to sell baskets, he'd never been off the island. The Geechee community was his whole life. What little he had seen of the mainland scared him. It was too fast and too noisy.

Of course, he would be catching the ferry with some other kids his age and Robin who was in the ninth grade. She loved going to Meridian because she loved anything new and different. Not like Bird.

It wasn't just the school that bothered him. Since classes were over at 3:00 and there was no regular afternoon ferry, students had to wait for a late ferry and sometimes it didn't run. The solution was for students to board with a friend or relative and only come home on the weekends. Bird didn't like the sound of that at all. He didn't want to be away from his family that long. He wasn't sure why, but he had a very bad feeling about the whole thing.

CHAPTER THREE

After he left Granny's, Bird ran as fast as he could to catch up with Robin. He was planning to ask her about school, but she beat him to it. "Can you draw a haint?" she demanded.

Bird looked at his sister and puzzled over the question. She was always asking about strange things nobody else would ever think of. "I don't know. I never saw one. You?"

"Maybe. If you go up that old road not too far from Granny's, you know, the one that leads off into the swamp, there's supposed to be a big old empty house way back there, something left over from plantation days. I heard Granny and Mamma talking about it. Belonged to the Donegan family."

Robin stopped and waited for Bird to ask for the rest of the story. But he didn't. He never did. He drove her crazy. It was like he didn't have any curiosity about anything. Robin, on the other hand, was curious about everything and everybody. Oh well, at least he was still listening.

"I went partway up there once and I think I saw something...or somebody. Scared me nearly to death. I'm going back again, but not without some root to protect me. That's why I got this." She pulled a shiny silver dime out of her pocket.

Now *that* got Bird's attention. He'd made a big deal of showing Robin the coins he'd made, but for the most part, actual money was hardly ever seen on the island. Most transactions involved barter. A mess of greens for a sack of potatoes. Their dad, Jacob, did carpentry work and neighbors paid him in vegetables or fish or oysters for jobs around Ibo.

Bird asked Robin where the dime came from and she just smiled. So, there was at least something that could get his curiosity up. She tried to come up with some long, complicated story about the coin, but in the end she admitted Miss Chalmers had hired her to help clean the little school house and paid her with the dime.

"I'm gonna take one of Dad's hammers and a nail and make a hole so I can run some string through it and wear it around my neck. Granny says that's supposed to bring you good luck." Robin was counting on the coin to provide some protection if she ever went up to the Donegan place again, but the truth was, she was so proud of earning the dime, she never, ever planned to spend it.

"Why don't you ask Granny to work some white root for you?" Bird asked.

"'Cause if I told her where I wanted to go she'd tell me, 'That ain't gonna lead to no good. Don't be getting yourself into a fix I can't get you out of.'"

The supernatural was as real to the Geechee people as the fish in the rivers. Like their language, they combined bits of the Christian faith with African traditions and belief in the root doctor, the conjurer. God was fine and prayer was fine, but there were limits. To begin with, God took his time and you couldn't ask God for revenge or to send bad luck to someone.

That was a job for Dr. Buzzard. That wasn't his real name, of course, but in the Geechee community, that's what they always called the conjure man. He was the one who could work a root on somebody. Or if a person had worked a root on you, Dr. Buzzard knew how to turn a spell around and throw it back on the one who started it. His work was mostly guaranteed and he was a lot faster than God.

There were also the spirits to contend with. The Christian faith spoke of the body, soul and spirit. The body dies and the soul rests in peace. But what about the spirit? Well, on Ibo Island everyone knew that the spirt never dies and those spirits stayed close by forever watching over the living. No Geechee person would think of throwing dishwater out the back door after dark without first warning the spirits. Dousing the spirits with water was definitely *not* a good idea.

Then there was luck, both good and bad. The best thing, of course, was to avoid bad luck by such things as holding your breath when you passed a graveyard, or always leaving a house through the same door you came in. But Robin knew if bad luck did happen, there was usually a way to reverse it if you acted fast enough, like turning around clockwise seven times.

Nature and dreams also played a big part in luck. The most serious form of good luck on Ibo centered on choosing the right numbers for the numbers man. Threes and sevens were known to be lucky, 13 and 666 were unlucky. Everything else was up for grabs.

Granny used the Biblical system. She'd open the Bible at random and then look for a sign. Maybe the chapter and verse numbers, maybe those numbers added together. Maybe the actual page number.

Ammee favored things she could count. How many eggs in the nest, how many pods on the okra stalk, how many peas spilled on the table. Other people believed in dreams. They'd buy a dream dictionary at the dime store. It not only listed the subject of dreams in alphabetical order and gave their meaning,

30

it also assigned a number to each kind of dream, a great advantage in making a winning selection.

Whatever the method, the rewards were worth the trouble it took to make a careful choice. The investment of a dime could have a $7 return. Spending a quarter might get you $25, which was more than a week's wages.

Robin was a big believer in the supernatural and she had hoped to involve Bird in a detailed discussion of haints and hags, but nothing came of it. When they got home, they found their mother bedding up some rows to plant sweet potatoes. Ammee had always kept a garden on Ibo, but since the war started, lots of folks in town were planting Victory Gardens. Gas rationing and the scarcity of tires meant there were fewer and fewer delivery trucks on the road.

The Hamlin's house was similar to Granny's, in fact, almost all the houses on Ibo looked alike. They were mostly square, one-story wooden buildings with a screen porch across the front. The tin roof looked like a four-sided hat plopped down on top. The windows all had wooden shutters which came in handy during the fall hurricane season. The houses were all build up off the ground which allowed air or water to flow underneath.

In addition to the house, Jacob built another small square building on the corner where his property joined the road. An overhang out front provided some shade and their dad added several benches along the front wall. Inside, open shelves lined all four walls and two tables end-to-end filled up the middle. Everyone on the island called it The Store. Even with shortages, Jacob managed to keep it fairly well stocked with canned goods, basic hardware, a few school supplies, kerosene for lamps, matches, flour, sugar, rice, needles, thread, fishing hooks and Bayer aspirin, the only white medicine on the island.

Ammee looked up. "Y'all better get busy with your chores. Bird, I'm almost out of wood for the stove and I need you to pump some water and tote it into the house. Sister, you go feed the chickens and slop the hogs."

Robin hated feeding the hogs. "Bird, I'll pump the water if you'll take care of the pigs."

Bird was already on his way into the house with an armload of wood. "OK." He dumped the wood into a box beside the cast-iron stove, which had four eyes and a big oven next to the fire bin. Bird used a poker to open the door and stuff in more wood. A couple of cast-iron skillets and a pot or two hung on nails driven into the wall. Summer and winter, the house always smelled like wood smoke.

"As soon as you finish up, I want y'all to go get dinner," their mother called from the yard.

That meant fishing and it was one chore both children were glad to do. In addition to woodworking, their dad knitted casting nets for himself and almost everyone else on Ibo. Jacob made nets of different sizes for different purposes. Some of them were ten feet long, twice that size when they were thrown open.

He had made smaller nets for Robin and Bird and taught them how to cast as soon as they were tall enough to lift the net with all the lead weights along the edges. The trick was to hold one of the sinkers in your mouth and then let it go just as you threw out the net.

Folks on Ibo depended on Jacob because he made nets to order. Mullet nets for big fish, tighter knit nets for shrimp. Jacob also made what he called a poor man's net. If that was all a man could afford, Jacob could make a net that would catch both fish and shrimp. Fish from the sea and the fresh water rivers not only fed families, it provided a crop to sell on the mainland.

As soon as they could, Bird and Robin got their nets and set off for the creeks which snaked their way through the swamps. The mullet ran as the tide was going out and the two children knew all the best places to catch them. Mullet fried in bacon grease with some onions and served over stiff grits was their favorite meal. Let other folks worry about wartime meat shortages.

Jacob usually came home on the late ferry from the mainland. The 20-minute ride through the open water along the salt marshes gave him time to relax and settle into the rhythm of the island. It wasn't like he worked in a big city, but even Meridian moved at a faster pace than Ibo. For one thing, there were only two vehicles on the island and no electricity.

For several years Jacob had been employed by Reeve's Sawmill and Lumber Yard. He worked mostly with George Madison (Matt) Reeve, the eldest son of the owner, George Washington Reeve. Matt was a lumber buyer and a contractor and Jacob was a builder. He and Matt shared a love for woodworking and he often stopped by the shop at the back of the sawmill to use some of the tools he didn't have at home.

Jacob loved the sight of the sun setting over the marshes which cast everything in a golden glow. He breathed deeply and thought he caught the faint aroma of mullet and onions. "You're a lucky man, Jacob Hamlin," he thought.

Ammee counted on Jacob to bring home the news of what was happening on the other side. "They're saying the oyster cannery may shut down, but then they been saying that for a year or more. Mayor Dupree is pushing the school board to add a room to the schoolhouse over there. If that goes through, I reckon I might end up working on that one." Conversation slowed down as everyone ate fish and grits with fried okra and fresh tomatoes and lots of sweet tea.

"Daddy we went over to see Granny today," Robin said. "She was telling some of those old stories ...again. At least she didn't tell any flying African stories today."

"Did she tell you the one about how we built the church?" Jacob asked with a smile.

"Oh yeah. The hurricane knocked down the church on the mainland and the ocean washed all the lumber over here and we used it to build our church, which just goes to show..." Jacob, Bird and Robin said together... "sometimes good comes from bad." Robin laughed. "If I didn't know better, I'd think Granny came over here on one of those ships from Africa herself."

"Watch your mouth, child," Ammee said. "That old woman's done a whole lot of livin' and seen things you don't even want to think about. Don't you be makin' fun of flying Africans. After what our people went through, it's no wonder they wanted to fly away."

"Ah come on Mamma, you don't really believe..."

Ammee cut her short. "Don't you tell me what I believe! I believe the Bible and it says that Elijah went up by a whirlwind into heaven."

"Yes, but..."

"And it says that Ezekiel saw a wheel in the middle of the air. Lots of things don't make sense, you just gotta take 'em on faith."

"Your mamma's right. Y'all remember Ole Mr. Mott? He used to come sit out in front of The Store and he swore he saw people fly. Just rise up off the ground, turn into a bird and fly away. Granny'll swear to it too. Her second cousin had a friend who'd seen it. Now you tell me what's easier to believe, that they flew away or that they just disappeared?"

As far as Bird was concerned, Robin and everybody talked too much, which usually got them in trouble. He decided to rescue his sister this time, before she went too far. "Daddy, you reckon Granny knows everybody who ever lived on this island?"

"Pretty close," Jacob said. The woman his children called Granny was actually *Ammee's* grandmother, Bessie Johnson. His parents lived in Alabama now so the kids hardly ever saw them. Ammee's mother died before either Robin or Bird was born, so Granny Johnson was the only grandmother they knew. She had been old as long as Jacob could remember and he had no doubt she knew just about everybody and everything connected to Ibo Island.

"Reckon she knows anything about the Donegan place?" Robin asked.

Jacob laid down his fork. "Funny you should bring that up. Mr. Matt and me were talking about that earlier today. He's planning to come out here tomorrow to take a look at some of the timber land."

CHAPTER FOUR

Being the eldest son in a southern family came with strings attached. Expectations and responsibilities. For the most part, Matt Reeve had done reasonably well to live up to what was called for. Right after college he went to work with his father, George Washington Reeve. Mr. Wash supervised the lumber yard and Matt spent most of his time finding and buying timber for the sawmill. Reeve Sawmill and Lumber Yard employed a number of local people and was a fixture in Meridian.

Matt had gotten into his share of childish scraps and teenage shenanigans, but nothing serious. He was a slightly above-average student and had done well in both his college classes and in athletics. From the time he was a kid, he had loved the woods, so working as a lumber buyer for the family business was a good fit. Matt and his father got along well and enjoyed each other's company.

The girls in Meridian and surrounding towns also enjoyed Matt's company. He was six feet tall, with sandy colored hair, dark brown eyes, a quick smile and an easy disposition. All in all, the female population considered him a "real catch," which meant he was in a position to make a good living and therefore to provide for a family.

Matt, on the other hand, saw the situation a little differently. He dated his share—perhaps more than his share—of local beauties, but the minute he saw the gleam of matrimony in those pretty eyes, he made a hasty exit. Clearly, being "a catch" meant being pursued and like any normal, healthy animal that is being chased, his instinct was to run for his life.

It wasn't that his parents hadn't set him a good example, they had. With a few normal ups and downs they had what everyone would agree was a happy marriage. It wasn't the final outcome that bothered Matt; it was the decisive initial step that gave him pause. What if he picked the wrong girl? What if he made a bad choice? There were no second chances because divorce was out of the question. He had to get it right the first time or else.

Everybody talked about "tying the knot, getting hitched, taking the plunge." They all sounded threatening, if not downright dangerous. And the worst description of all was the one Brother Courtney at First Baptist Church used all the time, "being yoked together."

Nobody said what they really meant, which was if you wanted to make love to a nice girl, you had to marry her first. Well, Matt had made love to several girls he knew his mother would not consider nice and it had not been a totally unpleasant experience. Why couldn't everybody just leave it at that?

However, by the time he was 30, the old I'm-just-looking-for-the-right-girl excuse was wearing a bit thin. The truth was, unfortunately, he simply hadn't found anyone he wanted to be yoked to. Generally speaking, boys and girls either got married as soon as they got out of high school or waited until they got out of college. Either way, the group of eligible partners normally covered a four-year span, the people who were in high school or college together. Once out of college, the pickings got rather slim.

Matt, as fate would have it, had been out of college a long time, almost ten years. He liked the life of a bachelor, living on his own terms. He enjoyed his job, spent time with friends, played on the company baseball team, indulged his woodworking hobby and had an active social life. And best of all, he didn't have to answer to anyone.

However, he was well aware that his parents were getting a little concerned about his future, especially since his younger brother was already married and starting a family. "Matt's the first born, he is supposed to do things in a certain order," Mr. Wash said to his wife, Martha. She had heard it all before. "He was *supposed* to find a wife in college. By now, he was *supposed* to have a family. In my generation, we did what we were supposed to do when we were supposed to do it. Matt is a dutiful son and a good man, but I just don't understand his hesitation to choose a wife. For goodness sake, can't he just pick one and get on with it?" Wash was getting worked up.

"Pick one!?!? Is that what you did? Just pick me like some tomato off the vine?" Martha asked.

Wash thought she was joking, but he wasn't entirely sure. However, he had been married long enough to know how to think on his feet. "Of course not. I chose you because you were the prettiest girl in the county and I was afraid if I didn't ask you to marry me, some other young dandy would have 'picked' you."

Martha smiled. Wash had always been a sweet-talker. They had been in their early twenties when they got married and she had never regretted it. Well, there was one thing that bothered her. Most people who knew George Washington Reeve took great delight in referring to her as Martha Washington Reeve. She had tried to get people to use her middle name, Elizabeth, but it was no use. She had to admit, being Martha Washington was a small price to pay for her life with Wash.

The first time Matt saw Cora was a hot summer day and she was on crutches. He almost laughed. "At least that one won't be doing much chasing," he thought. He watched her for a while and when he realized she was having trouble opening a door, he stepped up to help. She thanked him nicely and went on her way. Matt didn't know whether he felt relieved or disappointed.

After that, he began to notice her around town. She was attractive, but not drop-dead gorgeous. He liked that. She was younger than he was, but that was OK too. She wasn't all smiles and giggles like most of the girls he had dated. In fact, she looked rather sad although she carried herself well and seemed to know where she was going. He hadn't known her in either high school or college, but in a town the size of Meridian it wasn't hard to find out more about her.

Her name was Cora Strayhorn. Her mother had passed on when Cora was very young and she had been raised by her father's sister. There was some talk about a car accident in Atlanta or Savannah, in which someone died. The details were a little sketchy. Either way, that explained the crutches. Cora boarded with a family in town during the summer and went to Agnes Scott College in Atlanta.

She worked part time at the local drugstore and Matt ran into her once when he stopped in to pick up a prescription for his mother. He said hello, but Cora didn't seem to remember him. That was a new experience. Girls didn't normally forget Matt.

Before he knew what was happening, the world spun around 180 degrees and instead of being pursued, Matt became the pursuer. He figured he better work fast because she would probably be going back to school in September.

Matt's family went to the Baptist church, Cora was a Methodist. Since churches formed the basis for much of the social life in small towns, he began showing up at Methodist services. Cora didn't notice. OK, now what?

He decided to ask his brother Jeff who was closer to Cora's age if he had any ideas. "Just go talk to her," he advised.

"About what?" Matt asked.

"Gee, I don't know. She works in a drug store, tell her you've got a rash and ask what she'd suggest you do about it."

"You're no damn help." Matt was sincerely puzzled. He'd never had a problem talking to women and he approached customers and contractors all the time in the lumber business. What was it about this girl that had him so off his game?

Finally he decided to think of it more as a business deal and just take the direct approach. The next time he saw Cora at the drug store he introduced himself and asked if she would like to go get coffee or a Coke or something with him. She didn't fall all over herself, but she did say yes. He commented on the fact that she wasn't using the crutches anymore and she quickly cut off that line of conversation. He was curious, but he dropped the subject. After all, Matt didn't really want to talk about crutches anyway.

Since he knew about lumber and trees, that's what he talked about. Rather than being bored, Cora seemed interested. He relaxed a little. So far so good. Dating in small towns was governed by a long list of unwritten rules. Going for coffee or a Coke was casual. Lunch was more serious. Dinner and a movie—if it happened on consecutive weekends—could be considered a major commitment and was therefore dangerous.

Matt decided to take another tack. The next time he had to go check out a wooded area where his father might want to buy timber, he asked Cora to ride along. They chatted easily and when lunchtime came, Cora surprised him by taking two sandwiches and a thermos of ice tea out of her oversized purse. "I thought we might have a picnic," she said. Matt felt himself slipping but it was no use. He had no more control than a pig on ice.

The first time he kissed her, he knew he had finally found the one. He wanted to make love to her immediately, but she was a nice girl and he knew what *that* meant. Still, he just couldn't bring himself to take that final step and "settle down."

Cora didn't seem to be in any hurry to settle down either. September came and she went back to college to finish her senior year. Things were definitely not going the way Matt expected. He moped. He missed her. He wanted her. He finally admitted to himself that he loved her.

When she came home for Thanksgiving, he told her how he felt and tried to talk her into bed. Instead she talked him into waiting until she finished school. Two weeks later, he drove to Atlanta, presented her with an engagement ring and insisted they set a date. With her usual reserve, Cora agreed, but it would have to wait until she graduated.

Matt's parents were so overjoyed they were willing to help out in any way necessary. Since Cora had no close family, Matt's mother stepped in and she and Cora spent the next several months planning a wedding by long distance.

Most girls would have taken advantage of the Reeve's position and Martha's generosity to have the most elaborate wedding possible. Cora said no. No big church wedding, no bevy of bridesmaids in ugly pastel dresses, no expensive reception. She wanted something small and simple. Martha suggested the Reeve's garden with just family and a few close friends and Cora happily agreed. So Matt and Cora were married the day after Cora graduated.

Wash and Martha breathed a sigh of relief. Matt was happy and they were delighted with his choice. Cora was ten years younger than their son, but she was obviously a sensible young woman and Matt was completely taken by her. "It looks like he's 'picked' a good one," Martha said with a mischievous smile. Wash kissed her on the cheek. "So it does, my dear, so it does."

The one extravagance Matt insisted on was their honeymoon. They spent two weeks at the Hotel Monteleon in New Orleans, ate at all the best restaurants—their favorite was Commander's Palace—and rode the streetcar named Desire. Cora fell in love with beignets at Café du Monde and Matt fell more in love with her. He also discovered that nice girls could be very nice indeed. Cora embraced him and marriage with an enthusiasm that took him totally by surprise. She taught him a thing or two that aroused more than his curiosity and she had been teaching him things ever since.

Nine months and two days later Katie was born.

CHAPTER FIVE

As he and Jacob had agreed, early the next morning Matt and Katie took the ferry to Ibo. Because the ferry didn't carry cars, Reeve's Sawmill left a beat up old pickup on the island. Matt used some of his gas ration to keep the truck running. Jacob could use the truck when he needed it. The island wasn't very big, but having the truck on hand made it a lot easier to get around and to haul supplies up from the ferry when he restocked The Store. The truck was in its usual place and Matt used it to drive over to the Hamlin's house. When he got there, Jacob was sitting in the shade on one of the benches in front of The Store.

He got up and walked toward Matt, but before he had a chance to say good morning, Robin darted out the door. She wanted to talk to her dad before he and Mr. Matt left, but she was a little too late. So she waited, silently bouncing from one foot to the other. Geechee children knew it was bad manners to look a grownup in the face without permission and even with members of your own family, you didn't barge into a conversation. So she held her tongue.

Since she almost always had something to say, waiting wasn't easy for Robin. Bird, on the other hand, never seemed to mind. He was comfortable with his pencil and paper, words just didn't seem necessary. And he surely wouldn't have approached his dad with Mr. Matt standing there. In fact, Mr. Matt was probably the only white man Bird had ever seen on Ibo.

Finally, Jacob looked at Robin. "You want to see me?"

"Yessir," she nodded in Matt's direction. "Good mornin' Mr. Matt. Dad told us you were goin' over to the Donegan place this morning and if it's OK with you, I sure would like to go along. I promise I won't be any trouble, and besides I know just where that old road is."

Jacob looked at Matt, threw up his hands and shook his head helplessly. Matt smiled. "Don't worry, I understand. Katie's on summer vacation too. She's in the truck. Once she knew I was headed over here, there was no way I was going to come to Ibo without her." He turned to Robin, "Go on. Get Katie out of the cab and you girls sit in the back. We'll be there directly."

Although the girls hadn't met before, they instantly realized they were kindred spirits, two Miss Nosey Britches. In no time, they took care of formal introductions, discovered they were the same age, they were in the same grade and they both liked to fish—although Katie had never fished with a net. Robin promised to teach her.

"Have you been out to the Donegan place before?" Katie asked.

Robin hesitated. She'd just met this new girl and she wasn't sure what she ought to be telling her. "My Granny lives close by and one day I walked part way down the road, but I didn't go too far."

Katie was all ears. "Why not?"

"We're not supposed to go back there. Besides, I could feel this haint sneaking up on me." Robin watched Katie closely to see if she was going to laugh.

"I'd have been scared to death. What'd you do?"

"I ran all the way home," Robin said and they both laughed. "But don't tell my brother that. I've been trying to get him to go over there with me because if he saw the haint, then he could draw a picture of her. He's a real good drawer."

"I wish I had a brother," Katie said. "There's just me and that's not much fun."

Robin assured her brothers weren't always a lot of fun either. But it was neat that Bird drew pictures all the time. "Sometimes he'll draw stuff for me to take to school." The girls chatted on until their fathers finally got in the truck and headed off across the island. Matt drove but he looked to Jacob for directions. "Funny how little I actually know about his island," Matt thought. "It's close by, but in many ways it's a world apart." The girls stood up in the bed of the pickup, holding on to the cab the best they could. Matt would have driven right by the turn-off if Robin hadn't pounded on top of the cab.

Matt slowed down to a crawl and sure enough, there actually *was* an old gravel road under all the underbrush. About half a mile in, the gravel road turned to packed sand and then even that gave way to nothing but tall weeds and brambles.

On the trip across the backside of the island, the sun had been warm and bright, but now the air was heating up and the light came through the towering pine trees in hard, quick flashes. Pretty soon the long leaf pines ended and from there on the road was lined with ancient live oaks evenly spaced and thick with long fingers of Spanish moss.

It was clear at one time this had been a formal driveway which someone had carefully designed to impress visitors. Judging from the blackberry bushes crowding the roadside, no one had tended the land for what...decades?

Matt had come to Ibo at Jacob's suggestion to survey the trees and determine whether his father might be interested in doing some logging there. Things looked promising and Matt wondered how far the property went and how many acres of old growth there might be.

The road made a graceful curve and when he came around the final turn, Matt stopped the pickup dead in its tracks. There was a house where Matt had not expected a house to be. It was surrounded by what had in bygone days been a well-tended yard. For a minute, no one spoke. Then Matt turned to Jacob. "Did you know there was a house back here?"

"Sorta. I remember Granny telling stories about a big old rice plantation back here before the Civil War. As far as I know, once the slaves were freed, the owners left. That would've been after the war. I reckon you've heard about Sherman's Order #15? That's where he divided up the land the planters left and gave 40 acres and a mule to the freed slaves who stayed behind. The government reneged on the land grant, but some of us do still own land here on the island. What wasn't tended to, eventually just went back to the swamp."

They sat still for a moment and listened, but there was no sound other than the dry rustle of the palmetto leaves and the call of birds. The house in front of them was typical of older houses in the area. It stood on pilings four or five feet above the ground, a form of natural air conditioning. A spacious porch across ran across the front and down the right side. Wide wooden steps divided the porch in half, but the bottom two or three steps were hidden by the knee-high grass. Double front doors were outlined by leaded glass panels, amazingly still intact.

The old house still retained patches of the original white paint, but for the most part the exposed wood had faded to the same weathered gray as the moss on the trees. Still, the house was solid. Even deserted, it stood straight, level and square as the day it was built. Matt and Jacob both made note of that.

Each in his own way knew about the craftsmanship that went into building those old houses.

Finally, Matt put the truck in gear and slowly drove around the side of the house where they discovered another surprise, the Tin Lizzie. With the exception of the Reeve's truck, the model T was the only vehicle on the island. The story was that one time in 1925 a rich college boy had paid to have it brought over by ferry and then just left it there.

A metal key about three inches long was always hanging in the ignition. However, it was so difficult to start the old Ford, only the brave ever drove it. The procedure involved standing in front of the car, pulling the choke and at the same time cranking a lever under the radiator to prime the carburetor. Then the driver got in, turned the key, adjusted the timing stalk, the throttle stalk and the hand brake. Finally, he got back out to crank the lever and at that point, the car was supposed to start. The few people who knew how to start it also knew to take extra care because if the engine backfired and the lever turned counterclockwise, it was possible to end up with a broken arm.

Assuming that the driver had mastered the art of starting the Lizzie, the one other requirement was to bring along some gas to put in the tank and drive the Lizzie back to the dock. Needless to say, the procedure was at best a two-man job.

Matt and Jacob got out of the pickup. Matt pointed at Katie. "You girls stay put until we can figure out what's going on here." Jacob gave Robin a look that clearly indicated he expected her to obey too.

The sheriff and Jessie, the mailman, were standing in the shade smoking. "What's up Sheriff?" Matt asked. "I didn't expect to see anybody back here. In fact, I didn't expect to see *anything* back here. Do you know anything about this old house?"

Sheriff Mayhew put out his cigarette and shook his head. "Not really, although I've heard stories. Jessie found it yesterday when he walked over here and tried to deliver the mail. He brought me over this morning. First time he could ever remember a letter coming here and he had the devil's own time finding the place with no more address than Donegan Hall."

"You mean somebody *lives* here?" Matt asked.

"In a manner of speaking. Reckon you better get the girls out of the sun and ask them to join us."

Katie and Robin were only too happy to obey. They scrambled out of the truck and ran to join the men. "Keep quiet and follow us," Matt said.

"If one of y'all would give me a hand startin' the Lizzie, I'm gonna get back on the road," Jessie said. "Don't mean to leave you stranded, Sheriff. Reckon Mr. Reeve could give you a lift back to the dock? If I leave now, I might get lucky and catch a noon ferry." Matt nodded. Jacob and Jessie worked to get the car started and Jessie headed off toward the main road.

Ferry service to and from Ibo was a chancy proposition. One ferry made a round trip from Meridian every morning about 7:30 to deliver a few folks to the island, but mostly to pick up passengers going to the mainland to work. In the late afternoon it made another round trip to bring the workers home. In between, it only ran when the captain decided there were enough people waiting on the dock to make the trip worthwhile. However, there were almost always fishermen in their small boats willing to make the trip for a fee.

After Jessie left, the sheriff nodded and the little group made their way through the weeds and onto the porch. The front doors opened to a large entryway with an elegant staircase about midway down the hall. The house had an unmistakable air of bygone elegance.

Rooms with pocket doors opened to the right and left. Matt looked around for a light switch before he realized there wouldn't be one. A number of kerosene lamps sat on starched doilies covering mahogany tables. Various pieces of cut glass caught a sunbeam that found its way inside.

To the left was a formal parlor with uncomfortable looking antique furniture. At first it seemed that the room was empty, then a small movement caught Robin's eye. She gasped and pointed. The only light came from two tall windows partially covered with heavy velvet drapes. As their eyes adjusted to the dark, Matt and Jacob realized they were looking at two, tiny old women sitting side by side on the settee.

They sat very straight, their ankles crossed, black lace-up shoes visible under their long black dresses. Their hands were folded and lay carefully in their laps. The only thing about them that moved was their eyes. Rather than the weak, faded eyes usually associated with the elderly, their eyes were surprisingly clear and astonishingly black.

Sheriff Mayhew approached the women and motioned for Matt to follow. "Ladies, I'd like to introduce you to Mr. Madison Reeve. That's his friend Jacob Hamlin and the girls are their daughters. These are the Donegan sisters, Miss Sarah and Miss Sally." The ladies acknowledged the introduction with a single nod, otherwise they remained perfectly still, making no move to shake hands.

The sheriff leaned in to speak to the ladies. "If it's alright with you, I'd like to show these folks around your beautiful home." The sisters exchanged a look, then again nodded in unison.

When the group was out in the hall, the sheriff walked toward the back of the house and motioned for them to follow. "I want y'all to see what's back here first, it explains a lot."

The kitchen could have been in Granny's house. In addition to a large oilcloth covered table, there was a cast iron stove that had obviously been top of the line in its day. An empty wood box sat nearby. The black iron of the stove was shinny and the brass hardware looked newly polished although on closer inspection, everything in the room was covered with dust. On the outside wall was a sink with a pump handle. That was too much for the girls to resist. They gave it a try and heard a gurgle as the mechanism engaged. A second later, cool water flowed into their out-stretched hands. "Wow!" they giggled. There were no dishtowels in sight, so they ran their hands over their faces and up and down their arms. A good way to cool off a little.

"Take a look at this." Sheriff Mayhew walked around the kitchen opening doors on cabinets. Cups, saucers, plates of all sizes, glasses, serving dishes, pots and pans. Things were stacked neatly. "Sure don't look like my mamma's kitchen," Robin said.

"Mine either," Katie agreed. "It's way too neat."

They walked into the dining room and in an ornate cabinet they found cut-glass pitchers, decanters, goblets, and wine glasses. Waterford crystal, Matt guessed. Another cabinet held what was obviously the "good china" as opposed to the everyday dishes in the kitchen. Dust had settled on everything in this room as well.

Matt's mother was extremely proud of her Royal Dolton china. Martha had generously given four place settings to Cora and Matt for a wedding present. "I still have enough for eight and that's more than I need. At my age, I'm not up to big formal dinners anymore." Matt picked up a saucer, turned it over and read the name, Limoges. He'd be sure to tell his mother and Cora all about this unusual adventure.

There were tea, coffee and hot chocolate sets each in a different pattern and each with cups, saucers and accessories. In another cabinet they found a custom-fitted silver chest with a complete set of Tiffany sterling. Matt glanced at the girls. Their eyes were big as saucers. Neither Katie nor Robin had ever seen such riches. Jacob was much more interested in the wood and the workmanship of the built-in cabinets.

Between the kitchen and the dining room was a huge pantry. "This is really what I wanted you to see," the sheriff said as he opened the door. The room was empty. The floor to ceiling shelves were almost entirely bare except for a few Mason jars filled with what looked like petrified green beans. The only other items were three metal containers of graduated sizes marked sugar, flour and rice. They were all empty.

"That's it," the sheriff said. "I've looked everywhere and there's no other food in this house and as far as I can tell, there hasn't been for some time. I think those two old ladies are starving."

CHAPTER SIX

Sheriff Mayhew allowed the significance of the word "starving" to sink in before he continued. "I'm really glad y'all showed up. I tried to talk to them, but, I don't know, maybe the badge scared them. I didn't want to make matters worse, but we need to find out what's going on. Clearly something has to be done."

Jacob stepped forward. "Reckon they'll talk to Ammee? You know, maybe they'd feel better with a woman."

A short discussion followed and they decided to send Jacob back in the pickup to get Ammee. The girls promised to be on their very best—and quietest—behavior if they were allowed to stay.

"Rather than bother the sisters again, let's just wait outside." As they walked out into the bright sun, Matt said, "Just look around, this yard tells its own story. Obviously it has gotten out of hand, but at one time it was probably a real show place. Come on, let's take a look around."

In the middle of the yard was a large overgrown area. The girls went to investigate and found it was enclosed by a wrought iron fence. A tall gate on one end was rusted shut and probably hadn't been used in years. It took some effort, but they got it open. Immediately the smell hit them. Roses and honeysuckle. "Dad, look what we found!" Katie called.

Matt and the sheriff joined the girls. "Back in plantation days, the big houses all had fenced gardens like this. Since there were no lawnmowers, the livestock roamed free and kept the grass nice and short. But if the ladies of the house wanted flowers, they had to fence in a garden spot."

The roses were in full bloom despite the honeysuckle vines that had invaded the beds. Huge old azalea bushes of pink, lavender, and white ringed the garden, hiding the fence and enclosing the area like a private room. In the center was a fish pond that had long since dried out and cracked.

"It's like *The Secret Garden*," Katie whispered. Robin looked blank. "Oh it's a great book about this girl who was living in India and her parents died and she gets sent back to England to live with her uncle and he's... Remind me later and I'll tell you the whole story."

Matt left the girls to explore and he and the sheriff walked back out into the yard. Years of scouting land and buying timber had taught him how to quickly survey a landscape. The old growth forest surrounding the yard took his breath away. It stretched as far as he could see in all directions and it was completely natural. His guess was that no one had made an effort to manage it in over a hundred years. Clearly it had never been logged. Unbelievable.

About that time they heard Jacob and Ammee approaching. The motor in the pickup was in about the same untended shape as the forest, coughing and belching smoke with every mile. Jacob had already explained what they knew about the situation to Ammee. Greetings were brief and the group quickly reassembled and went back to see the sisters.

Although the outside temperature had risen fast, the interior of the house was still comfortable, a tribute to high ceilings, cross ventilation and tall windows which opened from top or bottom. Jacob once again admired the craftsmanship and skill of the original builders.

Sheriff Mayhew took the lead and introduced Ammee. The sisters watched and waited. Ammee pulled up a low stool and sat facing them. She repeated her name and waited. The sisters hesitated uncertain about what to do. Then Sarah extended her hand. Ammee responded. The old woman's hand was dry and cool, but her grip was surprisingly firm. Ammee smiled.

Rather than ask questions she just talked to them in a low, even voice. The rest of the group quietly found chairs and sat down to listen. Little by little the story of the Donegan family unfolded. The ladies' memories were remarkably clear when it came to their history.

Patrick Donegan had brought a boatload of slaves to the island sometime around 1800. In order to grow rice, they selected swampland that was adjacent to the rivers that ran through the island. The slaves cut the cypress trees and cleared the stumps out of the swamp. They drained and leveled the land for cultivation, dug canals and built dikes for flood control. The tides pushed the fresh water from the river into the rice fields. Patrick Donegan was a brilliant man and he had harnessed nature to create a perfect hydraulic system for draining and flooding rice fields. He and Caleb Harding became two of the richest and most successful planters in the south.

The sisters were born into a life of luxury before the Civil War. Donegan Hall was the setting for many lavish parties, a center of culture and refinement. The Civil War and the Emancipation Proclamation changed all that. Almost all the plantation owners on the barrier islands along Carolina and Georgia abandoned the land. "Our great grandfather, Mr. Patrick, refused to leave Ibo Island," the ladies explained proudly. In order to maintain the ancestral home, the family sold off all their other holdings on the mainland. Each generation had done their part to maintain their holdings on Ibo.

"Papa played the market—that's what he always said—and he did very well," Miss Sally said.

"Yes, up until the crash of 1929," Miss Sarah added. "He lost a great deal of money, we're not sure exactly how much, he would never talk about it...and I probably shouldn't either."

"Sister's right. He was never the same after that. Oh, he was such a forceful man when we were younger. You just knew that as long as Papa was there, everything would be all right."

"He passed away two years after the crash in 1931. He's buried in our family plot over yonder," Sarah gestured vaguely toward an open window.

"After that, Brother took over. We were in much reduced circumstances, of course, but he said as long as he kept the taxes paid, we would be just fine. We had a yardman and a cook." Sally stopped abruptly and looked at her sister.

Everyone waited. Finally the sheriff asked where Brother was and whether they expected him home soon.

Silence.

Ammee gently said, "It's alright Miss Sally. We just want to help, but we need to know where your brother is."

"Dead," the sisters said in unison. Sally leaned into her sister's shoulder and began to cry softly.

"He passed on two years ago," Sarah said.

The Donegan men had always cared for and protected their womenfolk, but when the men were gone, the ladies were at a loss for what to do. Going through their brother's room, they found a cigar box with about $200. "We paid the yardman for a while, but we finally let him go, but we kept cook. She worked for us for a while longer, but then she died too."

Since that time, the sisters had been living on the canned food in the panty, some rice and beans and the last of the

55

vegetables in the garden. Miss Sally wiped her eyes and apologized for not being able to offer their guests any refreshments.

The sheriff came to sit close by and assured them it wasn't necessary. Then he informed the ladies that he and Matt would be taking care of things for a while. They smiled. That was as it should be. They nodded and waited for the men to work things out, just as they had been doing all their lives.

Back outside, the group discussed the situation. The first order of business was to feed the sisters. "I reckon we need to get them signed up for ration books. I'll check into that," Sheriff Mayhew said. Ammee volunteered to come back and cook up eggs, bacon and grits, something quick and filling. She also had a pot of gumbo to share. It would just need to be warmed up, although she was not sure the sisters had any idea how to use the wood stove.

Robin said she'd stay and gather enough wood to fire up the stove so it would be hot when her mother got back. Katie asked her dad if she could stay and help and Matt readily agreed.

Jacob and Ammee got into the pickup and as they were turning around Jacob took one last look at the house. No wonder it was solid as a rock. It was probably built entirely of bald cypress cut from the swamps. That wood was practically indestructible. It didn't shrink, it didn't rot and termites wouldn't eat it.

Quiet as two little mice, the girls explored the upstairs. In all, there were eight bedrooms, but only one of them looked like it was in use. One room had obviously belonged to the sister's brother. His clothes were still hanging in the chifforobe. They kept reminding each other not to touch anything.

When Ammee got back, she and Robin got busy in the kitchen. They volunteered to walk home when they were done.

Jacob drove the pickup to take Matt, the sheriff and Katie to the dock where Sheriff Mayhew had his boat. As they made their way back to the main road the sheriff asked, "Matt, how is it that you were out here on the island today?"

"Jacob suggested I come size up the timber land to see if there might be areas where we could do some logging. I never expected to find anything like this." He glanced out the window. "Some of those pine trees are well over 100 feet tall. If I'm not mistaken, we're looking at a virgin, longleaf pine forest. I'm guessing some of these trees may be more than 200 years old."

"Is that good?"

Matt laughed. "It's good for the Donegan sisters. Longleaf pine is the source of heart pine, the most expensive wood in this country. Generally speaking, it takes at least 150 years for the trees to mature." Matt had a tendency to get wound up when he started talking about trees. He'd always loved forests.

In the time it took to get back to the ferry, the sheriff got a history lesson about pine trees. There was a time when longleaf pine forests dominated the South from the coastal plains in Virginia all the way down to south Texas. Because it was so hard and strong, longleaf pine was called the "King's wood" and used for shipbuilding and fine Victorian houses.

The exciting news about the Donegan property was that most of the other original forests had been logged out of existence. Heart pine was no longer for sale and no one planted it because they didn't want to wait 150 years for it to mature.

"Did you notice the floors in that old house? That golden red color only comes from heart pine. I'll ask my father to come take a look, but unless I miss my guess, the Donegan sisters are sitting on a treasure as rare as pirates' gold. Selling off just enough trees to thin the forest and keep it healthy will take care of any back taxes they might owe and give them a nice income for the rest of their lives."

As it turned out, Matt was right. The Donegan property contained one of the last vestiges of old growth, heart pine forest in existence. He arranged for an official survey, and then brought his father, Mr. Wash, to Ibo to talk to the sisters.

While the men were making plans on the mainland, Ammee began taking care of business on the island. She made sure the ladies had food in the house and she stopped by to cook at least one meal a day. She happened to be there the day Matt and Mr. Wash came to visit. She introduced the older man to the sisters. From their usual place on the settee, they scrutinized Mr. Wash's well-cut suit and his carefully groomed white hair. They recognized him as a gentleman of the old school and graciously welcomed him and Matt into the parlor. Ammee got out the Limoges tea service and served freshly made pound cake and tea as the ladies listened attentively to what Mr. Wash had to say.

Once they were assured that no one intended to cut down all their trees, they politely asked, "So what exactly do you advise us to do?"

"We would like to enter into a formal contract to manage your timber," Mr. Wash said. "That would include removing any dead or diseased trees and cutting only enough of the others to keep the forest open and healthy. Do you have any family member who could help you with this decision?"

They assured Mr. Wash they trusted him and were happy to do business with his company, after their family lawyer—whose name they were sure they had written down and could find somewhere—looked over the contract. With each tree valued at approximately $1000, there was plenty of money to buy a generator, add electricity to the house, install modern plumbing and heating and hire the necessary help.

Folks on Ibo were always glad to make a little extra money, so Ammee recommended a family she knew to come on a permanent basis. The mother would cook, a daughter could take care of the housekeeping and the father would fill the spot vacated by the previous yardman.

Ammee spoke to Matt and he approached Cora. She was already working part time in the office of the clerk of courts, but she was intrigued by the Donegan's story so she agreed to visit Ibo two or three days a month. Her job was to write checks, balance the sisters' checkbook, make sure all the bills were paid and touch base with the staff to make sure everything was in order.

On her first visit to Ibo, Cora made a point of stopping by to meet Ammee. Of course Katie had to come along to see Robin again. The girls immediately took off to play. They saw Bird in the distance drawing pictures. The mothers had coffee and cobbler—a special treat—and talked about the budding friendship between their two daughters.

Later than night Cora told Matt, "You know it makes me mad that I can sit and eat with Ammee in her house on Ibo, but if I invited her to do the same thing here, this town would have a collective heart attack. We'd have to bury the whole lot of them, which might not be such a bad idea."

While Cora was letting off steam to Matt, the Donegan sisters were enjoying living in the 20th century, eating well-prepared meals on a regular basis and getting used to the idea that they were once again among the richest women in the state of Georgia.

But not everyone was so pleased. Back on the mainland, Mrs. Maurice Dupree, the wife of the mayor and president of the local bank, was none too happy. In fact, Lucile Dupree was royally pissed.

CHAPTER SEVEN

Like a screeching teakettle, Lucile Dupree stormed through the house, her high heels—she always wore high heels—beating a menacing tattoo on her polished wood floors.

"Maurice Obadiah Dupree! Maurice!! Where is that little weasel? Maurice!"

Lucile glanced outside and realized Maurice's black Ford sedan was not in the driveway.

Well, of course. He'd be at the damn bank. Lucile stamped her foot in frustration. How in the world had things gone so wrong?

In high school, Lucile had been a very pretty girl with dark hair, dark eyes and a figure that developed ripe and early. Maurice couldn't believe his good luck when she asked him to be her date for the senior prom. Her choice was no accident. Lucile had surveyed the local prospects and settled on Maurice because his family had owned the Meridian Bank and Trust for three generations, a tradition she assumed would continue to include Maurice.

When they started college, Maurice announced that he planned to major in accounting because his dream was to own a hardware store. He was totally hopeless when it came to building or home repairs, but he loved the fact that there seemed to be a tool specifically designed for each and every job. Take screwdrivers for instance. In addition to the common Phillips head and the slot head, there was a star head, and even a six-pointed star-shaped head, for things that needed to get really, really tight.

The way Maurice saw it, everyone needs hardware and the more proficient a man was, the more tools he would need. By his calculation, a hardware store was a good way to earn a comfortable living. Lucile smiled sweetly and pointed out how disappointed his family must be. She also planted the idea that if she ever became part of his family, she would be disappointed too.

Maurice held out for two years but it became clear if he ever wanted to get to first base—or farther—with Lucile, he had to make some concessions. Giving up the hardware store did have some advantages. His father was very pleased and Lucile was a lot friendlier. At the end of their junior year, they became engaged. Maurice offered Lucile his grandmother's ring with two small diamonds, but she smiled sweetly and said she had her heart set on something newer...and bigger. Maurice complied.

So far her plan was working well. Lucile's parents couldn't afford a big wedding. However, in return for what Maurice's parents perceived as her role in bringing Maurice back into the fold, they paid for a very lavish wedding and set the young couple up in a modest starter home.

A year later their son was born and they moved into a larger house. From the beginning, Lucile doted on Young Maurice. He was a cute baby with soft brown curls and big blue eyes. Despite her protests, his father insisted on calling him Butch, and to Lucile's vexation, the name stuck.

However, she did stand her ground on another issue. Since the boy's birthday was in mid-October, she refused to let him start school at five, which meant he was nearly seven when he started the first grade.

Maybe that was part of the problem. From day one, Butch was a handful. He was in constant motion, always getting into things and because he was older than the other boys in the class, he had no problem encouraging them to join him in whatever mischief he thought up.

In grammar school, he hid kids' lunch boxes, put a frog in the teacher's desk drawer, pretended a raisin was a fly and ate it to impress the girls, taped over all the light switches, ground up carrots in the pencil sharpener, and smeared glue on all the erasers. As he got older, the pranks got more ambitious, but Lucile refused to discipline him.

He was her darling boy. Although she would never admit it to anyone, she did secretly resent the fact that after his birth she was never able to regain her girlish figure. Not to be deterred from the path she had plotted for her life, she relied on well-chosen foundation garments from Fine's Department Store in Savannah to create the proper illusion.

Maurice thought that after the bank position, the diamond ring, the wedding and the big house, Lucile would be satisfied. Not so. When the old mayor died, Lucile started her campaign to convince Maurice to run for the office. He didn't want to be mayor, but he did want peace and quiet. So he gave in and became mayor, but with one concession. With uncharacteristic firmness, he informed Lucile, "If I am to do this job properly, I require one night a week, Wednesday, away from the house, on my own, no interruptions."

"And what exactly do you plan to do with your night off?"

"Think, Lucile. Just think."

Lucile was so shocked she agreed. Maurice was even more shocked. It never occurred to him that Lucile might actually give her consent. The idea had just come to him in a flash. He had no specific plans, but he sure as hell wasn't going to give up the time now that he had it.

The first Wednesday night Maurice found himself sitting alone in his office at the bank after everyone had gone home. He made his usual rounds, checked all the doors, and turned off all the lights in the public areas. Back in his office, he adjusted his lamp, propped his feet up on the desk and read a comic book he found on a table in the lobby. At 10:00, he went home. Lucile was in bed pretending to be asleep. Maurice pretended not to notice.

Despite Maurice's strange Wednesday night behavior, Lucile was more or less pleased with the way her life was going, except for one thing. They weren't rich enough. In a cruel turn of fate, the richest man in town owned the hardware store.

It just wasn't fair. Lucile was supposed to be rich. She deserved to be rich. Society rich. Savannah rich. Stinking rich like those two old Donegan sisters. What right did they have to all that money? They hadn't worked for it. Not like she had.

For heaven's sake she couldn't remember a time when she wasn't trying to come up with ways to make her life better. All they did was sit there and get old and rich. Life was definitely not fair. That's why she was on the warpath and looking for Maurice.

She snatched her pocketbook and car keys from the hall table and was about to open the front door when she realized she was not properly dressed to appear downtown. Not even in Meridian. After all, she had a reputation to maintain.

Back in their bedroom, she stripped off her housedress, wiggled into her girdle, put on stockings and changed her shoes.

She rifled through the plastic cleaners' bags in her closet and chose a navy blue suit and a white blouse. In the bathroom, she applied new makeup and adjusted her hair. She grabbed a purse to match her shoes and marched out to her car.

Even in her anger she had to smile at the sight of her car. It was a champagne-colored "Oldsmobile Series 90 Custom Cruiser Phaeton Convertible," a phrase Lucile had repeated over and over until she could rattle it off with casual abandon. At least she had done one thing in her life right. When Butch wrecked her old car, Lucile persuaded Maurice to buy her a new one. That was back in 1941 just before Detroit stopped making new cars. Lucile slid behind the wheel with a satisfied sigh.

As an added treat, she sometimes sacrificed her precious gas ration to drive as fast as the car would go along a deserted stretch of the Old Jackson Road. Since the new highway had been completed, hardly anyone ever used the old road anymore. She'd once gotten it up to 98 miles per hour. It was thrilling, all the better for being a secret.

However, when driving on familiar roads, she stayed under the speed limit. It was safer and it gave more people a chance to see her go by. Sometimes she wiggled her fingers to people watching, sometimes not.

Driving slowly to the bank gave her time to calm down, although she was determined not to waste her anger before she had the chance to properly chastise Maurice. Oh, what a disappointment he had been and after she had pinned all her hopes on him. At least he was mayor and president of the bank. That counted for something. "But for goodness sake, in his position he should have known about the Donegan property, that isn't too much to ask, is it?" Lucile totally ignored the fact that nobody knew the sisters existed before Jessie, the mailman, found them.

She and Maurice could have gone out there, sweet-talked those old ladies and bought that land for a song. She would have been glad to find them a nice nursing home on the mainland. From the stories she had heard, the china and crystal in that house was worth a fortune. She could have taken a few choice pieces and sold the rest. If only Maurice...

She had worked herself back up to a fever pitch by the time she parked in her reserved spot and walked into the bank. Maurice's office was at the rear of the building and as she walked past, the tellers all smiled. She graciously returned their smiles. She stopped at Maurice's secretary's desk.

"Lottie Mae, I just came downtown to do a bit of shopping and I thought I'd drop in on Mr. Dupree. Is he free?"

Lucile Dupree was being way too nice, so Lottie Mae was immediately on the alert. "I'll check," she said and knocked on her boss's door, two quick knocks, a pause and one more. When no one answered, she carefully opened the door. Maurice had gotten the message and was just leaving through the back entrance. "I'm sorry, Mrs. Dupree, he's not in his office. He must have stepped out for a meeting or something when I was away from my desk. Would you like to leave him a message?"

Lucile clenched her teeth and smiled. "No dear, that's not necessary. I'll see him at home later."

Maurice left his car at the bank and walked quickly over to the Elks Club which was housed in what had once been a small school building. The interior still smelled of chalk, old books, dust and talcum powder. Maurice found the smell and the quiet comforting. He had no idea what Lucile was on a rampage about this time, but he knew sooner or later he'd have to face the music.

Maurice was known as a reasonably good businessman. When it was absolutely necessary, he could take a hard line with customers at the bank. That pleased the Board of Directors, although he didn't enjoy doing it. However, when it came to Lucile, he had only summonsed up enough nerve to stand up to her once. Winning his Wednesday night freedom was a memory he cherished.

In the grand scheme of things, he was totally outclassed and he knew it. He had often thought they would have been much better off financially if she had been the one running the bank instead of him. They would probably both have been happier.

When Lucile realized Maurice had given her the slip, she went home. It was after 5:00 so she fixed herself a drink, sat down in the living room and waited. She tried to read her latest copy of *Ladies' Home Journal*, but couldn't keep her mind on any of the articles. An hour later, she heard the front door open. She waited as her husband took off his hat and coat and started toward the kitchen. "I'm in here."

Maurice sighed, and walked into the room where Lucile was sulking on the couch. He took his time pouring himself a drink and trying to figure out how much trouble he was in and why.

Lucile started slowly, "Maurice, I want you to know I'm not angry, at least I'm not angry anymore. I'm just..." she drew in her breath and let out a long-suffering sigh, "hurt."

Maurice waited.

"When I think of what we could have had...oh it just makes me want to weep. All that timber and all that money and those two old women." Her voice took on a knife-edge, "They had absolutely no idea in the world what they owned. If you had just acted, we could have been rich, I mean really rich. I could have had a real place in society, maybe even in Savannah. How could you let a once-in-a-lifetime opportunity like that slip through your fingers?" She downed the rest of her drink in one gulp.

"Lucile, no one knew about the property. If the mailman hadn't gone out there, they might have died without anyone knowing."

Lucile paid absolutely no attention to the logic of that remark. "Well, everybody knows now, don't they? The whole town is talking about how rich those old women are going to be. I'm telling you I will never get over this loss, absolutely never. I'm going to take a sleeping pill and try to wipe the whole thing out of my mind." She swept out of the room.

Maurice sat for a few minutes, then got up, freshened his drink and picked up the evening paper. He smiled slightly. He had weathered the storm, such as it was. He had certainly lived through worse.

He listened to Lucile banging things around upstairs. Eventually the house got still. Maurice relaxed. Nothing like a nice, quiet evening at home after a long day at the office. And there was still tomorrow night to look forward to. Wednesday, blessed Wednesday.

CHAPTER EIGHT

In the beginning, Maurice had been afraid to do much more on Wednesday night than sit in his office. He had gotten into the habit of smuggling a bologna sandwich out of the house in his briefcase. He'd get himself a Coke out of the refrigerator in the little kitchen off his office and spend a couple of hours reading a book. He was afraid to be seen in public for fear word would get back to Lucile and she would call a halt to his precious night of freedom.

Once in a while he drove up Highway 17 and looked at all the little stands where Geechee women sold sweetgrass baskets. The stands were closed because it was after dark, which was just as well, because Maurice couldn't stop and run the risk of being seen.

Just to put some truth to the lie he told Lucile, occasionally he actually did some thinking about town finances or city improvements. But mostly, he just relaxed and enjoyed not having to listen to and worry about Lucile's latest complaints.

And then, by nothing short of an Act of God, the answer to all his problems walked into Meridian Bank and Trust early on Monday morning July 6, 1942. His secretary, Lottie Mae, knocked on his door and said there was a lady out front who wanted to open an account. It was unusual for a woman to open an account, usually the men in the family took care of that. Maurice was intrigued.

The woman who Lottie Mae pointed out was wearing a sleeveless black dress, white sandals, no hat, no gloves and no stockings! Maurice smiled. Her auburn hair was pulled back and tied at the nape of her neck. Since she was seated, it was difficult to tell how tall she was. Maurice was a little self-conscious around tall women.

Before he walked across the lobby to greet her, Maurice made one further assessment. She was attractive in a tan, outdoorsy way. Nothing flashy to give the church ladies anything to talk about. She sat easily with her legs crossed holding her pocketbook in her lap. It wasn't until she looked directly at Maurice that he noticed her eyes, which were a remarkable shade of green. Somehow they changed her whole appearance. Maybe the ladies did have something to worry about after all. Maurice straightened his tie and walked over to greet her.

As was his custom with new customers, Maurice invited the lady into his office and got busy filling out the necessary paperwork. Her name was Hattie Tuscano. As a matter of course, he asked how much she wanted to deposit. She slid an envelope containing traveler's checks across his desk. He counted them and was visibly impressed with the total. "Oh my, well yes," Maurice said. "Welcome to Meridian, and welcome to Meridian Bank and Trust. We're lucky to have you as a new customer. Where were you living before coming to our fair city?"

"Oh, I'm just moving up here from...down south."

A number of possible locations crossed Maurice's mind. Valdosta? No, too ordinary. Probably Miami. Or Cuba? That was it. She definitely had the look of a world traveler. Maurice had heard stories about Havana and he'd always wanted to visit, but so far he hadn't made it.

One of the standard questions involved the customer's place of work. Maurice was a little reluctant to ask Mrs. Tuscano about her husband's business since the account was in her name. On the other hand, it didn't seem quite appropriate to ask *her* profession. Apparently she noticed his hesitation.

"Is there something else?"

"Well, yes. I just need to know the name of your husband's employer, Mrs. Tuscano…"

"It's Miss."

"Oh, I see." In spite of himself, Maurice made a mental note of that fact. "Could you tell me where *you* work…what your profession is?"

Hattie hesitated, then after some thought, she replied, *"Joueur."*

Maurice had no idea what that meant, but he wrote it down without comment and filled out the rest of the forms. "Just one last thing, I need your permanent address."

"I'm afraid I don't have one. I'm currently looking for something…off the beaten path. Somewhere out of the way where I can have some peace and quiet."

Maurice certainly understood the desire for peace and quiet and that's when an idea began to form in the back of his mind. Perhaps he had just the place. Years ago his father had acquired a small house when the owner defaulted on the mortgage. It was off the main road, back in the swamp along Cay Creek. "I might have something that would interest you. It's a small tabby house…"

"What's that?" Hattie asked.

Maurice smiled. He rarely had a chance to show off his knowledge of local history. "Tabby is a mixture of lime, sand, water and oyster shells. In the old days it was a favorite building material along the Georgia coast. Builders still use it. They pour it into wooden frames and when it sets, it's as hard as concrete. It makes great insulation and over the years it'll stand up to hurricanes a lot better than frame houses.

"My father planned to use the little house as a fish camp, but nothing ever came of it. However, he did have electricity and indoor plumbing installed. It's mostly one big room with a couple of large windows, a sleeping alcove and a small kitchen. It's more or less isolated and I'm sure we can come to some agreement about the rent."

As soon as the words were out of his mouth, he knew he had made a mistake. "Oh no, no, no. I didn't have anything unsavory in mind." She didn't seem convinced. "Don't be in such a hurry, Maurice," he thought. "Take your time and get your mind in gear before you open your mouth." He tried again. "Please, just hear me out." In truth, he was not quite sure how to approach the subject, but he figured as long as he'd gotten that far he might as well continue. In for a penny, in for a pound.

Maurice switched on the intercom and asked Lottie Mae to bring in coffee. "What I'm about to suggest might be a little unorthodox." Lottie Mae rolled in the coffee service. She filled their cups and then left.

Maurice took a deep breath and started once more. "I realize what I'm about to suggest might seem strange. It might even be considered a little bit on the...shady side." Hattie waited and as tactfully as possible Maurice explained his situation with Mrs. Dupree. "I don't mean to speak ill of my wife, but she's... well, she can be very strong-willed. And when she gets an idea, she has a tendency to hold on to it. And talk about it. A lot.

"That's how I got to be mayor, because Lucile talked me into it. I never wanted to be mayor, as a matter of fact, I never wanted to be a banker. I wanted to own a hardware store.

Anyway, once I was elected, I demanded—yes demanded—one night a week on my own. To think. And for some reason Lucile agreed."

Hattie sipped her coffee and continued to wait.

"At the moment my wife is still honoring our night-out agreement, but who knows how long that might last." Maurice savored a swallow of coffee to give himself time to figure what came next since he was working the plan out as he went along. "So far I've just been spending my time here at the office after everyone goes home." Maurice had talked himself into a corner. He had a vague idea of a way he could help his new customer with her housing problem, guarantee his freedom from Lucile and fulfill a dream he had not even realized he had until that very moment. The plan, when it fell into place, was simplicity itself.

Finally he blurted out, "I like to play poker. I would be glad to offer you the little house rent-free in exchange for a slight deception. All you have to do, Miss Tuscano, is to let everyone think you're running a cathouse." There it was. He had actually said it out loud. But now what?

He could tell from her expression that the plan demanded more explanation. "I know the women in this town might get together and complain to the preachers if they thought their husbands were gambling. But if word got around—and believe me it will get around—that someone was running a house of ill repute, well, no self-respecting, church-going woman is going to admit she even *suspects* her husband of visiting such a place. No gossip, no preachers, no problem. And of course, you would be totally blameless." He wasn't sure he was explaining things quite right, but he decided to stop talking and see what happened.

Hattie sat very still trying to process all the ramifications of this offer. She put on her best poker face, but her mind was whirling. "Lord God you never know what's gonna turn up in these little towns. Who would have suspected this little round man in his bow tie would come up with such a devious plan."

Still, peace and quiet and free rent wasn't a bad deal and although Maurice didn't know it yet, Hattie knew a thing or two about poker. Living with a professional gambler had taught her a whole lot of things. For one, he always said, "There is no such thing as a friendly game of poker. If you're not in it to win, don't play." Hattie smiled at the memory. She was, in a manner of speaking, holding a pat hand. She let Maurice sweat a minute longer, and then smiled. "Mr. Dupree, I think we have a deal."

Maurice was so relieved he nearly tripped over his feet getting around the desk to shake her hand. "I am so glad you were not offended and that you can see the benefits of this arrangement to everyone."

They were about the same height and Hattie looked directly at him with those green eyes. "Yes, Mr. Dupree, now that you've explained exactly what you have in mind, I think I can. After all, I wasn't planning to join the Ladies' Aid Society anyway." She smiled with all the innocence of a cat playing with a mouse, "So, I guess from now on, this makes me Cathouse Hattie, doesn't it?"

Lottie Mae heard what sounded like loud laughter coming from Mr. Dupree's office. She stopped typing to listen closer, but when she didn't hear anything else, she decided she must have been mistaken.

And so it began. Maurice had been right. When the word got out about a mysterious woman renting a house on the edge of the swamp, the rumor about a cathouse rolled through town like fog off the water. Lucile couldn't imagine Maurice being involved, but still she sniffed his jackets and checked his collars for telltale smudges of lipstick. She didn't find anything, of course.

For several weeks, Maurice actually did use his Wednesday nights to think…about the poker games. They would need a proper table, so knowing Matt's interest in woodworking, he shared his secret and invited Matt to be a charter member of the group. Matt, in turn, suggested that Maurice hire Jacob to build the table. For his part in the enterprise, Matt would donate the wood. Jacob went to work and created a masterpiece worthy of any gentlemen's gambling club in Savannah.

Hattie was only too happy to take over as dealer and set the house rules. Chips, no money on the table. The buy-in was $10 with chips valued at a nickel, a dime and a quarter. Keep the stakes low and the game as friendly as possible.

Maurice carefully selected three other men to round out the group, Sheriff Mayhew because he knew the best places in the county to buy moonshine. He added Doc Fletcher just in case of emergency and Judge Munson to handle anything Doc and the sheriff couldn't. The need for secrecy was impressed on each new member.

Both Doc and Matt had been married long enough to know they had better come clean to their wives up front to avoid serious—perhaps fatal—consequences later on. The sheriff wasn't married, so no chance of trouble there and Judge Munson's wife spent most of her time in Florida.

Of all the cathouse regulars, Maurice was by far the worst poker player in attendance. He never took a risk with other people's money at the bank, but when it came to poker, he checked his common sense at the door and could be counted on to raise on a pair of twos.

The only thing that saved him from total destruction was that he genuinely enjoyed himself and was so guileless, it was hard to tell when he was bluffing. Occasionally he'd get over-extended, but Hattie always bought his markers so he could stay in the game.

With his Wednesday nights secure, Maurice finally relaxed. Secretly he thanked God for sending Hattie his way.

CHAPTER NINE

As the oldest daughter in a family of 12, Hattie became a second mother to her younger brothers and sisters by the time she was six. It was *not* her choice, that's just the way it was. One of the few things she *did* have a choice about was her name, Hortense. She was convinced someone just found that name lying around somewhere and attached it to her by mistake. So she changed it to Hattie.

Life on the family farm didn't change much for her first 15 years. Almost every season her mother got pregnant and each year there was another baby to care for. Somehow in her heart Hattie knew there had to be more to life than that. The hard part was, if she wanted a better life, she was going to have to leave home. So the day after her 16th birthday—which no one had noticed—she packed a suitcase, left a note, left the farm and left her old life behind.

She walked out to the road and started hitchhiking. The last couple who gave her a ride dropped her off on Canal Street in the middle of New Orleans. After a farm in the middle of nowhere, New Orleans was a shock, a big, beautiful shock. Canal Street was the widest street Hattie had ever seen. There were two lanes on one side going up town and two lanes on the other side going down town. There was also a wide green space in the middle where two lanes of trolley car tracks ran. She later learned folks who lived in New Orleans called that space the "neutral ground."

She was afraid to try to cross all those lanes of traffic on Canal Street, so she just wandered along in front of Maison Blanche looking in all the store windows, each one a little fairy tale all by itself. Through the main doors, she saw marble columns, crystal chandeliers, polished floors and more beautiful things than she could ever imagine. When the doors opened, she realized even the air smelled beautiful.

She didn't dare go in. Instead she just wandered along and eventually found herself standing in front of a small millinery shop admiring the fancy hats. The owner, Esther Rosenthal, came out with the intention of shooing her away. But Hattie spoke up first. "These hats are very beautiful. Do you make them?" Esther was very proud of her creations and her shop and she wasn't immune to a little honest praise.

Hattie blurted out that she was new in town—which was more than obvious—and needed a job and a place to stay. "I can sew real good and I'll do all the cleanin' up and...I can cook too...and iron...and wash..." Esther scrutinized the frumpy child standing in front of her. "I wonder if I can make a silk purse out of this sow's ear?" she thought. The challenge appealed to her, and on an impulse, she hired Hattie.

She gave the child a sandwich and while Hattie wolfed that down, Esther talked about her shop. Originally she had called it Hats by Esther and she was struggling to get by. But when she changed the name to Des Chapeaux by Madame Suzette, wealthy clients flocked to her door and she couldn't make hats fast enough.

Hattie smiled. She understood about names. For the next seven years, the hat shop became Hattie's finishing school. She learned how to dress, how to speak properly, how to behave in fancy restaurants, how to listen to her clients and most important of all, how to make sure Esther made a profit on every hat they sold.

Her forte was "refurbishing" hats. Hattie used bits and pieces left over from new hats to remodel old ones. A clear profit for Esther, a bargain for the customer and good training for Hattie. One of her first and most loyal clients was Mrs. Broussard, the matriarch of an old French family who had a house in the French Quarter. She had been quite a beautiful girl in her younger days and Hattie knew just the right touch to bring out the color of her eyes or to accent her high cheekbones.

Each summer Mrs. Broussard booked passage from New Orleans to New York on the *SS Momus*, owned by the Southern Pacific Railroad. She would never reveal her age, but she did finally give in to her family's concerns and agree to travel with a companion. She chose Hattie. Although she was sorry to lose her, Esther congratulated herself on the fine job she had done turning Hattie into a proper young lady.

Mrs. Broussard always traveled first class, of course. She occupied a large stateroom and Hattie had a smaller room next door which was normally occupied by children and their nanny. The voyage put the finishing touches on Hattie's education. From their first day out, she observed the women as they sat with their backs perfectly straight, their ankles crossed, their hands folded in their laps. They talked about books and plays and operas and places they had traveled.

Once she had Mrs. Broussard settled in her deck chair with her rug, Hattie had free time. She discovered the first-class reading and writing room, part of which was reserved for women. The library, which was in the same area, was open to all. On her first visit, she thought she was alone until a man spoke quietly. "Are you lookin' for somethin' in particular?"

She immediately recognized the soft accent of a fellow Southerner. She turned around to see a clean-shaven young man with dark curly hair and hazel eyes. She knew it was considered brazen for a woman to look a man in the eye, but she couldn't make herself look away. His voice sounded like the low notes of the washtub basses the street kids in New Orleans played.

"I'm just trying to learn about...about everything." She dropped her head to avoid looking into those eyes. He took the back of his fingers and tipped her chin up to see her face. "A noble endeavor. May ah offer my assistance?"

"Oh please, offer anything you like," Hattie thought with a sigh, but she was careful not to be too bold. "Yes, thank you."

If ever there is a place in the universe that distorts time, it is aboard a ship. For those going to meet a loved one, time drags. For those who have just met someone to love, a whole lifetime can go by in a matter of weeks.

His name was Julian Barrington, JB to his friends. He never made a date, he just showed up. "Walk with me," he said. It wasn't a command, it was an invitation. He tucked Hattie's arm into his and they walked easily together.

After their first encounter, Hattie saw him often around the ship. He moved in the same way he talked, with the slow confidence of a man who knew where he was going but had no reason to hurry to get there. Sometime he would catch her eye across the room and nod his head slightly in a silent, private salute. When he said, "Talk to me," she told him everything.

One evening he said, "Dance with me." When she said she didn't know how, he smiled. "It's just like when we walked together, only you have to walk backward." They danced until 9:00 when he excused himself. "Ah have to go to work now." She watched as he went into the next room and sat down to play cards as he did every night.

When she saw him later, she said, "I thought you said you were going to work last night."

"So ah did. Playing cards is my work."

Hattie said she had grown up in a home where cards were considered sinful. JB smiled.

"In a way, my family feels that way too. All the men in old Virginia families play cards, it's just part of being social. However, my family has disowned me, not because ah play, but because ah win. That makes me a professional gambler, and according to them, that's common."

"I thought maybe you were a doctor, since I hear the men you play cards with call you Doc?"

"Just a nickname. Ah'm Southern, ah play poker, ah win a lot. That reminds them of Doc Holliday."

Hattie looked up Doc Holliday. In several books she found references to the fact that he had tuberculous, which eventually killed him. Obviously that didn't have anything to do with JB. She dismissed the information as ridiculous.

Sandwiched between Doc's nightly card games and Hattie's daily duties taking care of Mrs. Broussard, they still managed to spend time together. On the last night of the voyage when JB went to play cards, Hattie went to her room to pack. She knew once they docked in New York she would never see him again.

After midnight, she heard a faint knock at her door. She opened it to find JB standing there, smiling slightly. He looked directly into her eyes and said, "Be with me." She never hesitated. Doc took his time. When she woke up the next morning, he was gone.

Mrs. Broussard left a note for her saying she wanted to be on deck to see the Statue of Liberty as they sailed into New York harbor. Hattie had already planned to be there and she was a little surprised that someone as well-traveled as Mrs.

Broussard considered Lady Liberty worth the special effort. On deck, Hattie scanned the crowd looking for JB, but he wasn't there. At the first glimpse of the statue, tears ran down Hattie's cheeks. She wasn't sure who she was crying for.

As she had done many times in the past, Mrs. Broussard took a short-term lease on a suite of rooms at the Plaza Hotel and another phase of Hattie's education began. For three seasons, she observed the top echelon of high society. With Mrs. Broussard she attended Broadway plays, went to the New York Philharmonic, even attended the premier of *Il tittico*, three one-act operas by Puccini at the Metropolitan Opera. Hattie thought it was wonderful, Mrs. Broussard did not think it was up to Puccini's usual standard.

Dinner parties and after-theatre suppers were the order of the day and Mrs. Broussard was a frequent guest at some of these occasions with the likes of Rockefellers, Carnegies, Vanderbilts, Fords, Astors and even an occasional Roosevelt. From time to time during the year, the elite abandoned the city for their homes in healthier locations like Newport, the Hamptons or Martha's Vineyard. Mrs. Broussard had a cottage in Southampton. It seemed to Hattie that each new location was grander than the previous one.

It was at a party in some mansion—Hattie was never quite sure who owned what—that she saw JB again. He was sitting at a table playing cards with a group of older men. In the last three years, he had lost some weight and he looked paler than she remembered. She knew better than to distract him, so she waited until the game broke up. When he saw her, he smiled and patted his heart. He was staying on their host's estate and in his usual way invited Hattie to, "Stay with me."

She told Mrs. Broussard she had been invited to a late party with some young people and asked for the rest of the night off. Mrs. Broussard smiled knowingly and agreed.

Happily Hattie joined JB in his rooms. "I didn't think I'd ever see you again," she said.

"Oh my dear, you don't know how many times ah wanted to ask you to leave with me, but the truth is ah never know where this life will take me next. The trick to being a successful gambler is never to stay in one place too long. Once ah've taken their money, it's time to move on. In fact, ah'm going to be leaving for Chicago at the end of the week." He paused and looked into her eyes. "Oh God," Hattie thought. She knew what was coming.

"Come with me."

Hattie wanted nothing more than to go with him, but she was also a responsible young woman so she discussed the situation with Mrs. Broussard. The older woman cautioned her about taking such a drastic chance, but she could tell by the look in Hattie's eyes, that logic was not going to play a part in her decision. So, being a woman of the world, Mrs. Broussard gave her blessing and Hattie packed her suitcase.

If New York had been elegant, Chicago was wild. Jazz, speakeasies, gangsters, it was life lived fast and hard. JB had no trouble finding gambling partners, the only problem was he and Hattie lived on different time schedules. He played most of the night, she was free during the day.

Eventually they worked out a schedule. They explored the city in the afternoons, and had supper together. Then JB went to work and Hattie went to sleep. In the mornings, she visited museums and art galleries and even took several classes at the local YWCA.

During their second year in the city, Hattie heard JB coughing more and more, deep wet coughs that frightened her. She remembered the book about Doc Holliday and realized the real significance of the nickname.

One evening at dinner, JB said, "Hattie, ah do not have much to give you, except my experience. A'm going to teach you about poker, you never know when it might come in handy. Just remember, you don't have to be the best player at the table, you just have pay attention. Know the odds and read the players, that's the trick." JB was amazed at how quickly she caught on.

As JB's condition got worse, Hattie reverted to her days of caring for her family. She lovingly nursed Doc until the end and she never regretted a single moment of her life with him.

JB might not have left her much, but what he did leave her was priceless. No one expected a woman to know anything about playing poker. Hattie followed his rule of not taking all their money all the time, so for a year or two, she got along fairly well. She met interesting people, visited Detroit, St. Louis and Nashville.

Things went fine until she beat Memphis Big Al once too often. That's when she packed her suitcase and her memories and went in search of somewhere she could find some peace and quiet.

CHAPTER TEN

From the time her son started to crawl, Lucile realized there was no more peace and quiet for her. Controlling Butch was out of the question and containment was only remotely possible. Despite the fact that Lucile insisted on calling him Young Maurice, it was obvious Butch was not going to be the Little Lord Fauntleroy she had in mind.

Early on, Lucile discovered the only way to keep him quiet and still was to read to him. It didn't seem to matter what she read, he was curious about everything. One afternoon when he was five, she was in the kitchen fixing supper when she turned around and there stood Butch, naked as the day he was born and a vivid shade of blue. "Baby, what's wrong, what happened?"

Butch smiled proudly. "It's innego, to keep me safe from the blue hag." Lucile was frantically trying to maintain her composure and make sense of the situation. She knelt beside him and tried to keep her voice even. "Oh, do you mean indigo?"

Butch nodded. "And the blue hag."

Lucile remembered an article she had been reading about island superstitions that mentioned indigo as a protection from the *boo* hag. She wrapped Butch in her apron and followed his wet footprints back to the bathroom where she found several empty boxes of navy blue Rit Dye and a bathtub full of blue water. She had no idea how he managed to find the dye in the laundry room or how he knew what to do with it. Maybe he thought it was like the bubble bath she sometimes put in his bath water.

What she did know was that she was getting a very severe headache. She called Maurice and Maurice called Butch. They had a serious talk and Butch promised never to dye himself blue again.

Almost every year, Butch got into some kind of trouble. However, his next major adventure came five or six years later and was much more public. The Duprees were members of First Baptist Church where Lucile sang in the choir and Maurice was on the Board of Deacons. Butch was very curious about the way baptism worked, which Lucile took as a good sign. He was particularly interested in the fact that the baptistery was always filled the night before a service so the water had a chance to warm up a little.

Armed with this information, Butch hatched a plan. He also did a little exploring. The front doors of the church were always open, but they were too visible. A little more searching revealed that the outside door in the choir room was never locked. It was on the side of the church, well out of public view.

Brother Courtney's sermon the next Sunday morning was mercifully short to allow plenty of time for the baptism of Katie Reeve and two of her friends who had made a public profession of faith as part of Vacation Bible School. It was an important day and the church was full. There were even a few Methodists who had come to see their friends get baptized.

Butch and his friends were scattered throughout the sanctuary, sitting quietly with their parents...waiting. The choir sang, "Shall We Gather at the River," and the curtain in front of the baptistery was pulled aside. The congregation gasped.

The pool was full of big round green blobs with silly faces painted on them. The look on Brother Courtney's face and the reaction of the congregation was well worth the time Butch and his gang had spent visiting a number of watermelon patches and stealing all the young melons.

Brother Courtney, in his black robe, white shirt and black hip boots, stormed back to the pulpit, mad as the proverbial wet hen. When he calmed down, he called Maurice and Maurice called Butch. The boy proudly admitted that it was all his idea. Maurice grounded him for two weeks. "I hope you'll use the time wisely to consider your actions." Butch did put the time to good use thinking about the incident and as far as he was concerned, his actions had produced exactly the results he hoped for.

Like most children in small towns, Butch learned to drive early. By the time he was 13 he was allowed to take his father's car on short errands to Piggly Wiggly or to get gas at J.M. Pure Oil. His mother's car was strictly off limits.

Unfortunately his father's Ford sedan didn't have the same allure as his mother's "Big Boy Hudson." Butch loved to sit behind the wheel and pretend he was driving a tank. One afternoon he and six of his buddies were sitting in the car and someone suggested just starting the motor so they could hear the low rumble of the engine. The keys were in the ignition, so Butch complied.

From there it didn't take much encouragement to back out of the driveway and go for a little joy ride. The only problem was the Hudson was much bigger and heavier than his dad's Ford. Butch had a hard time seeing over the hood and it was much harder to steer. However as long as he went straight, he was fine.

Then one of the boys in the back seat yelled, "Turn here," and Butch did. Unfortunately, he didn't slow down first. Thank goodness they hadn't been going very fast, but they were going fast enough to end up nose down in a ditch.

Nobody was hurt and they all crawled out of the car to survey the damage. Butch saw a man plowing a field near by and hiked over to ask him if he would bring his tractor and pull the car out of the ditch. Even the big John Deere had a hard time getting the Hudson back on the road.

The radiator was broken and water was leaking onto the blacktop. However, just because they couldn't drive the car didn't mean they couldn't ride in it. Butch told the farmer he was sure his father would be glad to pay him to tow the car into the J.M. Pure Oil station. Butch and the boys got back in the car, rolled down the windows and waved to everyone they passed on the way into town. When they got there, the farmer called Maurice and Maurice confronted Butch.

"Butch, how much do you think we should pay this nice man for his trouble?"

Butch was surprised and pleased to be consulted. "Ten dollars."

"Good," Maurice said. "I'll pay him now and you'll pay me back out of your allowance *and* you will explain to your mother what happened to her car."

Butch didn't mind so much about losing his allowance because his mother could usually be counted on for extra money. However, that was now out of the question and the very thought of explaining that he was responsible for wrecking her precious car scared the bejesus out of him.

The episode might have had a much worse ending, but Lucile found a way to forgive Butch and turn the situation to her advantage. She prevailed upon Maurice to buy her a new car, which was how she came to get the Oldsmobile Series 90

Custom Cruiser Phaeton convertible. It just went to prove an old Geechee saying that good comes from bad.

For a while Butch was on his best behavior. However, there are few things as tempting to a boy's imagination as a school building closed for summer vacation. Just to walk the empty halls was daring. When Butch broke in and was alone inside, he made believe he was Superman stalking bad guys on his way to saving the world.

But Butch preferred having an audience. He liked the fact that the other boys looked up to him and expected him to come up with things to do. Left on their own, they'd never have thought of anything fun or interesting. The challenge, of course, was to cause trouble without doing any real damage...or getting caught.

Unexpectedly, it was his mother who planted an idea in his head. She mentioned that the Saturday before school started again in September, the School Board was planning an open house to show off the new addition to the school building and the renovations that had been completed during the summer.

The night before the event, Butch and his buddies pried off a screen, forced open a window and climbed into the building. Butch told each of them to bring a flashlight, a hammer and a large screwdriver. As usual they waited for Butch to lay out the plan.

First they got a short ladder from the janitor's closet. Then they walked into the nearest classroom and closed the door. "Henry, grab the door handle and hold the door steady. Now watch," Butch said. He climbed on the ladder and carefully put the end of the screwdriver under the edge of the top hinge pin holding the door in place. With a couple of taps, the pin popped out.

Like lacing the fingers of two hands together, the hinge on the door fitted into the hinge on the frame. "Keep holding it

steady." Butch got off the ladder, squatted down on the floor
and repeated the process to take the pin out of the bottom hinge.
"Don't let go yet. Be real careful and open the door just enough
for us to get out in the hall." When they were safely outside, he
told Henry to shut the door.

They looked puzzled. "So now what?" Henry asked.

"Open the door," Butch said.

Henry turned the knob and pushed. At first the door
wouldn't budge, so Henry gave it a shove. That's all it took.
The door slipped off its hinges, fell backward and came
crashing down flat on the floor. "Wow!" the boys said.

"OK, get busy. We've got a lot of doors to fix." Working in
twos, it took several hours to sabotage all the doors in the
school. Finally tired and dirty, they left the same way they
entered. "Be sure to come with your folks tomorrow night or
you'll miss all the fun."

The following evening, the principal made a speech and
then sent each of the teachers to their room to open the door and
welcome visitors. One by one, the doors fell off their hinges
making an astonishing amount of noise. The event was a
smashing success, at least from Butch's point of view.

The next morning the principal called Maurice and Maurice
called Butch. Once again Butch confessed. He was quite
pleased when his father said, "It must have taken you a long
time to dismantle all those doors." Butch smiled proudly.
"Yessir. It took us a couple of hours and it was real hard work."

"Well, now that you understand hinges, you can get the rest
of your crew together, go back to the school and repair all the
doors. I think it would also be a good idea if you gave each door
a new coat of paint while you're at it."

Dealing with the consequences wasn't nearly as much fun
as setting up the trick. After all that work, the boys decided to
take a breather.

On Friday nights, they usually got together and went to the picture show on Main Street. They could always count on a serial, usually *The Adventures of Superman,* and a Western. Then Saturday afternoons they would meet with their cap pistols and relive the movie. The smoke and noise from the toy guns stoked their imaginations and added to the illusion of danger.

As a rite of passage, most boys in small southern towns got a .22 for their birthday when they turned 12. By the time Butch turned 14, all his gang had passed that milestone and most of them hunted with their fathers or brothers or cousins. It was Butch, of course, who came up with a daring idea prompted by all the Westerns they had watched.

"You know how cool it is in the movie to hear the bullets go whizzing by in the middle of a shootout? Well, I've figured a way we can do that for real, without anybody getting hurt. Bring your .22's and meet me back by the garbage dump where those two old boxcars are."

The plan was for two teams of two boys each to be stationed at opposite ends of the boxcars. One boy would get a chance to shoot each time and the other one would be the lookout who signaled when it was time to fire. The team at the other end would stand back out of harm's way, but close enough to hear the bullets go whizzing by.

They played several rounds and were having a great time until someone got their signals crossed and Jimmy got shot in the arm. He screamed and everyone came running. He was holding his arm, blood seeping through his shirt.

"I'm shot. You gotta do something!"

"Lemme see," Butch said. They all crowded around and sure enough there was a bloody hole in Jimmy's arm. "We've got to get the bullet out. Anybody got a pocket knife?"

Jimmy was having none of that. "No sir!! You're not gettin' anywhere close to me with a knife."

"We've got to get him to a doctor before he bleeds to death," Henry said.

Up until that time, Jimmy just knew his arm hurt. It hadn't occurred to him that he might bleed to death. "Do something! I don't want to die."

Butch took charge. "Calvin, you've got the fastest bike, you go get Doc Fletcher. We'll stay here with Jimmy." Calvin left in a hurry. "Somebody give me a handkerchief." Butch might as well have asked for a bowling ball. In exasperation he took off his t-shirt. "For gosh sake, just give me your belt. We've gotta stop the bleeding."

He folded the shirt, put it over the wound and cinched it tight with the belt. "Ouch!!" Jimmy looked a little pale which was definitely not a good sign. "Henry, hold his arm up," Butch said.

Doc Fletcher drove up shortly. Calvin was sitting in the front seat, his bike was in the trunk. Doc had already heard the story of the accident so he was reasonably sure Jimmy wasn't in mortal danger. He and Calvin found the other boys huddled next to the boxcar. "You boys ought to be ashamed of yourselves. I'm gonna do my best to save that young man's life, but you scalawags better do some serious praying. Now get this boy into the front seat of my car and be careful with him. The rest of you get in the back."

For a little added drama, Doc took off in a cloud of dust spraying gravel in all directions and drove at top speed all the way to his office. He sent Jimmy into the examining room with his nurse, then he turned to the boys and sadly shook his head. "I've already called the sheriff and I'm sure he's called your parents. I'll do what I can, but if Jimmy doesn't make it..." He left the threat hanging and turned on his heel.

He gave Jimmy a shot of Novocain, removed the bullet and dressed the wound. "You're gonna be fine. I want to keep you here for a while, so I'm going to give you a mild sedative to help you sleep."

Then he walked into his private office and called Maurice. "They say God takes care of fools and idiots and those boys were both today. They're in my front office now fervently praying. They think Jimmy's life is hanging in the balance and I don't plan to tell them otherwise, at least for a couple of hours. I called the sheriff and I imagine he's called their parents. Lord God, Maurice, were we ever that young or that stupid?"

This time Maurice didn't call Butch. He took action on his own and informed his son, "When school starts in September, you're going to Georgia Military Academy in Valdosta."

CHAPTER ELEVEN

Matt and Katie sat a little nervously at the kitchen table while Cora banged pots and pans around fixing supper. She usually said working in the kitchen settled her nerves, but it didn't seem to be working at the moment.

Butch's latest escapade, The Shoot Out at the Dump, was probably the topic of conversation in most Meridian homes that night. Lucile was telling everyone that Butch had been *invited* to attend Georgia Military Academy in Valdosta, but no one was falling for that one.

"Valdosta is not nearly far enough away," Cora said as she slammed the oven door on the biscuits. "Butch'll probably find a way to come home every weekend." She stopped long enough to flip the pieces of chicken frying in the cast iron skillet. "I'd feel better if they sent him out of state. I'm telling you that Butch Dupree doesn't think any farther than the end of his nose."

"Believe me, that's what Maurice had in mind," Matt said. "But before he could get everything worked out, Lucile intervened. He was going to send Butch up to Carlisle Military School in South Carolina, but Lucile wouldn't hear of that. Valdosta was kind of a compromise."

Wham! went another pot lid. "And just so you know," Matt continued, "Butch will only be home one weekend a month and that depends on whether he can get a ride or not. Maurice says he's not going to run a shuttle service between here and South Georgia no matter what Lucile wants."

"Lucile! Don't even get me started on her. That woman just gets up my nose."

"What's that mean?" Katie asked.

"She annoys me, pretending to be nice when she wants something and acting like she's too good to associate with you the rest of the time. I don't think she's got a real friend in this town." Bang! went a cabinet door.

"Speaking of friends," Matt said with a gleam in his eye, "Hattie mentioned that the two of you had lunch in town last week. How did that go?"

Cora shot him a look, then turned her attention back to destroying the kitchen. "Fine."

The truth was, lunch *had* gone very well. The two women got along easily and Cora wasn't sure why she hadn't just told Matt that. Maybe it was because she recognized in Hattie a possible ally. Someone who was willing to kick against the traces from time to time. Lord knows, Hattie was a lot more interesting than the other women in Meridian. Even from their casual conversation Cora could tell Hattie had a lot more worldly experience than she did.

Right on cue, Katie asked, "Who's Hattie?"

Matt put on a poker face and waited for Cora to answer the question.

"She's just somebody who's new in town and I thought we should get acquainted."

Matt smiled. He wasn't buying that any more than Cora was buying the story of Butch being invited to attend Georgia

Military Academy. After hearing about the cathouse plot, he had no doubt Cora would want to meet Hattie. Furthermore, he suspected the two women would like one another. He also knew Cora was sometimes prone to poke a hornet's nest just to see what would happen.

Although no one in Meridian had formally met Hattie, the timing of the rumor of a cathouse opening and the appearance of a new, rather exotic looking woman in town were enough to get tongues wagging. Cora, of course, knew that Hattie was innocent of the crime, but she rather enjoyed seeing the commotion it was causing. With the exception of Doc Fletcher's wife, Cora was the only woman in Meridian who knew the truth.

The situation was tailor-made for a little mischief. Matt halfway expected to hear his wife singled out for special attention in Wednesday night prayer meeting. In fact, maybe she had been. Lately his Wednesday nights had been spent elsewhere.

The kitchen and supper both survived and eventually the family sat down to eat. Between bites, Cora turned the conversation back to Lucile. "You know I keep seeing her down at the courthouse digging through old deeds and legal papers. That's not the section I work in, so I'm not sure what she's looking for, but you can bet she's up to no good.

"As a matter of fact, I heard her talking to one of the clerks out front about Sea Pines, that huge resort they're building out on Hilton Head. Lucile is hoping some investors will come down here to our islands." Cora set her ice tea glass down so hard it splashed over the sides. "I swear that woman sees dollar signs on everything. Can you imagine what would happen if they decided to buy up all the land and build one of those big private golf clubs on Ibo?"

"Are they gonna do that?" Katie looked at her mother.

"Who knows? Ammee says some of the younger people have already sold Geechee land that's been in their families since the Civil War. If the next generation doesn't want to follow the old ways, there's really not anything for them to do on Ibo. There aren't any jobs, so they have to come into town and when somebody offers money for their land, it probably seems like a good idea to sell."

"Do you think that's gonna happen to Robin and her family?" Matt heard the distress in Katie's voice.

"I wouldn't worry about it, Peanut," Matt said to Katie. "Jacob loves Ibo and he has a good job with the lumber yard. He does work for other folks out there too and they've got The Store. I don't think they're in any danger of leaving."

"I know life out there might not be easy, but I kind of envy them," Cora said. "Ammee talks a lot about how Geechee people look out for each other and share things," she paused. "Did you know there's not a doctor on the island? Ammee's a healer, which is the closest thing they've got. And they don't have a sheriff or a policeman. Not one and they still get by just fine."

"You want to move?" Matt asked.

"No, I'm not trading electricity and indoor plumbing for peace and quiet, but still..."

Matt knew only too well that peace and quiet didn't exactly match Cora's temperament. In fact, he had to admit—if only to himself—that Cora's righteous indignation about things had always amused him. He tended to take the world and life as it came. Not Cora. She had never seen a problem or a mess she didn't think she could fix. That and her mischievous streak were part of what had attracted him to her in the first place.

When he remembered what it was like when they first got together, he had to smile. He was ten years older than she was but although she was young, Matt's parents had taken to Cora right away. Initially Matt had wondered if they weren't just glad *someone* was going to marry him and give them grandchildren. Twelve years later he still thanked his lucky stars for Cora and Katie.

When they finished supper, Matt said he and Katie would clean up the kitchen. It seemed the kindest thing to do for all concerned. When they finished washing the dishes, they joined Cora in the living room and listened to Art Baker and *People Are Funny* on the radio. The show was all about contestants asked to do crazy stunts. One time they had a man go into the Knickerbocker Hotel and try to register a trained seal that he said was his girlfriend.

"Butch oughta be on that show," Katie said. "He's always doing wild stuff like putting the watermelons in the baptistery. I know Brother Courtney got all upset, but I thought it was pretty funny."

"Maybe, but not everything he does is funny," Cora pointed out. "He doesn't think things through, like that shooting stunt. Or the time he stole his mother's car…"

"He didn't really steal it," Katie protested. "I mean, it was his mother's car, he just drove it."

"…and had a wreck. With all his friends in the car. He was lucky. He could have killed somebody…like I did."

Everything stopped. It was as if a flash bulb had gone off, momentarily blinding Matt and Katie and freezing them in place. It took time to blink the world back in focus.

"Cora, what do you mean 'like you did?' When did you ever kill anybody?"

For a moment, Cora hesitated. Although she was the one who brought up the subject, she looked guilty, the way Katie looked when she got caught doing something wrong. They waited. Then little by little the story unfolded.

When she was 18, Cora's father had left Meridian early one morning and driven to Atlanta to pick up her and a friend from Agnes Scott College. It had been raining all day and by the time they loaded all their belongings into the car and left Decatur, it was late afternoon. Although a new highway linked Atlanta to Savannah, they still had to contend with all the little towns in between so the 250-mile trip usually took at least seven hours. On top of that, the rain slowed them down.

"By the time we got to Savannah, Dad was exhausted. He wanted to stop and spend the night, but I convinced him I was fine and I could drive the rest of the way. We made it as far as Richmond Hills and that's when this truck came out of nowhere and hit us head on. My dad and my friend were thrown out of the car and they both died before the ambulance got there. I had a broken leg and a concussion.

"As it turned out, I lost more than my dad and my friend that day. You know my mother died when I was born. Well, Dad had an older sister, Teletha. She moved in with us and was like a mother to me. She was 17 years older than Dad, so she had pretty much raised him too. They were very close." Cora smiled at the memory.

"I thought she was very sophisticated. She never married, she lived upstairs in our big house, but she had her own private entrance. She worked for the telephone company, bought all her clothes in Savannah and owned her own car. I loved my dad, but it was Aunt T. I took all my 'girl' problems to.

"She always gave me something pretty for my birthday and Christmas because she knew Dad would only think of the practical things. Before I went off to college, she took me to Savannah and bought my whole wardrobe."

Cora's voice got softer and slower as if she were running out of energy. "After the accident, she moved out of our house and never spoke to me again. She blamed me for her brother's death and she was right. It was my fault. If I hadn't insisted on driving, it never would have happened. I sold the house to pay for college and I rented a place in town each summer. After the funeral, Aunt T. moved to Atlanta. Several years ago I heard from a distant cousin that she was living somewhere up north." Finally Cora stopped talking all together.

Katie came to sit beside her. "I'm sorry Mamma."

"It's OK, it all happened a very long time ago."

Matt crossed to sit on Cora's other side. "I thought I knew everything about you. Why didn't you ever tell me this story?"

"I don't know. I was so happy when we started dating I didn't want to ruin it by bringing up something so sad. And I felt guilty and embarrassed. Then we got married and Katie came along and I just pushed it to the back of my mind.

"I hadn't thought about Teletha for years. I guess when I mentioned the accident, that brought it all back. Sad the way people just fade out of our lives sometimes."

CHAPTER TWELVE

Cora looked forward to her visits to Ibo Island. Even at the end of summer, she still enjoyed the walk from the ferry to Donegan Hall. Every yard, no matter how poor, sported some kind of wild flower that made it through the heat of the summer.

Once she turned off what passed for a main road on Ibo, the trees closed over and around her and without any artificial noise, she was transferred back to her childhood when she couldn't wait for summer days so she could go barefoot. Even at her age, she couldn't resist the temptation to take off her shoes and walk on the warm sand.

The Donegan Sisters were an island of tranquility with their quiet, formal ways. No matter when she arrived, they always had a pitcher of ice tea ready and something sweet to eat. They were always interested in news from "over there," but never upset by any of it. Cora wondered if all their lives they had lived at arm's length from the clamor and commotion of the real world. She wondered if they even knew there was a war going on.

Cora got her first inkling that something was up when she went through the bills and prepared to balance the checkbook. She noticed a number of bills for magazine subscriptions to

Saturday Evening Post, Colliers, Ladies' Home Journal, Redbook and *Reader's Digest.* There was also a bill for a case of Community Coffee, drip grind, shipped from New Orleans. "A case of coffee! How in God's name did they manage that? Nobody has enough coupons for a *case* of coffee." Cora puzzled over these developments for some time. The sisters might not know much about the outside world, but apparently they had figured out how to fill out mail-order forms and get around wartime shortages.

As it turned out, Cora wasn't the only regular visitor to Donegan Hall. Their house was the only one on the island to have an official mailing address. After his initial delivery, Jessie, the postman, and the sisters had become good friends. At his suggestion, they subscribed to the weekly newspaper, the *Meridian Herald,* which he delivered faithfully and they served him their special coffee and whatever homemade sweets they had on hand.

When Cora questioned them about the bills, they sweetly explained. "When Brother was alive, he used to bring home all those lovely magazines, but then, of course, that stopped. So we've just been reading the old ones until we found this card that we could send in to get new ones. Jessie has showed us how to order a lot of things...like the coffee. We hope it's not too much."

Cora had to smile. With all their newly found wealth, the sisters were still worried about spending money. When she thought about it further, she wondered if they had ever bought anything for themselves. The house, the food and the servants were all taken care of by the men in the family. They probably had a seamstress to make their clothes. It was a miracle they survived as well as they did. The current miracle was that they had found a source of coffee, which like sugar was carefully rationed and very scarce.

When Cora asked about the old magazines, the sisters said, "Oh we saved them, they're in the back room." And so they were, hundreds of them stacked floor to ceiling nearly filling a downstairs room that had probably been a spare bedroom at one time. Cora couldn't resist examining several nearby stacks. Some of the magazines were covered in mildew, some water damaged, some in pristine condition. The publication dates went back 30 years.

Taking turns, the sisters explained. "Now that we get new ones... we don't have to read these old ones anymore. We have plenty of room in the house... so we just keep them in here. We did think about taking them outside... but we were afraid if we tried to burn them, we'd set the house on fire. Would you like to take one or two home with you?"

"Oh yes!" Cora said. She found two copies of *Photoplay* in good condition. "I'll take one of these for Katie. I know she'd love to see it."

"If you plan to see Ammee before you leave the island, why don't you take some to her too?" Sally offered. Cora selected a *Ladies' Home Journal* for Ammee, a *Saturday Evening Post* with a Norman Rockwell cover for Bird and another *Photoplay* for Robin. The dates ranged from 1924 to 1934. The sisters seemed happy to share.

Later that afternoon Cora visited Ammee and distributed her gifts to everyone. "There must be at least a thousand magazines in that room."

"Lord a'mercy," Ammee said. "Do you suppose they'd be willing to give some of the magazines to the school? I'm sure Lucy Chalmers would be thrilled to have them for her students. I'll bet most of the kids on Ibo have never read a magazine."

On her next visit, Cora presented the idea to the sisters but they were a little reluctant to agree. "I'll tell you what," Cora suggested, "why don't I take you to see the school and then you can make up your mind."

"How would we get there? We don't have a carriage anymore."

Cora explained she was driving the Reeve Company pickup and she thought there would be room. The sisters were a little dubious at first, but Cora pulled the truck up parallel to the front porch steps so they could get in easily. It took some effort to get their long skirts tucked in and the door closed. Once Cora got behind the wheel, she realized she didn't have access to the gearshift on the floor which was buried under Sarah's dress.

"Oh," Sarah said as she pulled up her skirt, turned sideways and plopped her legs in her sister's lap. "How's that?" Laughing like naughty children, Cora drove across the island with the sisters urging her to "go fast, go fast."

When they got to the schoolhouse, they tumbled out of the pickup to go inside and make a proper inspection. The white frame building was one large room with a waist-high divider down the middle. The front of the room contained the teacher's desk, a cast iron stove and two flag stands. It was Sally who pointed out the obvious. "Where are you going to put the magazines?" Clearly there was no simple solution.

They got back into the pickup and Cora started the engine. "We don't want to go home," Sarah said. "We want to see the island," Sally added.

"Where do you want to go?" Cora asked.

They both started talking at once; two voices making up one conversation. "Anywhere. We've haven't been exploring in years. We used to take carriage rides with our gentlemen callers. Sometimes we went to see where the old Harding house was. But there was nothing left but the chimney and some charred wood. We were never allowed to go out on our own.

Papa took us to the beach once when we were little. Can we go to the beach? Oh yes, to the ocean. Can you take us there?"

Their childish enthusiasm touched Cora. She found it impossible to imagine what their lives had been like. There would have been no other families to visit, no young friends, no way to go anywhere unless someone took them.

Although drivable roads were scarce on Ibo, Cora did her best to re-introduce the sisters to the island they had lived on all their lives. They insisted on getting out and walking on the beach. They even took off their shoes and stockings and waded in the water. It was late afternoon by the time they got back to Donegan Hall, but it had been a great day all around.

That night Cora talked to Matt about the situation and Ammee talked to Jacob. Eventually they got together and decided the obvious solution was to add a room to the school. Out of courtesy, they visited the sisters and told them about the plan. Immediately they volunteered to donate the trees to be processed into lumber.

On Sunday, Jacob presented the plans to the church elders. A serious discussion followed and at the end of the service the congregation voted unanimously to help with the building. In typical Geechee fashion, everyone brought their time and their talent to get the job done.

Matt had the lumber delivered along with the necessary hardware. The tin roofing material was also shipped over from the mainland. Ibo men showed up with saws and hammers and every other kind of tool they had on hand. The women brought pots, built fires and cooked gumbo. The children ran errands and carried water to the men as they worked.

Jessie knew of an old post office which was being dismantled and he arranged to have all the open shelves donated. They were perfect for holding stacks of magazines.

The Donegan sisters were busy too. Somehow they managed to go through their collection, weed out the damaged magazines and separate the rest into types and years. Each bundle was tied with heavy twine so the stack could be easily lifted.

On moving day, everyone who had a wagon and a mule showed up to help haul magazines. Jessie drove the Lizzy packed with magazines. Matt drove the pickup and Katie, Robin and Bird rode in the back to make sure no magazines were lost along the way. Miss Lucy Chalmers supervised the moving in. At the end of the day, everyone went home exhausted. Cora and Ammee announced that there would be a formal dedication the following afternoon.

A good night's sleep, a bath and clean clothes transformed the tired, dirty work force into a holiday crowd. Bird had drawn a picture of the last wall going up and Jacob helped him frame it. For his contribution, Jacob carved a sign to put over the door. Donegan Free Library.

Cora, Matt and Katie took the early ferry. Matt dropped the ladies off at Jacob's and went to pick up the sisters. To his surprise, they had abandoned their usual black dresses for something more befitting the occasion. They were resplendent in purple and blue taffeta.

The ceremony was short. The students sang a hymn, "A Charge to Keep I Have," Pastor Goodall said a prayer, Jacob tacked the sign over the door, the Donegan sisters were introduced and received a tremendous round of applause. They accepted Bird's drawing and then the doors were opened and everyone got to go in and see the new library.

Several benches had been carried over from the church so folks could take their time to sit down and look through a magazine. As it turned out, the adults were as fascinated by the variety of publications as the kids. Miss Chalmers explained the checking-out process and made sure that everyone who wanted one went home with a 3 x 5 library card. The Donegan sisters were seated in a place of honor and they accepted praise and thanks like royal benefactors. It was nearly dusk when Matt took the sisters home. "You've done a wonderful thing for the island," he said. "Folks will enjoy the Donegan Free Library for many years to come." They smiled. "And they have done a wonderful thing for us. Who would have thought so much joy could come from a room full of old magazines!"

CHAPTER THIRTEEN

Age changes perspective. A six-year-old boy starting school for the first time may be scared or excited. But from the second grade on, the end of summer comes with a profound sense of sadness and loss shared by all his gender. Where there had been days open to all kinds of possibilities, now their days were structured, monitored, scrutinized and controlled by figures of power and authority.

In the normal scheme of things, Bird and Butch had absolutely nothing in common. But as September and a new school year approached, they both were dreading school. Their lives were being controlled by forces far beyond them. They were being forced to leave their home territory and abandon their normal circle of friends. Butch was going to Georgia Military Academy in Valdosta and Bird was off to the Glynn County Colored School on the mainland for the first time.

Because the Ibo ferry did not have a regular afternoon schedule, Jacob and Ammee made arrangements for their children to board with friends in Meridian. Robin was to stay with the Boone family where she had stayed the previous year and Bird was staying with the Todds who lived just down the street. The arrangement allowed the children to walk to school together each morning.

On the first day of school, Jacob rode the ferry with Robin and Bird. Robin was so excited she couldn't sit still. Bird, on the other hand, loved his life on Ibo surrounded by his Geechee community. He had never had to deal with a stranger. He had never spent a night away from his family. There was no way he could possibly get lost on Ibo. If he got hungry, there were nine other homes where he was welcome to drop by and share a meal. He had already learned how to read, write, do his numbers and draw, so he saw absolutely no reason why he needed to go to school anymore. And on top of that, there might not be anything on the mainland to draw.

He sat close to his father clutching his lunch bag. He also had a sweetgrass basket Granny had made especially for him to hold a few extra school clothes. Before he left the house, Ammee gave him a new tablet and a new pencil, but even those didn't make him feel any better. He was sure the whole enterprise was going to be a disaster.

Butch was equally unhappy. He knew he was being punished, but he wasn't exactly sure why. The shoot-out was a good game and everybody was having fun until Jimmy zigged when he should have zagged. It wasn't like he'd died or anything. "It's totally unfair to ship me off to that stupid school."

With all the kids safely back in school and off the streets, Meridian settled down a little. The fact that Butch was miles away definitely added to the sense of calm and made dealing with the late summer heat and humidity slightly less oppressive.

Bird was pleasantly surprised to find that he liked his new teacher, Miss Tipton, especially when she gave him a box of colored chalk and asked him to draw some pictures on the board and help her decorate the room. Another point in her favor was that she knew about the Harlem Renaissance, although she didn't know about Palmer Hayden. Bird decided to forgive her for that when she offered to help him find a book in the school library about drawing. Maybe he was going to survive after all.

Friday afternoon, Jacob met his kids at school and they all rode home on the ferry together. For once, Bird was the one to monopolize the conversation at supper. He told his parents that Miss Tipton knew about Harlem just like Miss Chalmers. Until then, he had thought Harlem was just something Geechee people knew. And he told them about the great school library. To anyone else, the library would have looked sad indeed, there were so few books.

Ammee and Jacob smiled as Bird chattered on about his first week at the big school. Robin had told them how scared Bird was to leave the safety of Ibo. Rather than make a big deal out of it, they decided to just let it play out and see what happened. Geechee people were, by nature, independent and resourceful. Given some time, his parents were sure Bird would find his way and apparently he had made a good start.

"Miss Tipton found two books for me and helped me get a library card, just like at the Donegan Free Library" Bird said. He was surprised to learn he was allowed to check books out of the school library on the mainland and bring them home over the weekend. Libraries, he decided, were a wonderful invention.

The rest of the weekend, Bird walked around with a book in one hand and his sketch tablet in the other. He studied the pictures carefully trying to figure out how to put more than one thing in a drawing and have everything come out looking normal. It was a lot harder than drawing one thing at a time.

"Miss Tipton said if I wanted to learn more about drawing, she'd stay after school on Friday sometime and help me. It means I'd have to stay over an extra night in town, is that OK?"

Ammee and Jacob had never seen Bird that excited about anything. They quickly gave their consent. Rather than dragging his heels, Bird was up before Robin and ready for school Monday morning.

Butch wasn't having such a good time. He had to sleep in a dormitory with a lot of other boys and he had to wear a uniform with a hat and a *tie*. He thought wearing a tie on Sunday morning was bad, now he had to wear one every day. And the hat! No matter how he put the thing on, it still looked stupid.

He was required to keep his shoes shined, his buttons polished, and his hair cut short. Someone was always telling him what to do. Get up, straighten up, march, pay attention, don't talk, go to bed, get up and do it all over again.

Georgia Military Academy really took the "military" stuff seriously. There were regulations about every little thing. Not only was Butch expected to obey the rules, he was expected to memorize them and be able to quote them word-for-word whenever any upperclassman demanded it.

He still held out hope that he would find kindred spirits among other new boys who were ready to have some fun at the school's expense. But no! Everyone was too afraid of getting demerits and losing privileges. As far as Butch could see the only privilege he had was being allowed to breathe without someone telling him to.

Although Butch was gone, things in Meridian were not exactly running smoothly. Lucile had stepped into the role of town troublemaker. She and Cora had locked horns at a PTA meeting when Cora made a motion to share the high school library with the colored students. Lucile took that as a personal affront and threw a hissy fit. "If they are allowed to take the books home, I'm not at all sure we'd want to put them back on the shelves." Cora took that as an insult to good sense. *Robert's*

Rules of Order went right out the window and in a split second the two of them were in a regular shouting match.

No one was sure why Lucile continued to come to PTA meetings since she no longer had a child attending the high school. Cora pointed that fact out loudly and often during the argument. Lucile threatened to get "my husband, the mayor" involved. No one paid any attention to that threat, because everyone knew Maurice stayed as far away from Lucile's tantrums as possible. Finally the PTA president decided to table the motion and deal with the subject later. Cora just smiled. She hadn't had that much fun at a PTA meeting in a long time.

Having lost that battle, Lucile moved on to other topics. She informed Maurice that she planned to present a petition to the church at Wednesday night prayer meeting. Her idea was to get the church ladies involved and have the local cathouse closed.

Maurice wasted no time in putting the kibosh on that one. "Lucile, do you have any proof that such a thing actually exists? Have any of your friends been complaining that their husbands have been visiting a...house of ill repute? Are they willing to say that publically?"

Looking at it in that light, Lucile decided to drop the idea. The best she could manage was to cross the street whenever she saw Hattie coming. For her part, Hattie never missed an opportunity to approach Lucile in public and speak to her as if the two of them were old friends.

Cora still saw Lucile at the courthouse digging through old records, but since that wasn't against the law, there was nothing she could do about it. "I make it a point to go look over her shoulder whenever I can," she told Matt. "I can't stop her, but at least I can make her uncomfortable." Matt just smiled.

By the time Butch got home at the end of the first month, he was primed for mischief. Friday afternoon he managed to get the whole gang back together. They had been idle in his absence so they were looking forward to whatever adventure Butch proposed.

"Thank goodness I won't have to put up with that military place long. I'm going to graduate this year, and my family's gonna send me away to college next September, if I don't get drafted first. My daddy's talking about getting me a summer job with one of his brothers down in Florida. So we've got to do something now. Something big. Something that folks will remember." The boys waited.

"I've been thinking about this all month and I finally came up with something. We're going to make someone disappear."

"Ahhh that's crazy, Butch. How're we gonna do that?"

Butch explained that he got the idea from a magician who performed at the school in Valdosta. He made his assistant disappear. Butch enjoyed the show, but he couldn't leave well enough alone. He had to know how the trick worked. So he hid out until everyone left the auditorium and then inspected the equipment and the stage.

"The magician didn't really make anybody disappear, he just dropped him through a trap door so he ended up under the stage where nobody could see him. The end of the trick was when the assistant came walking down the aisle. It was great!"

Henry, who was getting a little tired of Butch's craziness, wouldn't let go. "And how are we gonna get somebody on a stage to go through a trap door?"

"Use your imagination, Henry. We don't need a stage. We're gonna really make him disappear, 'cause we're gonna put him on a bus. Now you see him, now you don't. The bus will take him away so nobody can see him, get it? Then the bus will bring him back. I'm telling you, I've worked it all out. I saved enough money to buy a one-way ticket to the end of the line, that's just for show. Then I plan to give the bus driver enough to buy the kid a ticket to get him back from Savannah. We just need to find somebody to be the assistant."

Calvin immediately volunteered.

"No, it can't be any of us. It has to be a stranger."

"Butch, we don't know any strangers." Jimmy said.

Butch had to admit that was the one flaw in his plan. However, he was confident if they talked about it long enough, they'd come up with a solution. The boys spent the next several hours sitting on the pier talking about the plan and working out any details Butch had overlooked. Along about dusk, people started to congregate waiting for the last ferry to Ibo Island.

That's when they saw Bird.

CHAPTER FOURTEEN

The day had started out as most days in the early fall along the southeast coast: cool nights and warm days. It didn't take long for the morning sun to burn off the fog and for the temperature to start rising. To avoid the stuffy little waiting room at the back of the Greyhound Bus Station, several people were standing outside. Right on time, the bus made its scheduled stop at Jacksonville, North Carolina, along Highway 17.

Marine Corporal Leroy Hiram Jones got in line with the other passengers and handed the driver his ticket to New York City. As he walked down the aisle of the bus, Corporal Jones was aware that everyone was looking at him. That was a totally new experience since he grew up in a big family, in a small town. The only time anyone ever noticed him was when he got in trouble and he did that on a regular basis in his early teens.

His mother had always told him fighting was going to be the death of him. In a strange turn of fate, it was fighting that had changed his life. However, for once he wasn't the one to start it. The fight happened half way around the world when the Japanese attacked Pearl Harbor and suddenly the country needed everyone to fight.

114

It had taken Leroy a while to get used to having people notice him. After all, folks had never seen a colored Marine before. Not surprising since there had never *been* black Marines before. His was the first battalion to graduate from Montford Point, a segregated training base at Camp Lejeune, North Carolina.

Leroy held his head up and carried himself with pride. He knew he looked sharp in his form-fitting green and khaki uniform, polished black shoes and shiny black-billed service cap. The five-week training schedule at boot camp had been tough, but he'd been tougher. He knew the Marines were his ticket to a better life and he fought for it. Now he was on furlough to see his family before he boarded a train for Camp Pendleton, California, where he would ship out to the war in the Pacific.

From its beginning, the Marine Corps refused to accept colored recruits. However, in 1941 President Roosevelt created the Fair Employment Practices Commission which changed all that. After Pearl Harbor the choice for young men was basically get drafted or volunteer. And since the new law gave men a choice of the branch of service they wanted, Leroy volunteered for the Marines. In January of 1942, a record 22,600 men enlisted in the armed forces.

At 20, Leroy was slightly older than some of the recruits who had never been away from home and never been on their own before. He tried to help them when he could. Since he had grown up working on his family's small farm in South Carolina, he was used to early rising, long days and hard work. It didn't take him long to realize boot camp was going to be all that and a whole lot more.

The Marines had a few surprises in store, like shots for instance. It seemed to Leroy as if they vaccinated him for every disease known to man. Occasionally someone passed out. Leroy just gritted his teeth and closed his eyes. Shots were bad, but not as bad as what came next. Some guys actually had tears in their eyes when they got their heads shaved.

All of this was just a minor annoyance compared to the endless drills and endless marching. Everyone complained, so Leroy joined in. Although he knew better than to admit it, he liked being part of a group that moved in unison, turned on a dime, and never missed a step. It reminded him of a flock of birds.

Leroy had spent most of his life in cut-offs and old shirts. The marines issued him a uniform and told him exactly how he was expected to wear it. Every time he put it on, he smiled. He'd never been so well dressed. He especially loved his shiny new shoes. He'd never had a pair of new shoes before. He always wore hand-me-downs, if he wore any shoes at all.

In high school, Leroy had been a good student, when he found a subject that interested him. He loved history and he liked math. Everything had a place and numbers didn't change. Two plus two always equaled four no matter who added it up. Military instruction was a lot harder than high school and he had to work hard to stay near the top of his class.

In addition to regular classes, the Marines demanded he learn a whole new language. Some of the words made sense, some were just a collection of letters and some were one thing that meant something totally different. Chest candy for ribbons, made sense. So did fangs for teeth. He quickly learned that a BCD was a bad conduct discharge, something you did not want to get under any circumstances.

Some of the language was even funny. Like ARMY which didn't mean army at all. It meant Ain't Ready to be a Marine Yet. Then there were words like Alpha Charlie which were part of the phonetic alphabet, but really meant getting your ass chewed.

Through it all, Leroy refused to let anything or anybody—including the Drill Sargent—take the edge off his pride, although God knows the man tried. The Drill Instructor made it clear he considered *all* recruits to be worthless, sub-human, lily-livered, pieces of scum and he seriously doubted any of them would ever become Marines. Just to drive the point home, he screamed in their faces, "Back home your immortal souls may belong to Jesus Christ, but as long as you're here, you worthless asses belong to me."

The Marines had rules about everything. In addition to the manual of arms and close order drills, there were tons of naval regulations, customs of the service, military courtesy, VD prevention and those were just the ones written down.

There were more. A lot more. There were also all the traditions passed along by word of mouth. And the Drill Instructor, who spent all his waking hours with the platoon and seemed to be everywhere at once, knew all of them. Nothing—no matter how small—got past him.

Everything was expected to be perfect all the time. Recruits had to carry their rifles everywhere. What started out weighing 8.69 pounds—no generalities for Marines—ended up being a heavy burden. But no one in the platoon dared to complain because the unwritten law was, "Every Marine is first a rifleman."

Leroy was looking forward to "weapons training" because he had been hunting since he was a kid. When the DI asked if anyone had any experience, Leroy spoke up. "Yessir, I think I'm a pretty good shot with a gun." If he had expected to be praised for that, he was in for a surprise.

The DI threw up his hands in disgust. "God in heaven deliver me from idiots! A *gun* is a cannon with a relatively long barrel and a low angle of fire. For you brainless slime balls, I'm gonna put that into language even you can understand. Alright,

117

put your left hand on your cock and your right hand on your weapon. Now look at your right hand and repeat after me, 'This is my rifle,' now your left hand, 'this is my gun. This is for killing, this is for fun.' Have the rest of your numbskulls got that?"

"Yessir!"

"I can't hear you."

"YES SIR!!"

At least Leroy had sense enough to keep his mouth shut when they got to the firing range. The person conducting this training was the PMI, Primary Marksmanship Instructor. He started with the official "Weapons Introduction" during which the boots took their rifles apart, cleaned them and put them back together—repeatedly. They memorized their rifle's serial numbers and learned the Marine Corps four rules of rifle safety.

1. Treat every weapon as if it were loaded.

2. Never point your weapon at anything you do not intend to shoot.

3. Keep your finger straight and off the trigger until you intend to fire.

4. Keep your weapon on safe until you intend to fire.

And one more, just for good measure, "Be absolutely sure of your target and what is behind it."

Again Leroy expected to do well, but he soon discovered he couldn't just shoot something, he had to get into *position* to shoot. The Marines had four standard firing positions: standing, kneeling, sitting and prone. And each one of those was broken down in a zillion specific instructions.

Eventually they came to the actual qualification course. A marksmanship badge required 190 points out of a maximum of 250. To become a sharpshooter required 210 points. Some of the guys didn't qualify at all and were sent back to do the rifle instruction all over. Leroy scored exactly 210 points.

Even with all his good intentions, Leroy was ready to give up on several occasions. There was just too much to learn and too much to un-learn before he could move forward. But little by little his muscles grew stronger, his rifle became his friend, the manual of arms and close order drill became second nature. Without his even noticing, the smart-talking, girl-chasing, trouble-making Leroy Jones of his former high school days, disappeared.

For the graduation parade, the platoons formed one last time. Then the band struck up the Marine's Hymn, and when the standards of the battalion and the platoon dipped and the colonel returned their salute, every man there forgot the sweat and tears and humiliation. It was their moment to bask in the glory and the knowledge that they were now United States Marines, the first Black men in history to have that honor.

Corporal Jones walked down the aisle until he saw a free seat. "Mind if I sit here?" he asked as he put his gear in the overhead rack. "My name's Leroy Jones, what's yours?"

"Bird."

CHAPTER FIFTEEN

Serious readers of slick, quality magazines were unlikely to run across stories of parallel universes. That kind of thing was relegated to the pages of pulp magazines like *Amazing Stories.* Although very few people took the concept seriously, to a certain extent it did exist. People tended to live their lives along a straight line, unaware of what was going on in the lives around them. It was just the natural order of things.

The line of Maurice's life found him and his poker buddies reevaluating the accommodations for their Wednesday nights at Hattie's. In the beginning, it had all been a lark for Maurice, a temporary reprieve from Lucile. However, now he looked at it as a permanent situation and that demanded some changes. As the landlord, he decided what they needed was a separate room just for poker. He knew Hattie would be glad to have her living space to herself. If they installed windows on both sides, they could catch the evening breezes in the summertime and the room would still be cozy in the winter.

He mentioned the idea to Matt and Matt talked to Jacob about the building job. When they went to the house to take measurements, Jacob saw the poker table he had built. Matt smiled sheepishly and explained the Cathouse-Poker-Game scam. Jacob just smiled. That would be a choice piece of mainland gossip to bring home to Ammee.

The work went well and after two weeks, the room was almost finished. Jacob left on Friday afternoon to head home. His plan was to come back the next day and finish up. When he got to the dock, Robin and a group of others were waiting for the ferry. She waved.

Jacob looked around, "Where's Bird?"

"I haven't seen him. I guess he decided to stay over and take Miss Tipton up on her offer to help him with his drawing." Robin secretly hoped Bird wouldn't show up at the last minute. If he stayed in town, that meant she could spend some time alone with her dad, something that hardly ever happened. They made their way to the top deck of the ferry.

On the ride home, Robin asked her dad about his day, which she thought was a very grownup thing to do. Then they talked about her day, how she was doing at school and how she liked her teachers. In an effort to keep the adult conversation going, Robin said, "Bird's got some of his pictures hanging in the hall at school. I guess Miss Tipton put 'em there. You reckon Bird's gonna be famous some day?"

"I don't know about that, but it's good to see him coming out of his shell a little. He's always been the quiet one."

"Yeah, not like me, huh?"

"No, not like you," Jacob patted her knee. "What is it Granny calls you? Miss Nosey Britches?" They laughed easily and when the ferry docked, they joined friends and neighbors all anxious to get home after a long work week. Robin took Jacob's hand and he smiled down at her. Jacob loved his children, but he rarely had time to show it. Not for the first time he thought, "Jacob Hamlin, you're a lucky man."

121

When Ammee asked where Bird was, Robin reminded her that Bird had said he might stay over to work with his teacher. Having settled that, they sat down to supper. Saturday morning Jacob took the ferry to the mainland and caught a ride over to Hattie's to finish up and put a coat of paint on the room. Hattie made sandwiches and brought out a pitcher of lemonade for lunch. She asked about his family and finally realized that the Ammee Cora talked about was Jacob's wife. She recognized the description of Robin, but couldn't place Bird until Jacob mentioned his drawing.

"Oh, now I know who you're talking about. I've seen him around town, always with a pencil and a pad of paper. I used to dabble with watercolors a long time ago. I might still have some paper and brushes around here. Bird is welcome to them…if I can find them."

The first stop on Jacob's way home was the school. He had hoped to find Bird in the library, but instead he found Miss Tipton. He introduced himself and the teacher was quick to praise Bird's talent. When Jacob asked about working with Bird on Friday afternoon, she seemed surprised. "I haven't seen Bird since he left school at the regular time yesterday. Didn't he meet you at the ferry?"

Jacob felt a little stab of fear, but he pushed it to the back of his mind.

Miss Tipton saw his reaction and quickly added, "I did give him some drawing exercises to do, and some books to take home, maybe he stayed over at the Todd's house to work on those." That was Jacob's next stop. The Todds were sorry but, they hadn't seen Bird either.

"Maybe he stopped to draw something after school. You know how he just loses himself sometime," Mrs. Todd said.

Mr. Todd seemed anxious to help. "I'm thinkin' he mighta' slipped into his room late, he's got a door back there. If he did that, we wouldn't have seen him. He could have taken the early ferry back to Ibo this mornin'. Maybe y'all crossed paths and didn't even know it."

To save time, Mr. Todd drove Jacob to the dock to see if a mid-day ferry was running. They were lucky and Jacob made it just as the last passengers were loading. Rather than go to the upper deck where he would surely run into friends, Jacob sat in an inconspicuous corner downstairs. He forced himself to be still, to stop his mind from racing to dangerous places. "Just slow down and think it through. Don't go gettin' crazy about somethin' that hasn't happened yet."

Bird wasn't anywhere he was supposed to be. But there was no indication he was in any kind of trouble. If he had somehow missed the last ferry, then he would have made sure to catch the first ferry Saturday morning. "I didn't pay any attention to who got off, I guess I could have missed him. He's gotta be on Ibo, that's the only thing that makes sense," Jacob told himself. Although he tried to convince himself that was true, he knew in his heart if Bird had gotten off the early ferry, he would have seen him. Jacob felt another stab of fear. Rather than calm him down as it usually did, the 20-minute ferry ride seemed to take hours.

When he reached the island, Jacob hesitated. His first instinct was to walk home like he always did, but if Bird wasn't there, he didn't want to alarm Ammee. He also didn't want to waste time, if... "No, don't get ahead of yourself," he thought. "Like Matt always says, 'Just take it one step at a time.' Get the truck and drive around. You know all Bird's favorite places, check those out first."

Jacob drove slowly, scanning the roadsides. Unfortunately most of the sandy roads were just tunnels through briars, brambles and low-growing palmetto plants. A grown man standing three feet off the road would be totally invisible.

123

There were, of course, the rivers and the marshes, but searching them would require a boat. Jacob dismissed that idea because so far as he knew, no one had ever drowned on Ibo. Water, like fire, was taken very seriously. And besides, Bird liked walking on the sandy beach, but he did not like the ocean waves or wading in the river feeling mud between his toes. "No, water is just a waste of time."

Eventually Jacob ended up at Granny's. He talked to her long enough to find out she hadn't seen Bird in several days. Although it was a long shot, Jacob also stopped in to see the Donegan sisters. They were pleased to see him, and sent their good wishes to Ammee, but clearly they didn't know anything about Bird either.

Finally, he went home hoping and praying to see Bird sitting in front of The Store with his pad and pencil. He was not there. Jacob squared his shoulders and quietly asked Robin and Ammee to sit down with him in the kitchen. When he took her hand, Ammee knew something was terribly wrong. As gently as he could, he told them what he knew or more to the point, what he didn't know. He tried to keep his voice even, not to let the fear he felt show. He kept telling himself there had to be an answer, people didn't just disappear.

"I checked every place on the island where he might be, but I didn't find anything. Since there's nobody official over here to help, I think I ought to go back to the mainland, talk to Matt and get him to go with me to see Sheriff Mayhew. He'll know what to do next."

At the mention of the sheriff, Ammee started to cry. Not sobbing, that was not her nature, but tears ran down her face as she turned to Jacob. "I don't understand. Bird would never run away. He didn't even like staying on the mainland to go to school. He's just a little boy, Jacob, and you're telling me he's lost! How could that happen?"

Robin put her arms around her mother. "Don't worry, Mama, Bird's smart. He'll be OK and we'll find him, won't we, Dad?"

Jacob was not usually a praying man, but he prayed Robin was right. "I'll go down to the dock and take the late ferry back to Meridian." On his way, Jacob stopped by to see Chief. He explained that Bird was missing asked the older man to keep his eyes open when he went out fishing that night. Chief offered to take Jacob to the mainland in his boat, but he refused. "I have no idea how long I'll need to stay. Chief, I think you can help more here on Ibo. Tomorrow's Sunday and when the church hears what's going on, there's gonna be a search. They'll need somebody to take charge."

"You do what you need to do over there, son, and try not to worry. I'll get everybody organized back here." He watched sadly as Jacob headed for the dock.

Chief was actually Ezra Cathy. Folks on Ibo gave him the nickname because he had served in the 25th Infantry and been wounded in World War I. He was a tall man—well over six feet—with dark skin. His injury caused him to walk with a limp and regular canes were too short to give him any support. Jacob solved the problem by carving a special piece of heart pine into a staff as tall as Ezra. Striding around Ibo he looked like a cross between an African chief and a Biblical prophet.

Ammee had wanted to go to the mainland with Jacob but he pointed out that Bird could easily just come home on his own and she would need to be there in case that happened. After Jacob left, Ammee started to fix supper. Robin stopped her. "Mama, you don't need to do that. I'm not hungry."

"I know. I just need to keep busy. I can't just stand here wondering where Bird is."

"What we oughta do is go see Granny and tell her what's happened," Robin said. "Then we oughta go see Dr. Buzzard.

I'll write a note and leave it in the middle of the table. That way if Bird comes home, he'll know where we are."

The old folks on Ibo said the original Dr. Buzzard was a root doctor who came from Africa through the Middle Passage with the first captives. He was known to be a conjurer. He was a strong man, a patient man, characteristics common to a buzzard and everyone knows buzzards are a necessary part of life. So, they called him Dr. Buzzard and the name had been passed down through the generations.

Having somewhere to go and something helpful to do, made both Ammee and Robin feel better. They set out for Granny's right away. They found her sitting on the front porch, her strong hands working on a sweetgrass basket. One look at their faces told Granny something was wrong. As soon as they explained the situation to her, she agreed their best bet was Dr. Buzzard. Of course, they would testify at church the following morning, but right now there wasn't a moment to waste.

Dr. Buzzard lived in an old tabby house about half way between Granny's and the school. He invited them in and offered cups of a concoction he was drinking out of a fruit jar. They knew better than to refuse. Whatever it was, it tasted like sweet tea, but with a kick that probably came from a generous addition of moonshine. He settled back in his rocking chair and listened to their story. His first question was who might have worked a root on Bird.

"If you give me the name of the black-hearted person who put a spell on that child, I can lift that spell off Bird and he'll be home for supper. Even better, I can turn that spell around and throw it back on the one who is trying to hurt your boy."

Unfortunately, they didn't know of anyone who would want to hurt Bird. "You may not know who it is yet, but you will. 'Cause somebody done worked a powerful bad root on that boy and that kind of black magic will not stay hid for long.

When you find out who did it, you come see me and I'll take care of him.

"In the meantime, what you need is some good root, some white magic, which I can also do. Wherever Bird is, there are things you can do right here to keep him safe." Dr. Buzzard went into another room and came back to the front room with three pieces of burlap and some black string.

"Now I'm gonna make an amulet for each of you to wear, but you gotta help me build it. Bring me some of Bird's hair or a fingernail or some toenail clippings. Bring me three handfuls of gopher dust. Make sure you gather that graveyard dust from a spot just above the dead person's heart and dig it up right at midnight. The magic would be stronger if you gathered it at the full moon, but we ain't got no time to wait for that now. Then find me something Bird loved. Go on now, get a move on. We gotta get this spell working *tonight.*"

CHAPTER SIXTEEN

While the women were busy on the island, Jacob sat on the ferry feeling fear and sorrow as heavy and cold as the chains that had bound his ancestors. He tried to keep his fear in check and work out a plan. But to do that, he had to admit that Bird might actually be gone and he simply could not make himself deal with the reality of that thought.

Jacob had heard Granny Johnson's stories of the Middle Passage and the fear and sorrow his people felt being snatched from their homes and taken God only knew where. Up until now, they had just been stories, nothing that actually touched his life. Now he felt it in his bones.

As soon as the ferry docked, Jacob headed to Matt's house. Unlike on Ibo where someone was always willing to help out, Jacob knew it was unlikely anyone would stop to offer him a ride. As he walked along, he couldn't help but look down every street and into every alley. "Bird, wherever you are, be smart, son. The world can be a dangerous place."

Jacob hesitated a moment, then knocked on the Reeve's door. Matt was clearly surprised to see him standing on his doorstep. The minute he saw his face, Matt knew something was wrong. Cora met them in the hall and while Matt led Jacob into the living room, Cora hurried into the kitchen to get him a cup of coffee. "Jacob, what's going on? Has someone been hurt?"

Jacob poured out the story about Bird. "We don't have police on Ibo. I've been everywhere I know to go. Nobody's seen him, nobody knows anything. He's just...gone."

Matt thanked his lucky stars that Katie was safely asleep upstairs. He knew how he would feel if anything happened to her and his heart went out to Jacob. "Listen, you've done the right thing to come here as soon as possible. First thing we're going to do is call Sheriff Mayhew. He's probably still at his office and there might be something he can do right away."

For the first time since he realized Bird was gone, Jacob breathed a little easier. Matt was a good friend and he would know how to get things organized on the mainland. Suddenly, Jacob was hungry. In his hurry to search for Bird, he hadn't thought about food all day. In the way that women have of sizing up a situation, Cora guessed that might be the case. "We just finished supper. I've got some ham, black-eyed peas and corn bread, can I fix something for you?" Jacob gladly accepted.

While Matt went to call the sheriff, Cora set a place for Jacob at the kitchen table, heated up the leftovers and they sat down together. "How are Ammee and Robin? Is there anything I can do for them?"

"They're scared, but Granny's there and the church folks are helping out. There's a chance Bird might just come home so when I left, they were...they were just waiting." Jacob suspected they would probably do a lot more than that, but he didn't want to mention Dr. Buzzard.

It was about 2:00 in the morning when Ammee, Robin and Granny returned with the necessary ingredients for Dr. Buzzard. He placed leaves and bark and what looked like tiny, white

129

bones on each of the burlap squares. He added the gopher dust, some of Bird's hair and pieces of one of Bird's pictures. When that was done, he lit a candle, blew the smoke around and spoke an incantation or two in his magic, secret language. Finally he tied the pouches with the black string.

"Wear these around your necks and do not take them off until Bird comes home. Now there's one more thing to do." He handed each of them what looked like a small ball of mud. "You put this under your pillow every night and it's gonna open up your dreams so that Bird can come in. First thing when you wake up, write everything down. When he comes to you, you tell me what you dreamed and I'll tell you what it means."

Just in case Bird might have come back, Granny walked home with Ammee and Robin. It was 3:00 before they got back. No need to go to bed, so they just napped sitting up. Day clean signaled the birds which started up their early morning chirping and calling to one another. Ammee wanted to scream. How could they sing as if nothing were wrong? She tried to drown them out with her usual distraction of slamming pots and pans around as she fried bacon and made biscuits. They ate in a hurry and headed out through the early morning fog in order to get to the church before anyone else. They needed to ring the bell.

Without telephones, the church bell was used for quick communication. The ring for death and the one for disaster were different from the normal bell to call people to church. The toll for disaster was loud and sharp, that sounded like hurry, hurry, hurry. It was Communion Sunday so everybody would probably be at church anyway, but they were taking no chances.

When the congregation gathered, Brother Solomon called on Granny to testify about Bird. She explained that he had been missing since sometime on Friday and that Jacob had gone to the mainland to make an official report.

The Blessed Zion Prayer Group immediately called for nightly meetings to pray for Bird until his return. As president of the men's Brotherhood, Chief took charge of the search group. He sent some men to search the land while he organized every man who had a boat to cover the rivers and the marsh areas.

The church community wrapped their arms around the Hamlin family to offer whatever support they could. Although no one asked, it was assumed the family had already contacted Dr. Buzzard.

Matt and Jacob were doing all they could in Meridian. Matt finally reached Sheriff Mayhew at home. Although there wasn't much he could do officially that late on a Saturday, he instructed his deputy to make some extra trips around town and to keep a sharp eye out. He also promised to meet Matt and Jacob at his office early Sunday morning to get some information and organize a search.

"I imagine Ammee will be talking to the church on Ibo, but we need to get the churches over here involved too," Cora said. "Matt can speak to Maurice, he's a deacon at First Baptist, and ask him to speak to the congregation. It couldn't hurt to have the mayor on our side. Do you know anyone at the black churches here?"

Jacob said he had done work for both the Goodwill Baptist Church and the AME, African Methodist Episcopal Church. He planned to talk to those pastors and he was sure they would help spread the word.

"I'll give Hattie a call too," Cora said with a slight smile. "Not everybody goes to church, you know."

Having a plan of action and a full stomach made Jacob feel slightly better. Cora offered him their extra bedroom, but he declined. "I think I'll stay where Bird's been staying at the

Todd's. There's a back door into his room so I can go there without disturbing the family. That way if he comes back..."

Cora smiled. "I think that's a good idea, Jacob. Being around Bird's things may help you sleep. Tomorrow is going to be a long day for everyone."

Matt gave Jacob a ride to the Todd's house. The lights in the front of the house were all on, so Jacob knocked on the door, told them there was still no word about Bird and asked if he could use the room for the night. They were more than happy to have him stay. He thanked Matt for his help and said he'd be ready whenever Matt wanted to pick him up the next morning. Then he walked around the back of the house and opened the outside door to Bird's room.

He closed his eyes and turned on the light hoping beyond hope that Bird would be there when he opened them, but all he saw was an empty room. Bird's sketches covered one whole wall. Jacob recognized most of the people. Granny with her baskets, Robin and her fishing net, Cora working in her garden, there was even one of him building something. He smiled although there were tears in his eyes.

Dark, heavy thoughts started to fill his mind but he fought to keep them away. He was exhausted, but he was afraid to fall asleep because then he wouldn't be able to control his fear. He kicked off his shoes, lay down on Bird's narrow bed and picked up the book lying on the bedside table. It was a book of poetry by Harlem writers.

A soft knock on the door woke him at 6:30 the next morning. Elsie Todd said she was fixing breakfast and had made plenty to share. Jacob realized he had slept peacefully for several hours. Maybe Cora was right, maybe Bird had been looking out for him while he was asleep.

About an hour later, Matt came by and they headed down to meet the sheriff at his office. The deputy had turned in his report from the night before. No sign of Bird. Jacob provided the information the sheriff needed to file an official missing-persons report. He asked for a picture of Bird, but there wasn't one. Unfortunately Jacob didn't even know what his son had been wearing when he was last seen. The sheriff planned to get the missing-persons report out to neighboring towns, but he decided to hold off on that until they had a little more information.

Next the sheriff had Jacob write down a list of anyone Bird might have come in contact with on the mainland. Other than his teacher, the Todd's, the Boone family where Robin stayed and Matt's family, Jacob couldn't think of anyone else. Because the sheriff would be visiting and asking questions on Ibo, he asked for a list there too. Jacob hesitated. "Sheriff, everybody on Ibo knows Bird. You might want to start with Ezra Cathy, the one we call Chief. Bird likes to spend time talking to him and there's his teacher, Lucy Chalmers. Other than that, it's hard to say."

"What about the churches?" the sheriff asked. Matt said they had already discussed that. He would talk to Maurice at First Baptist, and Jacob would visit the black churches. The sheriff was a member of First Methodist and he volunteered to speak to them and his deputy said he'd take care of the Pentecostal church.

And so the search for Bird Hamlin began. Everyone on Ibo turned out. By contrast, hardly anyone in Meridian recognized his name and there was little physical description other than "a little colored boy, usually seen carrying a pad of drawing paper." It wasn't much to go on. Butch's gang was late coming into church, so they missed the announcement all together and Butch was far away in Valdosta.

133

CHAPTER SEVENTEEN

On Monday morning Jacob and Matt went with Sheriff Mayhew on his rounds. That way they'd all get the same information and avoid having to repeat everything three times. First they went back to the Todds because Sheriff Mayhew needed to establish a time line. They learned that Bird got up, ate breakfast and left for school at the regular time about 7:15. He was wearing his favorite red and blue shirt and a pair of old khaki pants. They hadn't seen him since.

The next stop was the Boones. They had seen Bird when he came by to get Robin and the two of them left for school together about 7:30. They hadn't seen him since.

The men spent about fifteen minutes with Bird's teacher, Miss Tipton, before school started. Bird had been in school all day, nothing unusual there.

"Was there anything different or unusual in Bird's behavior lately?" the sheriff asked.

Miss Tipton thought for a moment. "As I'm sure you know, Bird is very quiet, very shy. He never raises his hand even when I'm sure he knows the answer. He just doesn't speak up in class."

She cleared her throat and continued hesitantly. "The only time I ever remember him asking questions was when I talked about the Harlem Renaissance." She started to explain what that was, but thought better of the idea. "It's just a little thing and I don't know if that's helpful at all, but it's the only thing I can think of."

"Did he stay after school on Friday to work with you?"

"No. I did suggest some exercises he could do on his own and I gave him a book about drawing and a book of poetry by some Harlem writers. That's all. I haven't seen him since."

Jacob remembered Bird talking about Harlem at home and he wondered if that was important enough to mention. They stopped by the sheriff's office and they added what little new information they had gathered to the missing-persons report. That done, Sheriff Mayhew instructed the deputy to get the word out to all the towns in a 50-mile radius. Then they took "Beelzeboat," the sheriff's outboard that doubled as the police boat, and headed out to Ibo Island.

Although Bird wasn't in school there any longer, they made a point of talking to Miss Lucy Chalmers who had known Bird most of his life. She simply confirmed what Miss Tipton had said. Bird was a good student, but quiet and shy. She pointed out some of his drawings which were still hanging on the wall. They were just about to leave when she stopped them.

"You know there was one thing that seemed to catch his interest. I lived in Harlem for a while a long time ago and I was telling the class some stories about that. I told them about the Apollo Theatre and the Harlem Renaissance. When I mentioned an artist named Palmer Hayden, Bird really perked up. I think he was surprised to find out that Hayden had grown up in Virginia. Bird seemed to identify with that. He was really curious. I told the class the year Hayden was born and we figured out he would be 52 years old now. I said as far as I knew he was still living and working in Harlem."

"Sheriff, I remember Bird talking about all of that at supper one night," Jacob said. "Robin's usually the chatterbox, but Bird was talking a blue streak. You think that's important?"

"Could be. Do y'all have any relatives up there in New York?"

"Nosir. All our folks live right around here or over in Alabama."

"What about you, Matt? Any connection to New York that Bird might have picked up from Katie?"

"Not on my side and not on Cora's either as far as I know."

Their next stop on Ibo was Granny. She listened as they related what they had found out, but she had nothing to add. Their final stop was the Donegan sisters. Jacob had told them about Bird, so the sheriff decided to use that as an excuse to make a courtesy call on the old ladies to see how they were doing.

As usual they took turns speaking. "We are so glad you decided to drop by. We have been thinking about Master Bird ever since you told us he was missing. Sister and I would like to offer a reward. Isn't that what they do in cases like this? We were thinking of $100. Do you think that would be enough to help find him?" The sheriff assured the sisters that the amount was certainly generous, that he would circulate that information along with the missing-person report.

The men went by to share what they knew with Ammee before Matt and the sheriff headed back to the mainland. Jacob and Ammee watched them go. Neither of them moved. Ammee didn't want to go back into the house because everywhere she looked, everything she saw reminded her of Bird. The slow gentle life Jacob had always counted on was gone. He wouldn't allow himself to think that Bird might not ever come home, but he did know that no matter what happened, his life would never be the same.

That night they set up a makeshift table under the big oak tree and ate supper outside. It was easier than looking at Bird's empty chair. Robin had seen her dad, Matt and the sheriff talking to Miss Tipton at school and of course she wanted to know what they had found out. Jacob repeated what little they had learned and she broke into a big smile.

"That's it! I know where Bird is! He's up there on Harlem Island looking for that artist man. He told me he wanted to go. Said he wanted to meet that man. Wanted to be just like him. I know it! That's where he's gone."

Ammee and Jacob were so shocked it took them a minute to respond. "Robin, that's impossible. Bird would never run away and besides, how in the world do you think he'd get to Harlem?"

"He flew! Just like in Granny's old stories. Africans can fly. They didn't want to be here, so they flew back to Africa. Bird wanted to be in Harlem, so he flew up there." She set down her fork. "I gotta go tell Granny. I'll be right back!" Before they could react, she was gone.

There is nothing like coming face to face with the innocent faith of a child to make you re-evaluate your own beliefs. When Robin had questioned Granny's stories, Ammee remembered telling her about Elijah and Ezekiel. In fact she remembered saying, "There are some things you just have to take on faith." She looked at Jacob.

He looked a little uncomfortable because he remembered the same conversation. He specifically remembered saying it was a lot easier to believe someone flew away than that they just disappeared. So now what? Did they believe or not?

Robin and Granny had no such conflict of faith. Bird had flown away. Their amulets from Dr. Buzzard were keeping him safe and when he got ready, then he'd fly right back. In the meantime, they visited Dr. Buzzard again to share the good news and see if there was anything else they needed to do. Dr. Buzzard questioned them about their dreams. Granny recited hers, but nothing seemed helpful. "I got one," Robin said. "One night I dreamed Bird was in a boat all by himself. You know that picture in the big Bible, the one with all the people trying to climb into the ark during Noah's flood? Well, it was kinda like that, only the people were just floating. Nobody was scared or anything. Reckon that means anything?"

"Yes indeed. It tells us where to look for signs! That's what we got to do now. Search out the signs. Get my Bible and bring it over here to me." Dr. Buzzard went through his usual ritual of lighting a candle, blowing smoke over the book, reciting the secret incantation and letting the Bible fall open. Then he closed his eyes, and ran his finger down the page until it stopped. Then he opened his eyes and began to read. "And Jacob dwelt in the land wherein his father was a stranger..." He looked up, "Jacob! That's your father's name so we know we're on the right track. Yessir, the white root is workin'. This is a story about Jacob and his son."

Robin and Granny moved closer to see where Dr. Buzzard was reading. Genesis, Chapter 37. "Now he loved his son Joseph more than all his children because he was the son of his old age and he made him a coat of many colors. Do you remember that story?"

Robin and Granny nodded. "Do you remember what happened to Joseph?"

"His brothers were jealous and they sold him to some men in a camel caravan and they took him away."

"Yes, that is another sign. They took him away. Was he wearing his coat of many colors?"

"Yeah, his favorite red and blue one," Robin said.

"Good, good. The signs are getting stronger. Now, do you remember where Joseph went? I'll tell you. 'They took him to a great city that thronged with people.' That is the third sign, a great city thronged with people. When you get three signs together, that's powerful strong root and it's leadin' us along a straight and narrow path. Do you remember how the story ends?"

Granny spoke up. "Joseph stays gone a lot of years and lots of things happen but in the end he gets his family back together and everybody lives happily ever after...or something like that."

"That's close enough. Because that is the final sign. He is re-united with his family." Dr. Buzzard closed the Bible and sat back not only pleased with himself but a trifle surprised that things had actually fallen into place.

Granny and Robin wasted no time in reporting all these signs to Jacob and Ammee. "Bird's been taken away, he had on his coat of many colors, he's in a big city with lots of people, we've got some white root that's helpin' to keep him safe and he's gonna come back some day. Dr. Buzzard used the Bible to prove it, so it's gotta be true. We just have to wait until the time is right."

With the kind of faith that neither Ammee nor Jacob truly understood, Granny and Robin stopped worrying about Bird. He was just away and he would come back. For his parents, waiting was a torment. It was the little things that hurt the most. Seeing his empty shoes by the back door. Waiting for him at the ferry only to realize he wasn't coming. For his part, Jacob touched base with the sheriff every other day and kept his eyes open wherever his building jobs took him.

Cora needed someone to talk to, so she called Hattie. Although she wasn't family or a long-time friend of the Hamlin family, it was Hattie who came up with something she thought might help Ammee. She went by the town library and checked out some books. When Cora made her usual visit to Ibo, Hattie went along and they went to see Ammee.

"Cora told me about Robin and Dr. Buzzard. Now I'm not saying he's right or wrong, but I thought it might help to find out a little more about Harlem. It's definitely part of a great city thronged with people. It's a long shot, but you never know. The library didn't have much, but I checked out everything I could find so you could look at it later." With that she put a small pile of books on the kitchen table.

"In a nutshell, here's the story. Harlem is a lot older than most places around here. The Dutch started it in 1658. For a while it was mostly Jewish but now it's mostly colored. The Harlem Renaissance that the teacher talked about happened in the 1920s and '30s. Today about 200,000 people live there."

Ammee looked stricken. "I don't know how to think about a number that big. How many people is that?"

"About twice as many as live in Savanah," Hattie said before she realized that wasn't helping the situation any. "I know it sounds like a lot, but why don't you think about Harlem as a great big Geechee community."

"I was trying to feel better about all of this, like Robin and Granny are doing," Ammee said, "but now—oh Lord—if Bird *is* there, it's gonna take a miracle to bring him home."

CHAPTER EIGHTEEN

As usual Lucile paid little or no attention to anything that didn't directly involve her. She realized some child from Ibo had been missing for a while and she vaguely remembered hearing something about a search, but that had nothing to do with her. She was much more concerned with her own search.

Since Maurice's mishandling of the Donegan sisters, Lucile had decided to take matters into her own hands. She was convinced it was only a matter of time before some rich investors discovered Georgia's barrier islands and when they did, she was determined to be ready. One way or another, she was going to own land on Ibo.

She had spent days and weeks at the courthouse going through old land deeds and tax records looking for property that was in arrears. On the pretense of doing work for the Women's Missionary Union of the Baptist church, she had convinced the sheriff to let her search records for stills in operation on Ibo. She seemed to remember reading that anyone arrested for making or selling moonshine could have their property taken away. She found nothing.

So she went back to the courthouse. The files were always kept in the most uncomfortable rooms. They were dark and dusty. In the summer they held the heat. Lucile had thought about bringing in an electric fan, but that would have attracted too much attention. So through the summer she worked and sweated and Lucile *hated* to sweat. She prided herself on being able to stay cool and dry even on the hottest days. Only common people sweated and Lucile knew in her heart she was not common.

It was now getting colder and the rooms were clammy. As usual, everything conspired to make Lucile's life miserable. However, like a prospector with a serious case of gold fever, Lucile couldn't give up the search. There was too much at stake.

Why couldn't people just leave her alone? But no, it turned out that Cora Reeve worked part time at the courthouse and she seemed to be everywhere. Lucile was forced to smile and be pleasant and to invent reasons why she kept coming back. But the straw that broke the camel's back was when that Hattie woman from down in the swamps showed up. Lucile couldn't bring herself to even nod in her direction. People like that shouldn't be allowed in the courthouse. It just wasn't right.

Finally Lucile had to admit she was getting nowhere. She needed to try a new approach. She needed something specific, maybe a name. On her next trip to Savannah, she decided to visit Armstrong State College, on the off chance that they might have documents about the early history of Ibo. As she walked around the campus she looked with envy at the young girls in their plaid skirts, bobby sox and penny loafers. She remembered pretty dresses and tea dances. Oh, she had had such dreams at that age.

Well, she still had dreams and the determination to make them come true. As her mother often said, "There's more than one way to skin a cat." Rather than continue searching through court records, Lucile decided to start at the beginning, concentrate on the planters who first came to Ibo and see what turned up. That's when she hit the mother lode. Journals from 1805 to 1865 written by Roberta Harding, the wife of Caleb Harding one of the original owners of the island.

At first the entries were useless as far as Lucile was concerned. She did learn that Roberta was only 19 in 1805 when Caleb brought her to Ibo Island. She and Caleb had been married for two years during which she had lived with his parents in Philadelphia while he lived on Ibo building a house and getting ready for her arrival.

There was an early mention of Patrick Donegan and a trip he made from his home on St. Simons Island to Philadelphia where he met Caleb. Patrick, who Roberta always referred to as Mr. Donegan, already had a reputation as a "knowledgeable and inventive planter." Lucile assumed he was older than Caleb who was only 22.

Roberta's entries included facts about the work done to clear the swamps and how and where rice, cotton and indigo were planted. If there was information about money invested, money spent or money owed, Lucile made a note of that. She had expected Roberta's personal life to be boring, but she had to admit some of the entries were better than *Our Gal Sunday* or her other radio soap operas.

"I am lucky to have a kind husband who talks to me about the running of the plantation. For this I am truly thankful, for other than Maude Donegan, there are no other white women on the island. Unfortunately she lives a good distance from here and because I do not ride nor know how to manage a horse and carriage, I must rely on someone else for transportation.

"It is just as well, because I do not like visiting Donegan Hall. Mrs. Donegan is ten years my senior. She is a rather plain woman, stern in her bearing. I do not believe she likes me, although I can think of nothing I have done to give her offence.

In truth there is another reason. She has two small children and another on the way, while I remain childless."

Lucile smiled. So there was trouble in paradise from the start. Clearly Maude was jealous of the young, pretty wife of her husband's partner. Well, no surprise there. Lucile continued reading until another entry caught her eye.

"I do so miss Philadelphia. There is *nothing* to do here. Our slaves take care of the house and the garden. We have a library, but very few books...and I have read them all. I have done enough embroidery and cross stitch to adorn every surface in the house.

"I have a personal servant whose given name is Bessie. She was 12 years old when she was brought here on the *Windward* and she took Harding as her sur name. She is now 15 and follows me everywhere, however, she does not provide any company, for she rarely speaks. Today I was determined to engage her in conversation, so I began asking questions. At first she was reluctant to reply, but eventually she told me about her husband Calvin Johnson and the Geechee community on the island. When I asked her to spell the name, she could not for she is illiterate. Having little else to occupy my mind, I set myself the task of teaching her to read and write."

Lucile stopped. "I wonder if she knew that was strictly against the law? I wonder if she would have done it anyway?" Lucile read on. Apparently Bessie was a good student because Roberta describes teaching her not only to read and write but the basics of arithmetic, as well. She also taught her how to play cards and over time the two girls became close friends.

The teaching did not all go in one direction. Bessie taught Roberta about Geechee traditions, home remedies and folk tales. She even taught her some phrases in the Geechee language. "*See um da*, meant 'see it there.' *Bring em yah*, meant 'bring it here.' *Who pa you?* Who's your dad? *E been dam dead.* He's been dead a while. *Bacca chunk* was the big log at the back of the fireplace and *day clean* was daybreak."

Within the first year, Bessie gave birth to her first daughter, Sarah. To celebrate, Roberta gave both mother and child a ten-dollar gold piece. "Men can make their own way in this world alone, but we women sometimes need help. I told her to keep the money hidden away, because there might come a time when it would be her salvation. It is my intention, God willing, to make a similar gift to Sarah's first-born daughter and, if I am able, to each generation of girls."

Roberta was as good as her word. As a way to honor the gift and their friendship, Bessie demanded that as her daughters married, they keep the name Harding and add their husbands' sur name. According to a list slipped into the back of the journal, Bessie Harding Johnson begat Sarah Harding Davis, who begat Jasmine Harding Collier, who begat Rebecca Harding Collier who was five years old at the end of the Civil War. The boy's births went unmarked and unrecorded. Lucile jotted down the girls' names just in case they might be useful later on.

With minor setbacks, the next 55 years were the golden era for life on Ibo. The partnership between Harding and Donegan prospered. Patrick Donegan became a leader among the tidewater planters. In addition to having a knack for growing crops, he was also an amateur architect and a very good businessman with holdings not only on the island, but on the mainland and even in Philadelphia. While Patrick traveled, Caleb was in charge of the enterprises on Ibo.

In 1824 a strong hurricane hit the island causing tremendous flooding. A lot of the old wooden buildings were washed away. The rice and cotton crops were destroyed, but the sugar cane growing farther inland survived. Prompted by the storm damage, the partners went back to using tabby. The oyster shells, lime, sand and water were plentiful and when hardened they were as strong and heavy as concrete. Tabby was inexpensive and construction could be done by unskilled labor, rather than expensive carpenters using milled lumber. It was the best building material to withstand heat, humidity and hurricanes.

To further expand their wealth, Donegan and Harding built a small sawmill for use on the island and sold local timber which was resistant to disease and decay. It was ideal for maritime purposes. The yellow pines were used for masts and the natural curve of the live oaks along with the tree's weight and density also made it ideal for shipbuilding.

It seemed everything the partners put their hands to turned to gold. They truly had the Midas touch. Ibo Island became the site of sumptuous dinners, lavish lawn parties and holiday celebrations that drew guests from all over the tidewater area and from as far away as New Orleans and Philadelphia.

When Lucile read Roberta's account of this period of her life, she couldn't help but think of *Gone with the Wind*. She had read all 1037 pages twice and even persuaded Maurice to drive to Atlanta for the premier. Lucile was bereft. She couldn't decide whether she had been born too early or too late. Either way she knew she was destined for better things.

Then on April 12, 1861 Confederate troops fired on Fort Sumter. The Civil War began and life as Roberta had known it started to fall apart. There were crop failures, the price of cotton dropped, buyers now bought rice cheaper from Arkansas and Louisiana. Roberta noted these things but did not elaborate. Then this entry.

"We are now in the third year of this bloody war. There is much talk of freeing the slaves, which will surely be the end of us. I have copied the following article from the *Savannah Republican* dated January 1, 1863. 'As of this day, President

Abraham Lincoln issued the Emancipation Proclamation which declares that all persons held as slaves within the rebellious states are, and henceforward shall be free.'

"While the war still rages, my dear Caleb has decided to take action. He has vowed that none of our people, which number about 100, will be subject to the whims of any government. To that end, he has called a meeting of the Geechee community in what they call the praise house. I am to accompany him as this is a decision we made together.

"Caleb's message to those assembled was that although the Emancipation Proclamation officially made them free, the situation might arise when they would be called upon to produce written proof. Therefore he drafted and signed a letter for every man, woman and child on our land stating that by his hand and with his blessing they were free and therefore belonged to no man. He urged them to guard those letters with their lives."

Lucile skimmed through the next several entries. It took two more years to end the fighting and by that time Caleb was a broken man. When word reached the island that General Lee had surrendered, so did Caleb. He settled his debts and made plans to abandon Ibo. Roberta had made one final entry.

"I am leaving on the late ferry. Bessie and I have grown old together, she is my dearest friend. Caleb fears for what will happen to our slaves once we are gone. Land is the one thing that will make them truly free. So together we decided to give Bessie and her four daughters clear title to 40 acres each. He will deliver the papers before he leaves the island. I have grown to love Ibo and the Geechee people here. It breaks my heart to leave them.

"All the valuables from our home have been packed up and sent by boat to the mainland where they will be shipped to Philadelphia. As a small token, I have given Bessie and her daughters all of our bed linens which are made of the finest Sea Island cotton. It is only right that they should have them.

"Caleb will follow tomorrow. He does not know that I am aware of what he plans to do on this, his last night on this island. At midnight he will set fire to our house and leave nothing but ashes."

CHAPTER NINETEEN

Lucile closed the journal. For someone whose total interest and energy had always been focused on herself, she was surprisingly touched by Roberta's story. At one point, that woman had it all, big house, rich husband, wonderful life and then she lost it. The poor thing would have been in her '70s and she was headed back to Philadelphia with a sick husband and no money. Sad, very sad. Lucile vowed she would never end up poor like that.

Forty acres. Something about that had a familiar ring. Lucile had often heard the phrase "40 acres and a mule" and she thought it had something to do with the Civil War, but she wasn't sure exactly what. At any rate, it might be significant and it gave her an excuse to spend some extra time in Savannah. And as long as she was there, she decided to soak up a little more elegant Southern history and treat herself to luncheon at the Olde Pink House Restaurant. She rather liked the idea of being an interesting, well-dressed woman dining alone.

After lunch, she went back to the library. A quick search through the card catalogue turned up a document with the following information. "During the Civil War, General William

T. Sherman and Secretary of War Edwin M. Stanton met with 20 Black community leaders of Savannah, Georgia. Based partly to their input, Gen. Sherman issued Special Field Order #15 on January 16, 1865, setting aside the Sea Islands and a 330-mile inland tract of land for the exclusive settlement of Blacks. Parcels of not more than 40 acres were to be settled by approximately 18,000 freed slave families and other Blacks then living in the area."

Lucile consulted several other accounts and found there was conflicting information about whether or not the mules were ever made available. Frankly, she didn't care about the mules, but she was surprised at the broad scope of Sherman's order. Further reading in another reference book disclosed, "The orders had little concrete effect, as they were revoked in the fall of that same year by President Andrew Johnson, who succeeded Abraham Lincoln after his assassination."

Lucile returned all the books to the reference librarian, gathered her notes and papers, and returned to her hotel on Reynolds Square. Ever mindful of her figure, she decided to skip dinner and check out early in the morning. She loved driving along with the top down but it was too chilly for that now.

"So right after the Civil War there was a family group on Ibo who owned 160 acres. Wonder if any of them are still alive? If so, I wonder if they still own it. I wonder if they'd be willing to sell it?" It wasn't much to go on, but it was a starting place.

Back at the courthouse in Meridian, Lucile resumed her search. She looked for anything that might indicate the present ownership of land by Bessie Johnson or her descendants. She didn't find anything. Looking back over her notes she noticed something she had missed before. The first daughter in each generation continued using the name Harding. Maybe she was looking in the wrong place. So she started again.

Finally she found a document dated 1886 in the name of Harding and Company. That would have been about 20 years after Caleb and Roberta Harding left Ibo. Interesting. It was for a ten-year loan of $250 at six percent interest. According to the paperwork, the money was to be used to build a sawmill on Ibo and the borrower had put up 160 acres of land as collateral. Lucile held her breath. The principles were listed as Sarah Harding Davis, Jasmine Harding Collier and Rebecca Harding Johnson.

"This might be it. Dear God, just let there be some disaster that caused them to lose this land. If you let me find that, I'll never ask for anything else again." Lucile tackled the dusty files again but this time with renewed vigor and ecclesiastical hope in her soul.

Maurice was attending a banker's convention in Atlanta which gave Lucile a chance to visit the bank after hours and search through the records in peace and quiet. It took her a couple of hours, but she finally found a brittle old file for Harding and Company. She found the original papers concerning the mortgage and all the activity on the account. As it turned out payments were made on time up until July of 1893. Then there was a gap in the records. Damn.

She carefully put the files back where she found them and headed home. Early the next morning she visited the local newspaper. They didn't keep papers back that far, but they did keep a file of headline stories going back 75 years. In August of 1893 a category three hurricane hit Ibo Island during high tide, with 16-foot storm surges and winds over 120 miles an hour. It was known as the Great Sea Islands Hurricane. Lucile thanked the proprietor and made plans to visit the bank again that night.

Although there hadn't been any hurricanes along the Georgia coast that September or October, experience had taught Lucile that major storms tended to disrupt everything, at least

151

for a while. But eventually life got back to normal, so Lucile wasn't about to give up her search yet. Back at the bank she shuffled through several more years of records only to find that for two years there was no mention of Harding and Company at all. Then she found it.

The bank—Maurice's very own bank—put a lien on the 160 acres of Ibo property for non-payment. But that was all. There was no evidence of any further payments, nor had the bank ever called the loan. Just to be on the safe side, Lucile scanned through ten more years and found nothing. As far as she could tell, Meridian Bank and Trust owned 160 acres of land on Ibo Island and all they had to do was claim it.

Lucile couldn't wait for Maurice to get home so she could tell him the news. She made sure she had her ration book before she stopped by the Piggly Wiggly to pick up pork chops, Maurice's favorite. She fixed mashed potatoes, gravy, string beans, corn and apple pie for dessert. Just before he got home, she took a quick shower, washed her hair and put on a fresh dress. When Maurice walked in the door, she had a drink waiting for him. At a glance, Maurice knew to tread lightly, something was definitely up.

At dinner Lucile finally explained. "I have some good news, some very good news. You know how disappointed I was about the Donegan property on Ibo..." Maurice started to respond but decided against it. "...well, I've found 160 acres on the island that your bank holds a lien on. There hasn't been any activity on the account in...a long time, so I'm thinking you could just call in the loan and then we'd own some property out there. And when the investors come to build a resort, we'll be ready."

Maurice was curious but he decided to go slowly. "How did you find out about this?"

"I've been doing research...at the courthouse and in Savannah." She didn't elaborate about her late-night searches at the bank and Maurice wisely didn't press for details. "I worked really hard on this, Maurice, so please don't spoil it." Lucile went on to explain that the last payment on the initial loan of $250 was over 49 years ago.

Maurice agreed that was an unusual situation, but even so it wasn't as cut and dried as Lucile first thought. Very gently he explained he would have to check out the documents she found and if her facts were correct, then he would have to bring the information to the notice of the Board of Directors. He went on to say that even after such a long time it was bank policy to give overdue borrowers notice and allow them 30 days to pay off the loan. If that did not happen, then the bank would take ownership of the property and offer it for sale at auction. He expected Lucile to be upset, but she surprised him.

"So, that means we could buy it, couldn't we?" she said excitedly. Lucile was already making plans. She would have to remember to increase her gift to the Lottie Moon Christmas offering at church, just to say thank you for the Lord's blessings. Oh, she had so much to be thankful for.

Maurice didn't want to bring up the possibility that there might still be family members who could pay off the loan. It was a long shot and he couldn't see any reason to dampen Lucile's enthusiasm. So he agreed that it *might* be possible for them to buy the land. That made Lucile very happy and for the first time in a long time, she made Maurice happy too.

Maurice was still smiling when he showed up for his Wednesday night poker game. "Maurice, you are looking very pleased with yourself. Have you been up to something?"

Still smiling, Maurice said, "You could say that." He left the implication hanging in the air only long enough to get a reaction from the group. Then he changed the subject. He casually mentioned that Lucile had located 160 acres of land on Ibo for which the bank was holding an overdue loan. "I'm not sure how she found out because the loan has been outstanding since 1893. It's nearly 50 years old."

No one but Hattie paid much attention to that information. However for her, the very mention of Lucile and Ibo in the same sentence made her stomach hurt. She walked out of the room muttering to herself. "Leave it to Lucile to stick her nose in where it doesn't belong. I know Granny's family goes back a long way out there and I'll bet she's not the only one. Somebody on Ibo is about to be in big trouble." The next day Hattie called Cora and told her what she had heard. They decided to take the ferry the following morning to Ibo to talk to Ammee.

They were shocked by Ammee's appearance. It had been over a month since Bird went missing and she had lost a lot of weight and had dark circles under her eyes. When they approached, she looked at them with fear in her eyes. They assured her they had no news about Bird. Hattie quickly changed the subject. She related Maurice's announcement and their concern. Ammee listened but didn't seem to see the danger in the situation. When Hattie started asking questions, Ammee said they needed to talk to Granny.

As they walked across the island, Ammee's mood seemed to improve. She started talking about family history and explained that the person they all called Granny was actually *her* grandmother not her children's. Her own mother, Matilda, had died when Ammee was three.

As usual, Granny was delighted to have company and she was a wealth of information. Yes, she vaguely remembered something about a sawmill, and there might have been a loan, she couldn't remember for sure. However, she had a tin box which had been passed down from mother to daughter since

Bessie died in 1866. It held all the important family papers including the deeds to the four 40-acre parcels given to them in 1865 by Caleb Harding.

Cora finally said, "I'm sorry, but I can't keep up with all these generations. Granny, can you start with Bessie and just walk us through the daughters and their married names one more time?"

Granny laughed and began to recite her genealogy like a good Catholic reciting catechism. "First there was Bessie who took the sur name of Harding. She worked in the big house for Mrs. Roberta Harding and according to the old stories, they were close friends. Like I said, that's why all the first daughters in the family kept the Harding name. Bessie's first daughter was Sarah, who became Sarah Harding Davis. She was my grandmother. Her first daughter was Jasmine Harding Collier, my mother. Then her daughter was Rebecca Harding Johnson, that's me. My first daughter was Matilda Harding Cobb, and her first daughter was Ammee. She died when Ammee was just a little tot."

Hattie turned to Ammee, "So you're actually Ammee Harding Hamlin. Right?"

Granny spoke up. "After my mother died, I stopped using Harding except when I had to write my full name on something official. As far as people on Ibo know now, I'm just Rebecca Johnson, then there was Matilda Cobb, then Ammee Hamlin and then Robin...and Bird, of course. For most folks on the mainland, when they say Harding, they mean the white Harding family, but out here on Ibo, it's us black Hardings." Cora's head was still swimming in names, but she was beginning to get the picture.

Down in the bottom of the box Granny found the loan papers for Harding and Company with the signatures of Sarah, Jasmine and Rebecca. She also found the coupon book.

According to that, at the last payment, the company owed $84.24 on the loan. Ammee let out a deep sigh. "That's not so bad. Somewhere in that box there are six $10 gold pieces that Mrs. Harding gave to Bessie, Sarah and Jasmine. We can use that and come up with the rest of the money without too much of a problem."

Hattie was reading over the mortgage agreement and the lien which was attached. She shook her head. "Ammee, I'm afraid it's not quite that simple. According to this contract, this loan was signed in 1886. That's the year Bessie died, right. It was for a ten-year loan at six percent interest."

"What does that mean?" Ammee asked.

Hattie took a deep breath. "It's complicated, but I'll try to explain it. There are two parts to a loan. The principal is the amount you borrow. Interest is the amount of money the bank charges for the use of their money. They have a formula to figure out exactly how much interest you would owe over ten years. They add that to the principal and that's what you actually owe the bank.

"Now each of your payments gets divided between principal and interest. As you pay off the principal, what you owe in interest gets smaller. By the time you get to the end of the ten years, you will have paid off both principal and interest.

"OK, according to the coupon book, your family had been paying the loan on time until July of 1893, and had gotten the total down to $84.24. As long as you make each payment on time, the interest decreases. However there haven't been any payments for 49 years." She waited to see if that had sunk in. Ammee and Granny looked totally overwhelmed.

"What it boils down to is, if this is the property and the loan that Lucile found, that the interest you owe has been getting bigger each year for 49 years. I can't figure out compound interest without a mechanical calculator, but I'd guess by this time you may owe well over $1000."

No one moved. Finally Granny asked, "If we can't pay that back, could they take our land?"

Cora stepped in. "Right now this is all just second-hand talk from Maurice and we don't even know for sure it's the same property. If what Lucile says is true, then Maurice will have to notify the Board of Directors. And if that happens, I'm pretty sure they'll have to notify you and then give you some time to repay it."

"How much time|?"

"I don't know. Maybe 30 days."

"Thirty days! We could never come up with that much money in just 30 days."

Hattie took over. "If the bank gets in touch with you, bring me the papers immediately. Try not to worry. Just count on the fact that we'll do whatever we have to do to help you and Jacob get through this. We're not going to let anyone take your land, especially not that Dupree woman."

Cora hoped Hattie had a plan. They offered to walk home with Ammee, but she said she wanted to stay with Granny. They promised to leave a note for Jacob telling him where she was so he wouldn't worry.

On the ferry going back to the mainland, Cora debated whether or not to share what they had found out with Matt. She and Hattie talked about the unfairness of the whole situation. Bird was still missing, the holidays were coming up and short of asking Dr. Buzzard to make Lucile disappear, Cora couldn't see how telling Matt right now would help nor could she see any way out of the mess they were in.

"I'm the last one in the world to be superstitious," Hattie said, "but you know what they say, 'trouble always comes in threes.' First it was Bird and now this. I wonder what's coming next?"

CHAPTER TWENTY

Winter finally settled in and Thanksgiving, Christmas and New Year's all came and went with little or no notice. It was 1943 and Bird was still missing. It just hadn't seemed right to celebrate without him. In a way, the cold dreary weather made it easier to deal with his absence.

Late one afternoon, Cora dragged herself home from the courthouse and as soon as she opened the door Katie came running down the stairs. "You got a Special Delivery letter. You weren't here so the postman let me sign. It's on the table. Here, I'll get it. Aren't you going to open it?" All this came out in one breathless rush.

Cora took the letter. "It's from New York. I don't know anyone in New York...Oh my Lord, suppose it's something about Bird? I can't open it. Put it back on the table, we'll open it when your dad gets home."

"Mamma!"

"Katie, just do what I tell you. I can't deal with any more bad news right now."

"Maybe it's good news..."

"Katie!" Suddenly Hattie's warning about trouble coming in threes popped into Cora's mind. Logically she knew the letter wasn't about Bird because logically Bird couldn't be in New York. On the other hand, Ammee said both Granny and Robin had seen signs and Dr. Buzzard... "Cora, get hold of yourself. You are making a mountain out of a molehill. The letter's probably nothing. But if that's so, then why send it Special Delivery?"

Finally Cora gave in and called Matt at work. She told him that she and Hattie had visited Ammee and tried to explain the problem with their land. "It's really complicated and I'm worried. You think you might come home a little early today?" Matt said he'd be there shortly. Cora hung up. She hadn't mentioned the letter although she wasn't sure why.

Katie took care of that. As soon as her dad walked in the door, she grabbed the letter and shoved it at him. "Mamma got this Special Delivery letter and she won't open it. Here." Matt looked puzzled, took the letter and ripped it open. "You want me to read it?" Cora nodded. Matt scanned it quickly. "It looks like it's from a law firm," he said and read it out loud.

Jacoby and Rubin, LLP
4232 Grand Concourse
Bronx, New York
FOrdham 4-1800

Date: February 5, 1943
Re: Estate of Teletha Louise Strayhorn

Dear Mrs. Cora Strayhorn Reeve

On behalf of my firm, it is my sad duty to inform you that our former client, your aunt, Teletha Strayhorn, who lived at 125 West Tremont Avenue, Apartment 9-A, died on January 3, 1943. Before her death, I assisted her in the preparation and execution of her Last Will and Testament in which she named you as her Executrix and sole beneficiary. She also left instructions to be cremated. I have carried out her wishes and am in possession of her ashes.

As she died a resident of Bronx County, New York, we must file her Will for probate in the Bronx County Probate Court. Because you have been named Executrix, at the appropriate time it will be necessary for you to travel to New York and appear before the Bronx County probate judge to be administered the Executor's Oath, at which time the Letters Testamentary will be issued naming you as Executrix. After this is completed, you will be authorized to take possession of your aunt's estate.

I understand that you and your aunt were not close and you may not even be aware of her death. I also realize this information is a great deal for you to take in. You are welcome to call me at my individual number FOrdham 4-1822 with your questions.

Sincerely,
Julius Friedman
Attorney at Law

Cora was shocked. "That's Aunt T. I had no idea she was in New York and now she's dead and I'm supposed to go to New York..."

Katie was jumping up and down with excitement. As far as she was concerned, this was the sign Robin and Granny had been waiting for. They had said all along Bird was in New York. Now Cora was going to New York. She would find Bird and bring him home and everyone would live happily ever after. "I've gotta tell Robin."

Both parents turned on her at once. "No! You aren't to say anything to anybody until we figure this out."

At supper, Cora did her best to explain the hornet's nest Lucile was about to stir up. "Basically Ammee's family took out a loan way back when and they used their land as collateral. They paid on the loan for a while, but nothing's been paid for 49 years and the interest has accrued and at Hattie's rough estimate they owe over $1000. Matt, can you use the calculating machine at your office to figure out exactly how much they owe?"

"Yes, I should be able to do that."

Cora rushed on. "I'm convinced that's the 160 acres Lucile was telling Maurice about. Ammee and Jacob don't have that kind of money and if the land goes up for auction, I'll bet Lucile is planning to make Maurice buy it or buy it herself. We need to be here helping the Hamlins. Now before we know anything for certain, I have to leave and go to New York. What a mess." Cora was nearly in tears.

Matt understood how upset Cora was, he was worried too. As he saw it, the best thing to do was to take things one step at a time. That meant sending Cora to New York to deal with Aunt T's will. Depending on what they found out, he and Hattie could work with Jacob and Ammee while she was gone. His father might have some ideas too.

As soon as they started seriously talking about the trip, Katie begged to go. It would be a good experience. She would learn a lot. And, of course, she needed to be there to help bring Bird home. Cora gave in. She had too many things on her mind to put up much of a fight.

First, she had mixed emotions about Aunt T. Obviously the older woman still had some feelings for her and Cora was saddened about all the years they had missed. Years they could never get back.

Second, she was frankly afraid of what Lucile might do while she was gone. Cora knew how much time that woman had put in searching records at the courthouse and Lucile didn't do anything she didn't expect to pay off in her favor.

"Matt, I promised Ammee I would be here to help clear up this mess and now I'll be gone for...who knows how long. I have to go see her and try to explain." It wasn't a visit Cora was looking forward to, but she knew it had to be done.

"Mamma, can I go?"

"Yes, just make it snappy."

When they got to Ibo, they found all the womenfolk at Ammee's. Cora told them about the letter, and apologized for deserting the family when they needed her most. Granny started to laugh. "Mercy, Mercy. Oh Dear Lord, our prayers have been answered and you sit there apologizin'. You're like folks going to church to pray for rain but ain't nobody brought an umbrella. Ammee said we need a miracle to bring Bird home from New York, and the Lord and Dr. Buzzard done provided one. You!" Everyone got excited and Cora didn't have the heart to tell them how impossible the whole idea was.

Before they left Ibo, Robin slipped Katie her lucky silver dime. "I knew something good was about to happen so I had Dr. Buzzard put a special root on this charm. If you take it to New York, I know you're gonna find Bird and bring him home safe." She put the string over Katie's head.

As soon as Hattie found out about the letter, she called Cora. "We need to have a strategy meeting with everybody, your family, Jacob and Ammee, Robin and Granny. Can you get everybody together?"

Cora was almost afraid to ask. "Does this have anything to do with the loan?"

"No, it's just about New York, don't worry."

Although Cora didn't understand why her trip to New York required a strategy meeting, she assembled the group. When Hattie arrived she took over. She unfolded a large New York Manhattan Street Map, laid it out on the kitchen table and gathered everyone around.

"Now, everybody needs to have some idea of where you're going. This is Manhattan Island. It's between the East River and the Hudson River up to Randall's Island where the Harlem River separates it from the Bronx." As Hattie talked she pointed out rivers and streets and points of interest. "You said your aunt lived on West Tremont, well, that's in the Bronx. Grand Concourse is the main street in the Bronx. The lawyers' office and the Bronx Courthouse are both on Grand Concourse so you shouldn't have too much trouble getting around, you could probably walk."

"Where's Harlem?" Robin asked.

Everyone moved in closer and Hattie traced the area with her finger. "Harlem is part of Manhattan. Look here," she started at the bottom of the map, "it's easy to get around because streets in Manhattan are numbered from the bottom of the island and they run east and west. Avenues run north and south. Harlem starts at about 96th Street, and the East River. It skips over Central Park goes north to about 155th Street. The main street is Lenox Avenue.

"Now since Bird was used to going to church, you might want to visit the Abyssinian Baptist Church, it's the largest one in Harlem. It covers a whole city block on 138th Street. Just ask anybody, they can tell you where it is."

Hattie stepped back, apparently finished with her lecture. Cora confronted her, "How do you know all that? I thought you said you were from 'down south.'"

Hattie shrugged. "Yeah, I am from down south, but I've been up north too."

"You ever been 'out west'?" Katie asked. Cora gave her a smack on the arm.

Hattie just smiled. "Nope, never been farther west than the Mississippi River."

Throughout this exchange, Bird's family hadn't taken their eyes off the map. Up until that time, Harlem was just a name like Wonderland. Now it had boundaries and streets and churches. It was on a map, it was real. It was an actual place, a place where Bird might be.

It was also a place that got very cold in winter. Hardly anyone living on the South Georgia coast owned a coat heavy enough to stand up to a New York winter. Hattie managed to come up with a couple of extra sweaters and hats, scarves and gloves for Cora and Katie. They carried a strong scent of mothballs, but a day hanging in the wind took care of most of that. Boots would have been a good idea too, but the best Hattie could suggest was to wear several pairs of socks.

Two days later Matt drove Cora and Katie to Union Station in Atlanta and put them on the Southerner coming up from New Orleans and bound for New York City. Katie had brought a school composition book along to take notes. She wanted to remember everything so she could tell her dad and Robin when she got home.

They said tearful good-byes and boarded the train. As it slowly pulled out of the station, they settled in with suitcases and packages containing enough food to last the entire trip. No need to spend money to eat in the dining car.

Soldiers were everywhere, standing in the aisles, sitting on suitcases, even sleeping on the floor. As the train made its slow way north, Cora and Katie met most of the soldiers in the car. They shared their food and the men brought Cora coffee and Katie milk from the dining car. One special friend, Pete, even paid twenty cents to rent two pillows for them.

At first Katie tried to keep up with all the stations: Gainesville and Toccoa in Georgia, then they were into South Carolina and Spartanburg and Gastonia, then Charlotte, North Carolina. One of the soldiers gave her a map so she could trace the route which covered North Carolina, Virginia, Washington DC, Maryland, Pennsylvania, New Jersey and finally New York City. Katie carefully folded the map and put it in the back of her composition book. When they got home, she'd show her dad and Robin all the states they went through.

Katie confided to Pete that she was disappointed they weren't going into Grand Central Station. "That's my favorite radio show. I even know the whole introduction by heart. Wanta hear me say it?" Katie didn't wait for an answer. "As a bullet seeks its target, shining rails in every part of our great country are aimed at Grand Central Station, heart of the nation's greatest city. Drawn by the magnetic force of the fantastic metropolis, day and night great trains rush toward the Hudson River, sweep down its eastern bank for 140 miles, flash briefly by the long red row of tenement houses south of 125th Street, dive with a roar into the two-and-a-half mile tunnel which burrows beneath the glitter and swank of Park Avenue and then…Grant Central Station! Crossroads of a million private lives. Gigantic stage on which are played a thousand dramas daily."

When she finished everyone applauded. She blushed and clutched the silver dime hanging around her neck. This was going to be a great trip, she could just feel it.

Pete shook her hand. "That was great, but wait 'till you see Penn Station. You won't be disappointed, I promise."

When the journey finally ended and they walked into the main waiting area of Penn Station, Katie's mouth dropped open. The room was two blocks long and the ceiling was so high she got a crick in her neck looking up. "Wow! You could put all of Ibo Island in here and have room left over."

Pete walked out to Seventh Avenue with them, whistled down a cab and spent some time talking to the driver. "Was there a problem?" Cora asked. "Oh, they don't like to go out of their borough, but I told him I was on my way overseas and you were my mother and little sister. I shamed him into taking you to the Bronx." Cora and Katie both hugged him, wished him God's speed and watched as Pete ran to catch up with his buddies.

"You gonna get in or not?" the cab driver sounded impatient so Cora urged Katie to throw in the suitcases and get in quickly. The wind cut through their thin coats and they were glad for the warm cab. As soon as they slammed the door, the driver took off at breakneck speed.

As they were being tossed back and forth, Cora tried to remember all the things Hattie told her. "Everything in New York moves fast. Everyone is in a hurry. People think New Yorkers are rude, but they're not. They're just busy and there are so many of them the only way to get a little privacy is to ignore the guy next to you. Don't let that bother you, it's nothing personal. If you need help, ask. They'll help you every time, I promise."

Cora looked at Katie who was craning her neck to try to see the tops of all the buildings. She was having the time of her life. The whole thing was one great adventure to her.

Cora, on the other hand, was totally overwhelmed and teetering on the edge of panic. "Thank God Pete got us a taxi. If the cab driver had told me he didn't want to go to the Bronx, I would probably have apologized, walked away and we would have frozen to death right there on the sidewalk." She watched the fare build up on the meter and tried to remember how much she was supposed to tip the driver.

After a long ride, the cab pulled up in front of a large apartment house. As soon as they stopped, Cora shoved the fare and the tip at the driver and reached for the door handle. To her surprise, a doorman in a maroon uniform with gold braid opened the door and helped them with their luggage. Cora was so glad to see a friendly face, she almost hugged him.

She took a deep breath and explained that she was Miss Strayhorn's niece. "Ah, nice lady. We're gonna miss her. The lawyer left a key for you."

"Oh God," Cora thought. "We never lock doors at home. I didn't even think about a key. I wish Matt were here, or Hattie."

The doorman carried their luggage into the lobby. The floor was polished marble and there was a huge chandelier overhead. The elevator doors were brass filigree. The doorman pushed a button and seconds later the doors opened. He handed their luggage to the elevator operator who also wore a maroon uniform. "They're Miss Strayhorn's family."

"Sorry to hear about her passing. Her apartment is 9-A down at the end of the hall," the woman running the elevator said.

Cora thanked her and when the doors opened, she and Katie walked slowly down a long dimly lit hall with doors on both sides.

"Nine floors up. I've never been in a building this tall before," Katie said. "Can you imagine living up this high?"

Finally they found the right number, inserted the key, opened the door and turned on the light.

"Wow!" Katie said.

Cora sat down on her suitcase and burst into tears.

CHAPTER TWENTY-ONE

"What's wrong Mamma?"

"Nothing, it's just so big...and fast..."

"Yeah! Isn't it wonderful?"

Cora had to laugh. "Whose child are you?"

Katie looked puzzled. "What?" Cora waved her off. "I'm hungry," Katie said. "Let's go get something to eat."

"No!" Cora was surprised at the panic in her voice. "It's way too cold out there and I need some time to get myself together. First we need to call your dad to let him know we got here OK." They explored the apartment looking for a phone. The entrance hall held an oval table and four chairs. A mirror, almost as big as the tabletop, hung on the left-hand wall. An antique coat rack was to the right of the front door. Ahead of them down three steps, was a sunken living room with windows facing the street. Under the windows, between the radiators were build-in shelves crammed with books. "Wow," Katie said.

The light switch by the front door had turned on all the lamps in the living room. There was no ceiling fixture, just puddles of warm yellow light from the lamps. A dark green velvet couch was against one wall with a low coffee table and two wing chairs facing it.

Three steps up to the right off the living room was a breakfast nook with a built-in bench and a small table. Next was the kitchen which was about the size of a closet. They passed a bathroom in the hall leading to a large bedroom with windows overlooking the building's entrance. Katie had never seen a bed that big. It was covered with a dark blue spread and there were at least a dozen pillows of all sizes piled up against the headboard. Another door brought them back to the entrance hall.

All that but no phone. Finally Katie found it almost hidden in a little nook in the wall with just enough space for the phone and a shelf underneath for the phone book. They both stood there in disbelief. The phone book was four inches thick. "Wow!" Katie said.

Cora felt her heart sink. How in the world was she ever going to find her way around? Take it slow, that's what Matt would say. So she called home.

Hearing Matt's voice was reassuring. She told him they're had a good trip, which was true. She told him they'd met a young soldier who helped them, which was also true. She told him they had a wild cab ride, but they were safe, which they were. She told him they were fine and she realized that was also true. Katie took the phone told him she loved him, that she was having a wonderful time and hung up before Cora could stop her.

"Now," Cora said feeling a little better, "Let's see if we can find something to eat around here." She turned around just in time to see Katie climbing out a front window onto the fire escape. The cold air came rushing in. "Wow!" Katie said.

"Katie, can't you think of anything else to say?"

Katie smiled. Her mother sounded normal again. Whenever she was nervous, little things annoyed her. "Come out here,

170

Mamma. We're way up high and you can see forever. If you look down, it's like there's nothing between you and the street."

"Katie, come in and close the window, you're letting all the heat out," Cora said.

Reluctantly, Katie obeyed. In the tiny kitchen they found a can of Campbell's chicken noodle soup, some stale crackers, an unopened package of Oreo cookies, some tea bags, sugar and two bottles of Coca-Cola. There were ice trays in the freezer compartment of the refrigerator and pots and pans under the counter. Working in the kitchen helped Cora relax.

By Meridian standards, it was a poor excuse for supper, but they were so hungry, they didn't care. After they ate and washed the dishes, Cora said, "You know what? I bet we could find a couple of warm coats around here somewhere." With that in mind, they went through all the closets. It felt deliciously mischievous, like breaking all the rules, but it didn't matter because there was no one left to care. Best of all, they found a long, heavy wool coat for Cora and a warm jacket with a hood that came down to Katie's knees. "It's a little big, but it feels good," Katie said. Cora turned up the sleeves and they decided it looked fine.

Finally Cora sat down in the living room. It was only 8:30 but she was exhausted. Katie was running out of steam too. It had been three days since they left home although it seemed like much longer. "Why don't you take your bath first, then I'll bathe and join you in bed." Katie went without an argument. She loved the idea of sleeping in the oversized bed with her mother.

While Katie was in the bathroom, Cora wandered around the apartment trying to find something that looked familiar. Something her aunt had kept that would have reminded her of the life she had in Georgia. At first she found nothing. Then on the bottom of a bookshelf, she found a photo album. The first pictures were of babies in christening gowns. She had no idea who they were until she slipped one of the pictures out of its corner holders and checked the name on the back. It was her father.

She found pictures of him as a young boy, a college graduate and the smiling groom with his young bride. Cora had only one picture of her mother. She'd never seen this one. As she turned the pages she found her baby pictures and her high school graduation. The last picture was Aunt T. and her on the day she left for college. Then the pictures stopped. As Cora put the album away, several clippings from the Meridian newspaper fell out.

There was her engagement announcement, her wedding picture and a picture of her the year she had been elected to the School Board. Cora couldn't help but wonder, "If you kept up with me, why didn't you ever get in touch? Did you still blame me for your brother's death? What a shame we wasted all that time. How easily people slip away."

At that moment Cora made a promise to herself. She would not let the big city intimidate her. She would screw her courage to the sticking place and do everything she could to get Jacob and Ammee's family back together. If Bird was there, somehow she'd find him.

The next morning they slept late and woke up hungry. No hiding in the apartment, they had to go out for breakfast and maybe even look for a grocery store. "Let's ask that nice man at the door, I bet he'd know a good place." Clearly Katie was eager to go exploring. So they put on their coats, scarves and gloves. New York in January was one cold place.

The doorman told them his name was Sidney and proclaimed himself an expert on all things dealing with the Bronx. "For breakfast you could try the bakery down the block or how about the Automat, Horn and Hardart, dat's my favorite.

Yous don't have to wait in line and ya can take as much time as ya need to make a choice." He looked at their blank faces and realized they didn't have a clue what he was talking about.

"Lookit, the Automat is one big place with tables and chairs in the middle and the walls all around are covered with little doors. Back of the doors is the food. You just put your money in the slot, then open the door and take out the food. Simple. You got plenty of change?"

Horn and Hardart was four cold blocks away, but it was everything Sidney promised. No one paid any attention to them as they walked around the room. They got their trays, made their choices and had a wonderful hot breakfast. Cora started to relax.

"When are we gonna go looking for Bird?" Katie asked, wiping jelly off her mouth.

"I've been thinking about that. We have a lot to do here, so let's just take it one step at a time. Food first. While we're out, we need to find a grocery store. Then we need to call the lawyer, let him know we're here and find out what he needs for us to do. Let's just take care of that much and then figure out what to do about Bird."

From the warmth of the Automat, they surveyed the streets outside. They didn't see a sign for a grocery store, but they soon figured out people in New York had stores for everything. There was a bakery, a store with some vegetables in boxes on the sidewalk that must have been a grocery store, farther down the block was a butcher shop. They could make a start and ask Sidney for advice if there was something they couldn't find.

Back in the apartment, Katie put the groceries away while Cora called the lawyer and set up an appointment for later in the day. She gave him her address and asked the best way to get to his office. It wasn't too far, but he advised taking a taxi.

"Good," thought Cora. "I can handle that, and it'll be a lot warmer than walking."

Katie sat in the front window seat looking at all the buildings. She had never been up so high before. She could see people moving around in apartments across the street. One woman was pinning her laundry to a line stretched between two buildings. The one thing missing was trees...well moss and trees. Everything in New York seemed to be made of concrete.

Way in the distance she could see an elevated subway track and the cars driving underneath it. Katie fingered the silver dime amulet Robin had given her. So far the root was working.

Just then there was a knock on the door. Katie and Cora exchanged looks. When Cora opened the door she was greeted by a short, slightly round woman wearing a bright red sweater over a flowered blouse. She had on a black skirt, thick black hose and oxford-type shoes. She smiled and stuck out her hand.

"My name is Sadie Glanzrock, I live across the hall in 9-B. I was sorry to hear about Teletha, may she rest in peace. A shame, a real shame, she was a very nice woman and a good neighbor. Did they tell you how she died? It was a heart attack. I was the one who called the ambulance, but she was gone by the time they got here. May I come in?"

Cora was stunned. She stepped back and invited her in.

Sadie walked into the living room and sat down, completely at ease. "I always liked this apartment, you know it gets the sun. On the back, well, I don't get the noise from the street, but still, the sun is nice. You were Teletha's niece, right? She talked about you some."

Cora quickly introduced herself and Katie and offered Sadie tea.

"Tea would be nice." She pointed to the china cabinet. "That pot, that was her favorite, Wedgewood and she's got all the cups and saucers. Good quality, old, and not a chip anywhere. She knew how to take care. The tea's in the cabinet over the stove along with the sugar. I don't take cream."

Katie managed to find a tray and Cora added some pastries they brought home from the bakery. She did her best to serve tea the way she remembered Aunt T. doing it back home. Sadie seemed to be pleased. "So, how are you doing? I see you found the bakery. You got everything else? You need anything you just ask me. Teletha was my friend. So have you called the lawyer? I know them, Jacoby and Rubin. They're good. Simon my late husband—may his memory be a blessing—he did business with them. Who are you dealing with? Jacoby?"

Cora gave her Julius Friedman's name. "Junior partner. He's young, but he's alright. He'll take care of everything. I know Teletha was cremated. It's not our way. We Jews believe the body is sacred, the "temple of the soul," it's the way we do good in the world. But never mind. So, how long are you staying?"

Cora was a little evasive. She couldn't decide whether Sadie was a busybody or whether she would turn out to be their salvation. Katie didn't hesitate.

"We're here to find a friend of ours. His name is Bird Hamlin. He's a Geechee boy from Ibo Island and we think he flew up here to Harlem and we've come to take him home."

That statement demanded a very long explanation that included Bird's family, Ibo Island, the Geechee community, flying Africans, Dr. Buzzard, gopher dust, signs and faith. Cora sat back and listened as Katie and Sadie discussed the situation and came to an understanding and a plan of action.

"You take care of Teletha and the lawyer. While you're gone I'm gonna make some phone calls, talk to some people, get some advice. There's Mrs. Cohen, lives in the penthouse. She's got a colored maid, who might be able to help. She would know about these things. But first we'll order in Chinese for lunch."

While Sadie was on the phone, Cora quietly explained to Katie that in New York, people ate lunch at noon and dinner at night. Nobody ate supper. Katie added that to her list of New York things to tell her dad and Robin.

Whether they called it lunch or dinner, what surprised Cora most was that you could make a phone call and someone would deliver food to your door. While they were waiting, Sadie noticed Katie's notebook. "You like riddles? Gimme your book, I'll show you one." She turned to a new page and wrote "F U N E M? S V F M. F U N E X? S V F X. OK, M N X." She handed the book back to Katie. "So, can you figure that out? No, so I'll give you a hint, say the letters out loud."

Katie tried it, but it just sounded like gibberish. Sadie laughed. "OK, so I'll tell you. There's this guy who just got off the boat and he can't speak English so good yet, but he's hungry. So goes into this diner and he asks, 'Haf you an-y ham?' And the guy behind the counter says, 'Yes, v haf ham.' Then they go back and forth. "Haf you an-y eggs? Yes, v haf eggs. OK, ham n eggs."

They were still laughing when the delivery boy came. In no time, Sadie was serving up the contents of half a dozen little white paper boxes with metal handles. The food smelled wonderful, but Cora had no idea what most of it was. Katie tried her hand at chopsticks and ended up dropping more than she ate. Cora had better luck with a fork.

After lunch, Sadie went back to her apartment and Cora and Katie took a cab to the Grand Concourse. The cab left them off in front of the lawyer's address and they took the elevator to the eleventh floor and the offices of Jacoby and Rubin. Cora gave her name to the very stylishly dressed receptionist and shortly Julius Friedman appeared. He was a handsome man with dark hair and Cora could tell instantly his suit was tailored and expensive. He offered his condolences. "The first thing you will need to do is go to the county courthouse." He explained the procedure and directed them to the Bronx County Probate Court which was within walking distance. Once there, Cora took an oath, signed some papers and became the official executrix of her aunt's estate.

Back at the lawyer's office they learned the details of the will. Teletha left Cora the contents of her apartment on West Tremont Avenue and her accounts at the Chase Concourse Bank. The lawyer also gave Cora the key to a safe deposit box. Since the bank was close by, Cora decided they could take care of closing out the account while they were in the neighborhood.

Apparently Teletha was well liked. The manager at the bank said she had been a loyal customer for many years and he was truly sorry to hear of her passing. Teletha had a checking account with $273.45 in it and there was a saving account with $1,492, which was almost as much money as Matt made in a year.

"If I may offer a suggestion," the manager said, "why don't you take the total of the checking account in cash and we'll supply you with a cashier's check for the savings account balance. Cora readily agreed. "Thank God for the extra money," Cora thought. "Everything is so expensive. On top of that, I can't believe I came here to get Bird without taking into account how I was going to buy him a ticket home."

"Now, I'll show you where the safe deposit box is." The manager escorted Cora and Katie down a long hall, through an iron gate and into a room lined with boxes with numbers and two keyholes. The manager inserted his key and Cora turned over her key. He pulled the box out about two inches, then stepped back and waited for Cora. Finally he said, "You may remove the box." She did and he showed them both into a small room with a built-in desk. "Take all the time you need. Since you are closing out the account, I took the liberty of bringing some bank envelopes which may be helpful. When you're finished, just ring the bell here on the desk." With that he closed the door and left them alone.

Cora folded back the top of the long skinny box and took out the contents. The top layer was all official papers. On the bottom there was a small gold ring with three rubies, which Katie immediately slipped on her finger. There was also a cameo broach and a lady's wrist watch which Cora recognized.

Most of the papers looked ordinary but the words "Bell Telephone" caught Cora's eye. Teletha had worked for the phone company back home and apparently she had gotten a similar job in New York. The papers were stock certificates. Cora put everything into the large manila envelopes supplied by the bank. She rang the bell, and shortly the manager was back. They finished their business and he walked them out to the street and hailed a cab. Cora sat back clutching her purse with the cash, the cashier's check and the envelopes containing the stock certificates.

Not two minutes after they got back to the apartment, Sadie knocked on the door. "So, how did it go with the lawyer? He was helpful, yes? You got everything straightened out? Good."

Sadie had a way of asking questions and then supplying her own answers. "So, here's what I learned. You're not gonna find your friend."

"What?!" Katie was shocked.

"Wait a minute. You're not gonna find *him*, you gotta let *him* find you. It's like this. You drop a pin, you get a magnet. But you don't put the magnet on the pin, because you don't know where the pin is. You put the magnet somewhere you think the pin *might* be and let the pin come to the magnet. That's it, that's what you gotta do."

CHAPTER TWENTY-TWO

The next morning Sadie knocked on the door early. "Have you had breakfast? No. Good, get your coats."

They walked across the street and into a little store almost hidden in the basement of an old building. The air inside was hot and wet with steam and the smell of yeast. A tray of bagels was just coming out of the oven. Sadie wasted no time in placing her order and instructing the young girl behind the counter to add cream cheese, lox, a slice of onion and a slice of tomato to each one. Chewy on the inside and toasty on the outside. Delicious. "Today bagels, and before you leave you'll try cheese blintzes, potato pancakes and egg creams."

Back at what was beginning to feel like home, Sadie explained what she had planned for their day. "I talked to Mary, Mrs. Cohan's girl, she's from down in the south and she says everybody down there goes to church. Am I right? So, that's where you're gonna start. The biggest church in Harlem is the Abyssinian Baptist Church. They got a real famous rabbi over there. No, not a rabbi, what do you call them?"

"Reverend."

"Yeah, that's it. Reverend Adam Clayton Powell. Very famous. Everybody knows him. You forget the name of the church, just ask for him."

"Do you think it's safe for us to go to Harlem?"

Sadie laughed. "Who knows? It's like a Jewish boy what wanders into an Irish neighborhood." She shrugged. "Ahhh, you'll probably be OK."

Katie touched the silver dime good luck charm hanging around her neck. "You don't have to worry about us, Miss Sadie, we'll be OK, we've got Ibo Island root working for us."

"That's right, I almost forgot." Sadie had written out the directions and added her phone number just in case they got lost and needed help. Bundled against the cold, Cora and Katie took the trolley on Jerome Avenue to the 8th Avenue subway and got off in Harlem on the corner of West 137th Street. It felt like being on Ibo Island. They were the only white people around.

As soon as they came out of the subway, they saw the church. They needn't have worried about finding it. It looked like a gray stone castle, complete with towers on each end and a series of arched double doors, all painted red. It covered an entire city block. Neither of them could get over how big everything in New York was.

The church was so imposing, at first they just stood looking at it. Then Katie spotted a smaller door with a sign saying "church offices." That sounded promising. It was warm inside and smelled of lavender. At the end of a long hallway, they saw a young woman sitting at a desk working at a typewriter.

"Can I be of assistance?"

Cora stepped forward. "I hope so. You see, we're looking for a boy, a young Negro boy. His name is Bird Hamlin, he's about 12 and we think he may...may be here in New York." Cora knew she sounded ridiculous but she kept going. "He doesn't know anyone here so we thought maybe someone would have directed him to the church for help." Cora could tell by the look on the young woman's face, the whole idea was crazy.

"Did this child run away home?"

This at least sounded logical, so Cora decided to approach it that way. "Yes, we think he may have. He didn't tell anyone he was leaving and his family is very worried about him. They're back in Georgia, but since we had to come up here, they asked us to try to find him." Cora realized she was talking too much and not making much sense.

At that point Katie spoke up. "Bird is an artist. We brought some of his sketches," she took them out of her bag and handed them to the receptionist. "They're good aren't they?"

The young woman examined the sketches and smiled. "Yes, very good."

Katie rushed on, "What we were thinking...what we were hoping was that you might put some of these up...somewhere, like in the hallways or something. Somewhere people could see them and if Bird saw them, then he'd know someone from back home had been here. I put our phone number in the Bronx down at the bottom. If he sees it then maybe he'll call us and..." Katie was nearly crying. "We really, really need to find him. Can you help us?"

The young woman's face softened. "I'd like to help, but I don't see how..."

"Please, just try," Katie pleaded.

The receptionist looked at the sketches again. "All right, I'll do what I can." She turned to Cora. "Please give me your name and an address here in the city. And your phone number. I'll talk to the people who work with our after-school program and see if anyone knows anything. And I'll put up the pictures. Oh yes, put the boy's name down too, please. We do have children from some of the schools nearby who come over in the afternoons, but I don't want to get your hopes up." She looked at Katie's expectant face, "But I will try to help."

Cora and Katie thanked her and started to leave. Then Cora turned back. "Do you think it would be alright if we just stepped into the church to say a quick prayer?"

"Of course. The doors to the sanctuary are just opposite the main entrance. Just follow the hall back the way you came in."

Cora and Katie followed the directions and cautiously opened the double doors. They had never seen anything so beautiful or so large. The pulpit seemed to be miles away and the sun shining through the stained-glass windows made rainbows everywhere. They quickly slipped into a back pew and prayed for Bird. Katie smiled. Now they had the Ibo God, the Harlem God and Dr. Buzzard on their side.

When they got back to Tremont Avenue, they knocked on Sadie's door. Her apartment was smaller than Aunt T's and it didn't have a sunken living room. Her's was only large enough for a couch and two chairs plus a small drop-leaf table. Sadie insisted they stay for lunch and they were more than happy to accept. She showed Katie how to open up the table and Cora set places for the three of them. As they ate, Katie told Sadie everything that had happened and Cora finally asked something she'd been wondering about for some time.

"Sadie, if you don't mind my asking, why did you decide to help us. When I was talking to that young woman, I realized how foolish this all sounds. I mean we don't even know that Bird is here and if he is, the chances that he would come to that church or of our finding him are...pretty hopeless."

Sadie didn't respond right away, and Cora thought she might have offended her. Finally she said, "You wanta know, so let me tell you a story. My family, well, my mother she died a long time ago, may she rest in peace. My father lived a good long life, but he is also gone. I have two brothers, they stayed in our home in Munich, Germany... They got families, I got nieces and nephews, but since the war started...I haven't heard from them in three years.

"I came here when I was 18 to live with an aunt and go to New York University. After the First World War it was very hard on Germany. It was like we were being punished for the war. Then Hitler came along and he started to build up the army and build roads and he told people to stop being ashamed. He told them to be proud of who they were.

"My Papa was a very smart man. He saw what was coming before most people and he was afraid. He said what Hitler was doing might be good for Germany, but it wasn't going to be good for the Jews. He wanted to sell everything and leave, but my brothers wouldn't listen. They said, 'We are Jews, yes, but we are also good Germans. We have a nice house, a family business, we are part of the community, we pay our taxes, we drink beer, and we're safe.'

"Not long after that, Papa had appendicitis. Because he was Jewish, they wouldn't let his doctor operate at any hospital. Papa died of a ruptured appendix. But I think he saw what was happening to his country and died of a ruptured heart.

"Things have gotten much worse there, but I still have faith that my brothers and their families will survive and someday we'll be together again. I understand about hope even when it doesn't make sense. We Jews have a long history of believing in lost causes. But you know," she smiled slightly, "sometimes they work out. For us, it took 40 years wandering around in the desert, but we finally made it to the Promised Land. You just have to have faith and *savlanut.* Patience."

That night when Cora called Matt, she was full of news. She told him about the will and the bank account. "And Matt, we own stock! Did you ever hear of such a thing? We're *stockholders.* Just like in Monopoly. Aunt T. had stock in Bell

Telephone. The lawyer said I'd have to meet with Aunt T's broker and change the name on the stock certificates or something like that. Anyway, I have to do that so they'll send me the dividends. Can you believe that? We get money just for owning stock, we don't even have to do anything. I had no idea being rich was so complicated. The whole thing makes my head swim."

Finally she got around to talking about their trip to Harlem. She was about to tell him how hopeless everything looked when Katie took the phone. "We had a great trip to Harlem. We rode the subway and the church was almost as big as Penn Station. And we talked to this really nice lady and I gave her some of Bird's drawings and she thought they were great. She's going to put them up so people can see them. And maybe Bird too. And we went into the church. Wow! It was really big too and the colored glass windows were beautiful. And we prayed so now we've got our God, the Ibo God, the Harlem God and Dr. Buzzard to help us out. Did I tell you about Mrs. Glanzrock? Well, she lives across... I'm sorry, Mamma says I'm running up the long-distance bill so I have to hang up. I love you. Bye."

Cora tucked Katie in and then sat in the living room with a cup of tea listening to the city noises outside. Even on the ninth floor, she could hear them. Rather than being distracting, she found the sounds comforting. It meant people were out going about their business taking care of things even in the middle of the night.

Then she thought about Sadie and her family. Of course Cora knew there was a war going on, with ration books and shortages, but for her, the war was mostly an inconvenience, not a real danger. Matt was too old to be drafted and she didn't have brothers. She couldn't imagine what Sadie must be feeling.

She didn't understand what was going on with the Jews. Until she met Sadie, the only Jews she knew anything about were those in the Bible. And if they were God's chosen people, why did other people hate them? Maybe she would get a chance to ask Sadie...but that didn't seem quite right either. Finally, she took her cup into the kitchen, washed it out and went to bed. Just before she dropped off to sleep, she said a prayer for Bird and for Sadie's family.

CHAPTER TWENTY-THREE

Little by little they were making progress. They had learned to send the garbage down the chute to the incinerator. They had learned to carry nickels for the subway and change for the Automat. They had learned to say lunch and dinner, not dinner and supper. They—well, Katie—had learned to eat lox. They had learned to walk fast and not look people in the eye and Katie had even learned how to whistle for a cab.

The last official hurdle was dealing with the Bell Telephone stock. According to Julius Friedman, Cora needed a broker to get the dividends assigned to her. He gave her a recommendation, but Cora hesitated to call. It wasn't that she distrusted Mr. Friedman, the truth was she didn't have any idea what a broker did.

She and Matt lived a comfortable life. Up to that point, high finance to Cora meant making sure all the bills were paid, the checkbook was balanced, there was enough cash to cover budgeted items like food, clothing and household expenses. A little bit went into a savings account and Cora made sure she always had some walking-around money in her purse. Stocks and dividends were completely foreign to her.

The answer, of course, was Sadie. "They try to make it sound complicated. All that aggravation, who needs it? Here's what it comes down to. You need money now, you sell the stock, you take the cash. You don't need the money now, leave the stock alone and get the dividends later. So, tomorrow we'll take all the papers to the broker's office, he sorts it out, you sign your name, they send you the checks. Easy-peasy." And it was.

Cora was glad to get caught up in doing anything that kept her mind away from the silent telephone. She kicked herself for not getting the name and phone number of the young woman at the church. At least that way they could have called to see if she had any news. As it was, all they could do was wait.

Waiting wasn't any easier a thousand miles south. When Sheriff Mayhew publicized the reward offered by the Donegan sisters, he got a few responses, but nothing useful. One person said he thought he had seen a boy getting on a Greyhound bus, but since Bird wouldn't have had money for a ticket, there was no use to waste time following up on that.

Matt was the link between Cora in New York and Bird's family on Ibo. He made a special point of going to the island to tell them about the trip to the church in Harlem and that Bird's pictures were being displayed. Frankly he didn't know if that information made the situation better or worse.

Without knowing it, Maurice dropped a bomb at the next poker night. "I think I'm home free with Lucile. She showed me all her research and sure enough there is a lien from the bank on some land out on Ibo. Thing is, the loan was made to a Harding and Company and I can't find a record of any Hardings around here since right after the Civil War. Makes it simple in a way. Since there's nobody to notify, I'll give the information to the Board tomorrow. The bank won't want some worthless land out there, so they'll put it up for auction. I know Lucile thinks there's money to be made on Ibo, but then Lucile sees dollar signs everywhere."

"Will you buy the property?" Hattie called from the other room.

"Lucile asked me the same question. Can't be me, that would be a conflict of interest, but I'm pretty sure Lucile'll find a way to buy it. She's got some money from her family. Either way, it's out of my hands. Let's play poker!"

Hattie came in from the kitchen looking—she hoped—as sick as she felt. "Gentlemen, I'm sorry, but I don't think I can do this tonight. I'm not feeling well at all. Matt?"

He read her thoughts and took over. He managed to get Doc and the sheriff on their way then turned to Maurice. "I think you better stay behind, Maurice. You see, there's a problem with the land on Ibo." The three of them sat back down at the table and Matt continued. "As it turns out, Harding and Company is the name Ammee Hamlin's family used to take out the loan."

"Who's Ammee Hamlin?" Maurice asked.

"Ammee is Jacob's wife. That property belongs to her family."

"Jacob? Like the Jacob who built this table? I don't think I ever knew his last name, but whatever it is, he's not a Harding."

It was Hattie who had to explain the difference between the white Hardings who originally settled Ibo Island, and the black Hardings who had been given the land and had been living there since the end of the Civil War.

Matt picked up where she left off. "We know nobody's paid on that loan for a long time..."

"Forty-nine years," Maurice said.

"That's right. I've done some figuring and as far as I can tell they owe about $1450..."

"Actually $1463.88..." When the gravity of the situation began to dawn on Maurice, he looked stricken. "Lord God, Matt, I'm sorry. I had no idea. Y'all know I gotta give this information to the Board. I'll stall as long as I can, but with Lucile in the middle of this I can't stall for long. Once I tell them, it becomes official. Then they'll inform the Hamlins that they have 30 days to pay the loan. Reckon they can come up with the money?"

Matt and Hattie both shook their heads.

Maurice sat there staring at the table. "Damn Lucile!"

When he got home, Matt started to call Cora and then changed his mind. There was no reason to give her bad news when there was nothing she could do about it from so far away.

Cora was coming to the same conclusion. She almost picked up the phone to call Matt because she needed to get his advice, but there was no reason to trouble him when there was nothing he could do. She realized that everything she accomplished in New York brought her one day closer to the time when she and Katie would have to go home, whether they had found Bird or not. About the only item of business left was to sell the furniture.

"Not to worry. I'll take care of it," Sadie said. Cora was beginning to wonder if there was anything Sadie *couldn't* take care of. "I'll call my cousin Sol, he knows a man who buys furniture. He comes, he makes you an offer, you haggle a little, eventually you agree on a price. He takes the furnishings, you get the money."

"It sounds easy, but I'm not sure I'd know a good offer if I heard one. I don't know what any of these things are worth."

"You don't have to know, he knows. Here's how it works. Anything he offers you first, it's too low. So you ask for more and you hold back a few things. You can always throw them into the bargain at the last minute. But don't worry, I'll be here. Let me deal with him."

The two women started to go through the apartment jotting down what they thought each item was worth. Katie took notes. Sadie seemed to know what she was doing and the dollars started to mount up. By the time she was done, Aunt T's household goods and furniture came to nearly $500.

Cora was astonished. "Sadie, that's a fortune...at least for us. Do you really think we'll get that much?"

Sadie shrugged. "Close."

"Well, I want to pay you for this."

"You can't pay me. It's a *mitzvah*, a good deed. I'm doing you a favor."

Cora smiled. "Alright, I'm going to do you a *mitzvah*." She went to the china cabinet and began to unload the Wedgewood tea set. There was a teapot, a coffee pot, eight cups and saucers, a small tray for the cream pitcher and sugar bowl, and a larger tray for pastries. "Katie and I want you to have this. Use it in good health and know that we could never have gotten through this without your help."

Sadie threw her arms around Cora. "Such a table I'm gonna set. Even Mrs. Cohan and all her fancy-smancy friends have got nothing this grand." Katie helped carry the china across the hall, piece by piece. Then Sadie opened the drop-leaf table and they set everything out so she could see it in all its glory.

Sadie glanced at her watch. "It's getting late. I have to get ready for *Shabbos*." Before Katie could ask, Sadie said, "The Jewish Sabbath. So go. But you should come back at 4:15." With that she hustled them out the door.

Back in their apartment, Cora and Katie speculated as to what was involved in *Shabbos*. Their conclusion was that it was probably like getting ready for Sunday. So they each took a quick bath and then went looking for something nicer to wear.

They searched Aunt T's closets and found a black dress that almost fit Cora. For Katie, they found a dark red blouse and a matching shawl that looked nice with her good black skirt.

Promptly at the appointed time they knocked on Sadie's door. She had also changed clothes and was wearing a navy blue dress with a pretty white lace collar. She looked them up and down and nodded her approval. "Welcome to my home. I don't know if you know, but it's a custom with us Jews to invite a stranger to share the Shabbos meal. Usually this is a family celebration, but since my Simon passed, and my children are all the way out on Long Island, well, I take some liberties. But I do light the candles and say the blessings because that's important. So tonight we do that together."

She continued to talk as she made preparations. "When I first came here, I lived with my aunt on the Lower East Side. Lots of immigrants, Jews, Irish, Italians. The noise, you wouldn't believe. Peddlers and kids and traffic. But in our neighborhood, on Friday evening, the noise stopped. So quiet it got, from two blocks away we could hear the chants of the cantor."

On the sideboard were two silver candlesticks with tall white candles. There was also a silver goblet. Sadie pointed to them. "The candlesticks belonged to my grandmother. A wedding gift to Simon and me. The wine cup, we bought that one together." She glanced at her watch. "We light the candles a few minutes before sunset, but first we put a little money aside for the poor." She took some coins out of her pocket and laid them on the table.

Then Sadie carefully lit the candles and waved her hands toward her face as if she were washing it with the light. "I would normally say the blessing in Hebrew, but for you, I'll say it in English."

"Do it a little bit in Hebrew, please," Katie said.

191

Sadie covered her eyes with her hands and recited, "*Baruch Atah Adonai, Eloheinu Melech Ha'Olam,* that's the beginning of each blessing. It means 'Praised are you, Lord our God, Master of the universe.'" And then she continued the rest of the blessing in English, "...who has sanctified us with your commandments and commanded us to light the Sabbath candles.

"Now we each say a silent prayer for our families, their health, their peace and their honor." She turned and picked up the goblet. "Normally the father does this, but tonight it's just us. 'Praised are you, Lord our God, Master of the universe, Creator of the fruit of the vine'" She took a sip of wine.

Sadie then picked up the two loaves of bread on the table. "This is *challah,* egg bread." She held one in each hand in front of her and recited another blessing. 'Praised are you, Lord our God, Master of the universe, who brings forth bread from the earth.' Then she tore three small pieces from one of the loaves, sprinkled a little salt on it and handed them around.

"Traditionally there would be singing, but nobody wants to hear me, so now we eat. Matzo-ball soup and there is also roast chicken. Do you want to hear a little Jewish joke? I'm telling you. This is the history of the Jews in one sentence. They tried to kill us, we survived, let's eat." Cora and Katie smiled politely. "Oy, without the whole history, I guess it's not such a good joke."

But it was a good evening. The apartment was filled with the aroma of candle wax and spices and for the first time in weeks Cora felt a sense of peace. That night before she dropped off to sleep, Katie said, "You know, Mamma, we've added another one."

"Another what, Sweetie?"

"Now we've got our God, the Ibo God, the Harlem God, Dr. Buzzard and now the Jewish God all on our side. That's powerful root. Things are gonna work out, you wait and see."

CHAPTER TWENTY-FOUR

After breakfast Cora suggested they go back to the Abyssinian Baptist Church. "No, Mamma. That might ruin everything. We have to give the root time to work. Tomorrow is Sunday and everybody will come to the church and they will see Bird's pictures and then he'll call." Once again Cora was struck with Katie's unwavering faith. Part of her wanted to share in that certainty and part of her wanted to protect Katie from the disappointment of failure. Katie found the subway map Sadie had given them, "Let's go sightseeing."

"Oh Katie, I don't know. It looks really complicated." They spread the map on the table and studied it carefully.

"It looks like we can take the D Train and just stay on that all the way to Manhattan. Oh, come on Mamma, it'll be fine. Easy-peasy." They bundled up and set off on their adventure. They went through the turnstile just as the train was pulling into the station and they got carried along with the crowd headed for the subway door. It wasn't too crowded and when they found seats, Cora breathed a sigh of relief. "Now if we can just figure out when to get off..."

Katie turned to the woman sitting next to her. "We want to see Manhattan. Can you tell us when to get off?"

The woman seemed surprised at first, but then she smiled. "Sure. Just get off when I do."

Katie read the signs at each station. "Mamma, look! It says Yankee Stadium! I know about that. That's where they play baseball. Dad and I listen to the games sometime. I can't wait to tell him I saw it."

The trip flew by in stretches of black punctuated by the hard, white light of the stations. In what seemed like no time at all, Katie's new friend said, "OK. Rockefeller Center. This is our stop." Katie and Cora followed the woman up to the street. When they reached Fifth Avenue, she pointed, "The skating rink is right over there and you should see the Empire State Building while you're here. It's not far. Just walk down Fifth Avenue to 34th Street." With that she was gone and Cora and Katie realized they were standing alone in the middle of Manhattan.

They just followed the crowd and had no problem finding the skating rink. They stood along the edge and looked down at the skaters gliding around. Some of them were very good, some kept falling down, but everyone seemed to be having a good time. When they got cold, they walked into the Visitors Center on the corner just to warm up.

A young woman in a smart uniform asked if they needed any help. "We're going to see the Empire State Building," Katie said with authority.

"You've chosen a good day. It's clear so you should have a magnificent view from the observation deck on the 86th floor. It's all open air and you can walk all the way around. If that's too cold, go up to the deck on the 102nd floor. It's enclosed. You'll need to get your tickets in the lobby. Is there anything else you especially want to see?"

Without a moment's hesitation, Katie said, "I wanna see Grand Central Station. Is it far?"

The woman laughed. "That's an unusual choice, but I think it's a good one. Actually the name is Grand Central *Terminal*, but most New Yorkers just call it Grand Central. It's just a few blocks away. You're on Fifth Avenue now, so you want to walk a block over to Madison, then one more block to Park Avenue and then down to 42nd Street. Here, I'll show you where it is on the map. After that, you're going to walk back over to Fifth and down to 34th Street to get to the Empire State Building."

Armed with directions and a map, they walked along Park Avenue. Hattie had been right, the street was crowded with people and everyone was in a hurry. The wind was blowing and they were thankful for Aunt T's borrowed coats.

When they walked into the building, Katie could almost hear the radio announcer saying... "and then Grand Central Station!" The main waiting room was made of cream-colored marble and the ceiling was painted blue green with gold outlines of the constellations. Katie was sure the chandeliers were bigger than she was. There were troops in uniform everywhere and one whole wall was covered with military pictures. Underneath it said, "Buy Defense Bonds and Stamps Now!"

"Mamma, Mamma look, there's the terminal clock and the information desk where all the characters in the stories meet." They looked around for a place to eat and saw the Oyster Bar, but oysters were no big deal, they could get plenty of those back on Ibo. Instead they choose a small café and ordered hot pastrami sandwiches.

Back out on the street, they walked over to Fifth Avenue and headed south. It seemed that everywhere they turned there was another store window that caught their eye. From street level on 34th they could hardly see the top of the Empire State Building and couldn't believe they were actually going all the way to the top.

They got their tickets and were directed to a "bank" of elevators. "Wow!" Katie said looking around. She'd never seen so many elevators all in a row. The ride up was so fast their ears popped and when they got to the open-air observation deck on the 86th floor, Cora didn't want to go outside. However, there was no stopping Katie, so Cora ventured out the door, but stood with her back pressed up against the building. Katie, of course, walked all the way around the building. Along the way she heard a teacher pointing out landmarks to her students, so Katie tagged along.

"All right now, if you look north, you'll see a large green area. That's Central Park, of course. If we walk around to our right, that's East, you can see the East River. If we keep going we'll be looking south. There you can see the Brooklyn Bridge and out in the harbor is the Statue of Liberty. Now come around a little bit more and you're looking west. That's the Hudson River and if you keep going you'll be back where you started."

Katie insisted they go to the observatory deck on the 102nd floor. "You'll like it a lot better 'cause there are windows all around." She was right and Cora let Katie be the guide and point out all the highlights.

It was mid-afternoon by the time they headed back to Rockefeller Center to catch the subway. Cora had checked the map before they started out so she and Katie walked with confidence, just like real New Yorkers.

When they got home, Cora made scrambled eggs for supper. They were just finishing when the phone rang. Katie grabbed it. "Hello?...Oh Hi, Dad. I was hoping it might be Bird, but guess what? We went sightseeing and..." Cora smiled as she listened to her daughter relive the day. Finally she got a chance to talk to Matt.

"Sounds like Katie is having the time of her life," Matt said. "It's nice to hear her so excited. Things aren't going so well down here. You and Hattie were right. The land Lucile found does belong to Granny's family. Turns out they owe close to $1500."

"Oh Matt, I'm so sorry. Is there anything that will help?"

"Maurice had no idea whose land he was dealing with. Now his hands are tied and I guess, we all just have to let things play out and see what happens. Hattie and I are trying to come up with some way to keep Lucile from buying the land, but it's not looking good. How are things going up there?"

Cora made sure Katie was out of hearing distance. She explained that they had someone coming to buy the furniture and move it out on Monday. "Katie's still sure we'll get a call, but if we haven't heard anything by Monday night, we're going to have to leave with or without Bird. Oh Matt, how did our world get so complicated? Whatever happens I'll be glad to get home. I miss you."

That night Cora dreamed about falling off the Empire State Building. It was like she was lying face down on the air. She could feel the wind in her face, but for some reason, she wasn't afraid. She remembered thinking maybe that was what it felt like to fly.

Sunday it snowed. Big fat flakes that floated down slowly and melted fast. Katie put on all her warm clothes and sat out on the fire escape. By New York standards, it wasn't much of a storm, but for someone who had never seen snow before, it was a beautiful blizzard and Katie loved every minute of it. She held Robin's lucky charm in her hand, picked a snowflake way up high and made a wish for Bird as she watched it fall. She decided seven was the exact number of snowflakes she needed to make something good happen.

Although they had talked about Bird every day since they came to New York, neither Cora or Katie mentioned him at all on Sunday. To distract everyone, Cora invited Sadie over for a treasure hunt. Each of them was to go through the apartment and pick out three treasures to keep before the furniture man came to take everything away. Sadie chose three cut-glass wine glasses and Cora added the fourth for good measure. Katie chose the shawl she had worn for *Shabbos*, a snow globe with the Statue of Liberty which she found way in the back of a bookshelf, and a bright-colored shopping bag from Macy's. Cora's choice was easy. She picked three silver picture frames with pictures of her father and Aunt T.

Sunday came and went without a phone call.

Monday morning they had just gotten up and dressed when Sadie knocked on the door carrying a bag of bagels. "Eat fast. Then gather up everything that you wanta keep, put it in the bathroom and close the door. I called my cousin Sol and he said the buyer is gonna look at everything and give you a price for the whole shebang. Then we'll haggle a little. Not to worry, he doesn't deal in *schlock*. He knows good quality when he sees it. I'll get you a good price. Once you get your money, the moving guys come. They're gonna pack *everything*. I'm telling you, if you leave the garbage in the can, they're gonna pack it."

Cora hadn't actually announced to Katie that they were leaving, but selling the furniture made it all too clear. Katie's faith had been so unshakable, Cora wasn't sure how she was going to deal with the harsh adult reality that sometimes faith isn't enough. "I just can't stop to worry about that now," Cora thought. The immediate problem was to get their belongings together and stash them in the bathroom.

When the buyer showed up, Cora and Katie made it a point to stay out of Sadie's way. It took about an hour and most of the time they couldn't understand what was being said, but from all appearances, Sadie had the situation well in hand. Finally Cora was summonsed to sign a paper and receive a check for $650. "God bless Sadie, she's done it again."

199

Cora was astonished at how quickly the movers packed everything. Aunt T's whole life disappeared in less than half an hour. When the workmen were gone, Cora and Katie brought out what was left in the bathroom. A card table and two folding chairs. The bed frame was gone, leaving just the mattress on the floor. They had stored a tea kettle and two cups, and a few odds and ends of food in the refrigerator with a note saying "Do Not Open." Cora had also packed their suitcases the night before. The apartment didn't look like home anymore, it just looked empty and sad.

Sadie had one last surprise up her sleeve. "Have I got a treat for you. This afternoon we're going to the Paradise Theatre over on the Concourse. It's so beautiful on the inside, you wouldn't believe. Looks like you're in a courtyard, with stars and everything in the sky. Such a place, I'm telling you it's so grand, they don't even need to show a movie. But you get that too. *Jane Eyre* with that Orson Wells fellow and Joan Fontaine. Is she gorgeous or what? By the way, did you know she is Olivia de Havilland's sister? And for you, Miss Katie, they have Margaret O'Brien. So hurry up, I don't want we should be late."

The Paradise was everything Sadie promised. All three women cried for poor Jane when she found out the man she loved, Edward Rochester was already married. But in the end, she got her inheritance and married Edward and they lived happily ever after. It was getting dark by the time the movie was over and because no one was ready to go home yet, they stopped by Child's Restaurant for pancakes.

Sadie insisted they come by her apartment for a cup of tea and since there was nothing left for them in 9-A, they were glad to accept. They just stopped by the old apartment long enough to leave their coats. As they were headed out the door, the phone rang. "Mamma, you go on over to Sadie's," Katie said. "I'll get the phone, it's probably Dad."

Several minutes later, Katie burst into Sadie's living room. "Mamma! Come quick, it's Bird!"

CHAPTER TWENTY-FIVE

Cora dashed across the hall and grabbed the receiver. "Hello?...Hello?...Is anybody there? ...Bird?"

"Yes..."

"Bird, I'm so glad to hear your voice. This is Cora Reeve. Matt Reeve's wife...Katie's mamma. Are you alright?"

"Yes."

"Where are you?"

"Harlem."

"We came up here to find you...No, I mean we came here because my aunt died, but we...Robin was so sure you were here and Dr. Buzzard said...It's a long story. Anyway, we *are* here. We were planning to leave tomorrow and we want you to come with us. Can we meet you somewhere?"

There was a long pause and Cora wondered what was going on. She had expected Bird to be overjoyed to hear from someone back home. Maybe he *had* run away. Maybe he didn't want to go home. Maybe someone was there with him and he couldn't talk freely.

"We don't have to leave then, but we do want to see you. Is there somewhere we can meet?"

"The church." Cora heard someone whispering in the background. "About 11:30?"

"Yes, of course. We'll be there."

"Thank you." The phone went dead and Cora stood there holding the receiver trying to figure out what was happening. Katie and Sadie had followed Cora across the hall and were watching her now, so she smiled. "We're going to meet him at the church tomorrow at 11:30."

Sadie saw the look on Cora's face and knew something was bothering her. Katie, on the other hand, was whirling around the empty apartment like a Dervish. "We found him, we found him…"

"Katie, stop with the singing already," Sadie said. "Come, help me make the tea. Give your mother some peace and quiet to call your father and tell him the good news."

As soon as they left, Cora dragged a chair over to the phone and dialed home. Matt answered on the first ring. "Hello?"

"Matt…"

"Oh, Cora. I'm so glad it's you. Give me some good news, please."

He sounded so sad, Cora didn't want to start out with her misgivings. So she took a deep breath and tried to sound enthusiastic. "We found him! He's actually here. I just talked to him."

"Oh my God, Cora, that's wonderful."

Matt wanted to know all the details. He sounded so relieved and so excited Cora went back through the whole story again. Although she thought they had already talked about it, she relived all their sightseeing adventures. Then she told him about *Shabbos* with Sadie and getting the "Jewish God" on their side. She told him it snowed on Sunday and admitted she had given up hope when they didn't hear anything that day.

"That's not all." She told him everything that happened from the furniture man coming, to the movers and how fast they took everything away. "We made $650! I couldn't believe it."

"I can't wait to hear all the details when you get home. I wish I had a way to talk to Jacob and Ammee tonight, but I'll take the first ferry out in the morning."

Cora didn't want to dampen his enthusiasm, but she also didn't want to get everybody's hopes up until she knew the whole story. "Matt, you know they're going to have a million questions, and we haven't actually *seen* Bird yet, I just talked to him on the phone. We're meeting him tomorrow morning, so why not wait until you can tell his family everything. I'll call you as soon as we get back here and by that time, we should know what's been going on with him and when we'll be able to leave and…everything."

Reluctantly Matt agreed. Cora stood with the receiver in her hand after Matt hung up. "Ammee always said Bird didn't talk much, so maybe it's nothing to worry about." Up until this point, Cora had refused to dwell on how Bird had disappeared or what might have happened to him in the six months he'd been gone. Now all the possibilities played out in her head. "Maybe he was kidnapped. Maybe he's being held hostage. Maybe he's sick or he's been hurt. Maybe he's been living on the streets. Maybe he's been in jail. We've been praying to find him, we should have been praying to find him safe and sound."

Katie stuck her head in the front door. "Sadie said to tell you your tea's getting cold." Cora walked across the hall. Katie was in the midst of telling Sadie some long story about Bird and Robin and the Donegan sisters' library. Cora sipped her tea and waited. Finally she sent Katie off to get ready for bed.

Sadie looked her in the eye, "So what are you thinking? In my experience, too much thinking is not a good thing."

"When I talked to Bird, I expected him to be...happy to hear from me. Or at least to hear from someone from back home. But he hardly said two words. I know he's not a big talker, but still, oh I don't know..."

"Did he tell you something bad?"

"No, he didn't tell me anything."

"So, you're worrying about nothing? I'm telling you, forget about it. If there's a problem tomorrow, then you'll worry about the problem tomorrow. I'm going to bed."

The next morning Cora and Katie retraced their steps to the 8th Avenue Subway and got off in Harlem. They turned toward the church and Katie spotted Bird immediately. He was taller than she remembered, but he looked fine. He was standing with a light-skinned man who had his hand on Bird's shoulder. Katie started to run ahead, but Cora held her back. "Let him make the first move, we don't want to scare him away."

"Why would he be scared of us?" Katie demanded.

The man and Bird walked toward them and the man held out his hand. "My name's Marcus Jones." Cora introduced herself and Katie. "Bird's been staying with my wife Fay and me. Why don't you follow us to our apartment and Bird can tell you his story." With that, he and Bird turned and walked away. Cora and Katie followed.

They walked for several blocks then the man entered a brick apartment building. It looked all right on the outside, but the lobby was empty and there was an Out-of-Order sign on the elevator. "It's on the third floor," Marcus said as they started up the stairs. The stairwell was dark and it smelled like someone cooking greens too close to a bathroom. Down at the end of a long hall, he knocked lightly on a door and they heard several locks being unbolted. A woman opened the door a crack, peeked out, then closed the door again and removed a chain.

They walked into a comfortable living room with a couch, two armchairs and a small round table. The furniture was old, but well kept. Several of Bird's pictures were taped to the wall. Cora stepped forward and held out her hand to the woman. "My name is Cora Reeve. My husband, Matt, works with Bird's father, Jacob. His mother, Ammee, is my friend."

Katie chimed in, "His sister, Robin, is my friend too."

The Joneses looked at Bird and he indicated that what they were saying was true. "Please sit down," Fay said. For several moments no one spoke, then she said, "We saw the pictures at church, but Bird didn't recognize your name. We asked at the office and the receptionist described you and your daughter. It was her Bird recognized. That's when we knew it was safe to call you."

"Safe?" Cora said. "Why would you worry about that?"

Fay looked slightly uncomfortable. "Bird told us it was a white boy from where you live who put him on the Greyhound bus and sent him up here, so we didn't know whether to trust you or not."

"What bus? What boy?" Cora asked.

"You better let Bird answer that." Fay nodded at Bird.

"I was on my way to the ferry that Friday afternoon and this boy motioned for me to come over to where he was standing by the bus. He was real tall and he had on a uniform so I went over there."

When Cora heard the word uniform, she felt a chill. As far as she knew, there was only one boy in Meridian who wore a uniform.

"I didn't look him in the face or say anything. He just shoved this ticket and a package at me. He told me to get on the bus and somebody would ask for the package later. He said the bus driver knew all about it and if I made any trouble, he'd put me off in the middle of nowhere."

Cora could see the pieces coming together. Butch was tall for his age and even without the uniform, his attitude would have been enough to scare Bird. She doubted if Bird had ever been on a bus before and telling him to keep quiet was like telling the Sphinx to be silent.

The child had been forced into an alien world, isolated in silence, afraid to reach out to anyone for help. Bird was alone, without any money and as far as he was concerned, everywhere was the middle of nowhere. Cora realized she had been viewing the whole situation through the eyes of the people he left behind. When she looked at it from Bird's perspective, it was an entirely different story.

"I kept my head down and started walking to the back of the bus. Once I turned around to see if I could get off, but the boy blocked my way. Then he got off, the driver shut the door, said 'take a seat,' and he started down the road. I looked around, but nobody paid any attention to me. When the bus turned the corner, I nearly fell down so I just found a seat and sat down."

"Weren't you scared?" Katie asked.

"Scareder than I've ever been in my life. The bus started going faster and faster. Once or twice somebody flagged the bus down, and got on, but nobody ever got off. I held on real tight to my stuff from school and I cried, but not loud enough for anybody to hear. I knew I was gettin' farther and farther away from home, but I didn't know what to do. I didn't know where I was, I didn't have any money and I was afraid I'd never get back to Ibo or see my family again."

Tears rolled down Cora's cheeks. She wanted to reach out to Bird, but she knew better than to interrupt.

"Every time we came to a rest stop, I tried to get off, but the driver looked at my ticket, and said, 'This ain't your stop. I'm keepin' my eye on you and you better be back on this bus

207

before we leave.' One time I tried to hang back, but he sent somebody to get me.

"Finally we stopped in some town and a guy in a uniform got on. At first I thought he might be the police, so I ducked my head. Then he asked if he could sit in the seat next to me and he had a nice soft voice. He said he was a Marine and his name was Leroy Jones.

"When he asked me where I was going, I said I didn't know. He took my ticket and said it looked like we were both going to New York City. I had never looked at the ticket before. Part of me was still scared, but I was a little excited too...about New York City, I mean.

"It took us a long time to get to New York, but Leroy took care of me from then on. He bought me food, a hamburger and a Coke. Boy, that tasted good, I was real hungry. He asked about my family and told me about his family and he brought me home with him. He said everything would be alright and I tried not to be afraid anymore."

Bird indicated the two adults, "This is his mamma and papa. They took me in and they've been good to me. Leroy stayed a little while, but then he had to leave to go out to California and go overseas. I've been here the whole time."
Bird stopped as if he had used up all the words he knew.

"Why didn't you call us?" Katie asked.

Bird looked sad, then he shrugged and said quietly, "Who would I call? We got no telephones out on Ibo. And I didn't know Mr. Matt's last name or anything."

Katie wouldn't leave it alone. She asked Bird why he didn't write to tell his mamma where he was. Cora came to Bird's rescue. "Katie, think about it. You know what Ibo Island is like. Have you ever seen a street sign or a mail box?"

"We got no addresses on Ibo. We live at our house, Granny lives at her place. I wanted to get in touch, but we couldn't figure out what to do."

Marcus broke in. "We tried sending letters to his mamma at General Delivery, Ibo Island, but they all came back marked 'No Such Address.' We tried the same thing using Meridian, Georgia, but that didn't work either."

At this point, Fay entered the conversation. "Bird's been working on weekends at the candy store and saving his money and we've been tryin' to help too."

"I sold a few of my pictures. I figured when I got enough money, I'd buy myself a bus ticket back home."

"Bird's been going to school at PS 194 over on West 144th Street. At first he was way behind everybody in his class. But they keep some of the kids until 5:00 to get extra help and Bird caught up fast," Fay said. "His teachers all say he's smart and he has a lot of talent. They got him to work on the school newspaper and everything. When he gets in high school, there's a really good art program we've been looking into and…" She stopped suddenly. "Pardon my manners. I didn't offer y'all anything to drink. Would you like a cup of coffee? Or hot chocolate? Bird loves hot chocolate."

Without waiting for an answer, Fay got up and went into the kitchen. Cora saw her wipe her eyes as she filled the coffee pot and heated milk in a pan on the stove. Once again, Cora realized there was yet another side to the story. So far, all her thoughts had been with Jacob and Ammee and Robin. But now she realized there was another family involved. When she looked at the story from the Jones' point of view, she had to rewrite everything again.

They had sent their son off to war, and the Lord had sent them Bird, another young boy who needed their help. It was clear they cared for him and apparently Bird felt the same way.

Although Cora didn't want to dwell on it, she knew Bird would have a better education and a lot more opportunities in New York than he would in Meridian, Georgia.

"Oh my God, what if he thinks he has to make a choice? When Jacob and Ammee find out what's happened, will they think they should make a choice for him?" Then suddenly another thought struck Cora. "Maybe Bird was afraid to go home. Maybe he had a good reason to be afraid."

She wasn't exactly sure how to approach the subject, but she had to get an answer to the question that was at the bottom of everything. "Bird, you said an older boy put you on the bus. Did you know him?"

"No Ma'am. I never saw him before."

"Would you know him if you saw him again?"

"I don't know. I'm pretty good at remembering faces. In fact, I drew a picture of him while I was sitting on the bus. Want me to get it?"

With a gnawing fear in her heart, Cora nodded.

A minute later she and Katie were looking at one of Bird's sketches. There was no mistaking it. They were staring at a picture of Butch Dupree.

CHAPTER TWENTY-SIX

"Matt, it was awful. I couldn't believe my eyes although I don't honestly know why I should have been surprised. It was Butch, no doubt about it, it was him. Just when I thought things might have a chance of working out, this happens."

Bird hadn't shown much interest in who the boy was, so Cora let the subject drop. Katie wanted to see Bird's school and the Joneses said it was close by so the kids went off to explore. When they left, Cora tried to explain who—and what—Butch was. When she mentioned that he was the mayor's son, Marcus started pacing the living room. "It doesn't seem right to send Bird back down there and to get mixed up in all...that...stuff. Of course we want his folks to know he's alright, but..."

Fay said, "You don't know what it was like at first. That boy was scared of everything. After Leroy left, he hardly ever talked. He wouldn't leave the apartment, he wouldn't eat, he cried himself to sleep every night. It was just by accident that we got through to him. One night Marcus was trying to draw a picture of some shelves our neighbor was gonna build for us. Bird took the pencil away from him and drew this perfect picture of the living room with the shelves all in place. I'll never forget the smile on his face when he showed the drawing to us. From that point on, things got better."

The more Cora heard, the more confused she became. She had thought the big problem was going to be *finding* Bird, she hadn't stopped to think about what he had been going through in the months he'd been gone. Clearly things were a lot more complicated than they appeared at first glance. She wanted to make sure Fay and Marcus understood she and Katie were not there to snatch Bird away. But she also wanted them to understand what his parents had been through not knowing whether he was alive or not. And then there was Butch. How in the world was she going to explain Butch?

"There is no doubt that the Dupree boy did a terrible thing and he needs to be held accountable. But the only way to put a stop to him is for Bird to tell the sheriff in Meridian exactly what happened. I know it must sound scary, but Bird has a lot of people back home who care about him. People who will make sure he's safe and that Butch gets what's coming to him."

In an effort to further reassure the Joneses, she explained that Butch's father had already sent him away to military school. However, she could tell they were not impressed by that. "Would you feel better if one of you came home with us? I'd be glad to pay for your train ticket."

That didn't seem to be the solution either. They continued to talk and finally the Joneses asked for one more day to get used to the idea and then to help Bird get checked out of school, tell his boss at the candy store he was leaving and say good bye to his teachers and friends. Cora assured them she knew how hard it must be for them to let Bird go. Although there were no phones on Ibo, Cora promised to make sure Bird knew he was welcome at their house anytime he wanted to call the Joneses and let them know what was going on.

"It's not just that," Marcus said. "He's smart and we got better schools up here. Besides that, he's got real talent. There are lots more opportunities for a kid like that in the city. We know we got no right to keep him, but it's a lot to think about."

Cora knew he had a point, but there was no way she was leaving without Bird. When Fay invited them to stay for supper, Cora said she thought they ought to spend the last night alone with Bird. She volunteered to come by the apartment the next morning so they could all go down to Penn Station together.

"Matt, that's the way we left it. So we'll leave tomorrow morning. I know the Joneses realize Bird has to leave with us, but I can't help feeling sorry for them. They really do care about him and we all know there are some good reasons for him to stay here. Anyway, assuming it all works, we should be in Atlanta some time on Saturday. Can you check with the station there for the exact time?"

Matt said he would take care of everything. He wanted to immediately tell Bird's family he was safe and coming home soon, but he agreed that waiting one more day until they were actually on the train was a better idea. He and Cora also decided not to spoil the happy news for his family by mentioning Butch's involvement. There would be time for that later. However, Matt did call Hattie to give her the latest update.

Sadie was in much the same position as the Joneses. She had formed a close attachment to Cora and Katie and she hated to see them leave. When she found out they were staying an extra day, she planned one last adventure, to the Bronx Zoo. The latest excursion made Cora realize once again how much more there was to do in New York than back home. There were zoos and museums and art galleries, none of which existed anywhere close to Meridian or Ibo Island. What would Bird's life—or Katie's, for that matter—be like living in such an exciting city?

213

Cora loved her life with Matt in a community where she knew everyone and where life didn't go by so fast. She couldn't imagine herself living in New York City, but more and more she could see the advantages for the younger generation. And she could understand how the Joneses felt safe in Harlem and probably thought of the South as a dangerous place. What she had thought would be an easy decision, was turning out to be anything but.

After they got home from the zoo, they ate a light supper and went to bed early. Katie tossed and turned all night so neither she nor Cora got much sleep. The next morning Sadie went down to the lobby with them to say good-bye. The elevator operator said she would miss them. Sidney shook Cora's hand and gave Katie a Yankee's baseball cap. Sadie hugged Cora, "So, you'll write, you'll let me know what happens and call me from time to time, but only on Sunday when the rates are cheaper. *Shalom*."

Then she handed Katie a large brown paper bag. "Bagels, a knish or two or three and some deli for a nosh on the train. You're not gonna find food like that down South." She was right. It was going to be hard to go back to bologna sandwiches, white bread and Jell-O.

The cab driver blew the horn several times. "Hey Lady, gimme a break. I'm tryin' to make a livin' here."

That was the wrong thing to say. Sadie walked around to his side of the cab, stuck her face in the window and gave him a piece of her mind. "Don't be such a *schmuck*. You're givin' the city a bad name. What? It's gonna hurt you to wait a minute?" Just to make her point, she took her time helping Cora and Katie into the cab. Finally they headed to Harlem and Cora held her breath just hoping Bird would be waiting for them at his apartment building.

When they got there, she and Katie walked into the lobby. Bird and the Joneses were standing in a sad little group. Fay approached Cora. "I think you know how we feel about Bird, but we would never want to keep him away from his family." Her voice cracked and Marcus took over. "The boy's got a talent and here in New York he could go to an art school, get some proper training... Maybe he could come stay with us for a while... something..."

Cora reached out and took both Fay and Marcus by the hand. "Bird is a very lucky young man. Now he has two families. Once his parents know he's safe and hear how kind you and your son have been to their son, there has to be a way to work something out. Here is our address and phone number, we will keep in touch and let you know how things work out." By this time, everyone was close to tears. Another round of hugs and Fay handed Bird a large brown paper bag. "Fried chicken, biscuits and fried pies to eat on the train." Katie held up her paper bag, "I got one too, bagels." Everyone smiled.

"I promise to write," Bird said. "And call," Katie added, "but only on Sunday when the rates are cheaper."

The cab driver seemed determined to make up all the time he lost waiting for them. He drove like he was in the Indy 500, or maybe he was just making up for the fact that the race had been canceled because of the war. At any rate, they made it to Penn Station in record time. As it turned out, there was a train leaving in half an hour and they hardly had time to get their tickets, run down the steps to the platform, locate the right car and find their seats. As they pulled out of the station, Cora realized she hadn't called Matt. At the first stop, she found a pay phone and quickly told Matt they were on their way.

As soon as he hung up, Matt started making calls. Hattie first, then Sheriff Mayhew. Next, he went looking for Jacob and found him working on a job near the dock. Matt got out of his car in such a hurry, the left the door open. He saw Jacob around the back of the house and yelled across the yard, "They found him! He's coming home!"

Jacob looked up startled. "What? They found…oh my God, they found him? They found Bird? I gotta go tell Ammee," Jacob said as he ran toward Matt.

Matt laughed. "Yes, you do, but I think you should leave the saw here." Jacob looked down and seemed to be surprised to find he was holding a crosscut saw. "Oh, yeah," he said and dropped the saw on the ground. Then he bent over and picked it up, "No…" and put it back on his work bench. "I gotta go," then he doubled over, put his hands on his knees and started sucking in air like a long-distance runner who just finished a race.

Matt took him by the shoulders and helped him straighten up. "It's over, Jacob. We got him. He's with Cora and Katie and they're coming home."

When the reality hit him, Jacob broke into tears. "I was so afraid we'd never see him again…" Matt hesitated a moment, then gave his friend an awkward hug. "It's gonna be OK. Now you've got to go tell Ammee and Robin." Matt pointed Jacob in the direction of the dock. "I'll take care of this job, you get out of here. The sheriff's waiting with his boat to take you to Ibo. Go!"

Jacob saw the sheriff's boat and made a flying leap. "Damn man!" Sheriff Mayhew said. "It's a good thing you made it. I'd have hated to tell Ammee we found her son but her stupid husband drowned himself trying to fly over to my boat." They laughed and took off.

The 20 minute ride seemed to take forever. Before the boat docked, Jacob jumped off and ran all the way home. "Ammee! Ammee! They found him! Bird's OK. He's fine. He's coming home." Ammee and Robin ran to meet him and they hugged and laughed and cried and danced around the yard.

"I'll go tell Granny," Robin said and ran off shouting to the world, "Bird's coming home. Bird's coming home." When Jacob and Ammee caught their breath, they headed to the church. From the first sound of the bell, the good news about Bird spread to every corner of Ibo Island. Folks smiled and laughed and took a moment to give thanks to God. Robin went to give thanks to Dr. Buzzard.

While Ibo celebrated, Cora sat on the train and tried to relax and not count the minutes as they slowly ticked by. She watched and wondered if anyone would say anything about Bird sitting with them, but no one did. Again there were soldiers everywhere, young men headed to basic training in Georgia.

At one point the conductor motioned for Cora to join him. He explained that under normal circumstances once they crossed the Mason-Dixon Line the train would be segregated. But the official word had come down that no one was to ask a soldier to move, so everything would stay as it was. Cora breathed a sigh of relief.

This time instead of watching the cities get bigger, they watched the countryside expand. The dark, crowded cites up North had an air of suspense and mystery about them. The Southern cities were younger and more open.

"Everything looks different," Bird said. "On the bus, we went into the middle of all the little towns. Now we're going through fields and factory yards." Cora smiled. In six months, the silent, shy Bird had been replaced by this new version. He seemed older and he certainly talked a lot more.

When the solders in the car saw Bird making sketches, they all wanted one and they offered to pay for them. Bird said his "going rate" was 50 cents each. Oh yes, this was a whole new

Bird. They talked and ate and slept and slowly the miles and the hours went by.

At one point Cora saw Katie writing in her notebook. It was the first time she had noticed it since they left home. "Katie, what's that?"

She handed the book to her mother. "It's just some notes of all the stuff I wanted to remember to tell Dad and Robin." Cora read through the list and smiled.

KATIE'S NOTEBOOK

There is no moss in Atlanta. We must have passed the moss line when I wasn't looking.

I thought Union Station in Atlanta was big until I saw Penn Station.

I got to go to Grand Central Station! It was great.

Mamma was too scared to go to the edge at the top of the Empire State Building.

If you want to see the sky in New York City, you have to look straight up.

There are iron stairs on the outside of all the buildings.

A bagel is like a really heavy biscuit with a hole in the middle.

New York City is really, really, really cold. And noisy. And dirty.

The air smells funny. Mamma says it's because they use coal for heat.

Nobody has garbage cans. You dump your garbage down a thing like a laundry chute. It gets burned up in the basement.

The lights never go out even in the middle of the night.

You have to have keys for everything, even the mailbox.

Almost all the cars in New York City are yellow.

They keep all their trees in parks, or make them grow in little squares along the sidewalks.

Subways were scary at first, but now I like them. I like to stand in the very front car and look down the tunnel.

Here are some Jewish words I learned:
Schlep, carry
Mitzvah, a good deed
Shalom, hello or goodbye
Kvetch, to whine all the time
Bobbeh Meisseh, grandmother stories
Goy, that's me, a gentile
Klutz, a clumsy person
Maven, somebody who's really good at something
Mench, a good person

"You didn't write down anything about the Sabbath service with Sadie."

"I know. I'll tell them all about that. It was too complicated to write down."

Finally, they pulled into Union Station in Atlanta. They had been gone less than two weeks, but Katie was shocked at how small it looked after seeing Grand Central and Penn Station. "Someday," she promised herself, "I'm going back to New York City." She glanced over at Bird, "I'll bet he goes back too."

With a lot of screeching of wheels and hissing of air brakes, the train finally came to a stop. It took several minutes to get luggage off the overhead racks, say good bye, wish the soldiers good luck and line up in the aisles. Cora went first, then Katie, then Bird. As she started to step off the train, Cora scanned the crowd looking for Matt. He saw her first and waved. She ran to him. They hadn't told Bird his family would meet him in Atlanta so it took him by surprise when Jacob grabbed him in a bear hug like he used to do when his son was little. Even in his joy to have Bird home again, Jacob realized his son wasn't a little boy anymore. Ammee and Robin covered Bird with hugs and kisses and neither one of them gave a fig whether it embarrassed him or not.

People watching couldn't help but smile. That much joy was like the smell of popcorn, impossible to resist. Ammee and Robin held on to Bird as if they thought he might fly away again. Out in the parking lot, they climbed into Matt's 1941 Chevy sedan. It was one of the last cars to come out of Detroit before the car makers converted to munitions, trucks, tanks and planes in January of '42.

Normally, Katie would have called shotgun, but she waited for her dad to sort everybody out. She ended up in the middle of the front seat, with Bird and Robin sitting between their parents in the back. It was a tight squeeze, but nobody seemed to mind. The air was warm enough to have the windows rolled down a little and as soon as they got out of Atlanta, it smelled like pine trees. Glenn Miller's orchestra was on the radio and for the moment, God was in his heaven and all was right with the world.

Cora told Bird's family about the Marine who rescued him and the family he had been staying with in New York. Since they had never seen him any other way, no one was surprised that Bird just sat quietly.

It was Robin who peppered him with questions. "What was New York like? Did you like livin' in Harlem? Did you go to the Apollo? Did you meet that artist fellow? Did you have to go to school? What's livin' in an apartment like? Were there lots of people around? Dr. Buzzard said you were around lots of people, but you were safe. He was right, huh? Did you make friends? Did you draw lots of pictures? Did you bring some home? Do they have fish up there? Rivers? Could you go fishin'? Where'd you get that new jacket? Was it cold in New York? Does it snow up there?"

Jacob finally reached over and patted her on the arm. "Robin, that's enough questions for now."

A second later Katie and Bird both pointed out the window at the same time. "Moss!" They laughed. "We just passed the moss line, now we're really home," Katie said.

"Yes," Cora thought, "we're home." She wondered how long she could hold on to the good feelings before they had to tackle reality again.

CHAPTER TWENTY-SEVEN

It turned out that reality was like a puzzle with lots of interlocking pieces. Bird and his family on Ibo held some of the missing pieces. Robin was still wrapped up in her belief in Flying Africans and Dr. Buzzard's power to set things right. Jacob and Ammee were overjoyed to have Bird home and to find out that he was unharmed and had been taken care of by good people. They were ignoring the how and why. Granny sat quietly listening. She had dealt with the unpredictable nature of the world for many years and she knew there were more pieces to come. She was waiting for the who.

Bird finally got around to telling them how a boy asked him to do a favor and give a package to someone on the bus. Bird went on to explain that he was just trying to help, then the bus started to drive away and he didn't know what to do, so he just sat down.

"Who was this boy?" Jacob asked.

At that point, Bird showed them the sketch.

"That's Butch Dupree," Jacob said. "Bird, how do you know that boy?"

"I don't know him, I never saw him before."

"Then why did he pick you?"

"I don't know," Bird was almost in tears. He kept insisting he had never seen Butch before. Granny wanted to step in and save her grandson, but messing with other people's children was never a good idea. So she waited.

Finally Ammee spoke up. She didn't recognize the sketch either, but she recognized the name. "Jacob, that's the boy Cora talks about all the time, the one who's always getting into trouble, the one they sent off to that military school."

"I know who he is." Jacob's voice was tight and he took a deep breath and tried to calm down. He had heard about the shoot-out and he figured tricking Bird was the kind of thing Butch would do just for the hell of it. "God damn him. Mayor's son or no mayor's son, I'm gonna put a stop to that kid."

Both his children turned to look at Jacob. They had never heard him swear before.

Ammee reached for his arm, "Jacob! Don't you go doin' something you can't undo."

"Don't worry. He broke the law this time. I'm gonna get Matt to go with me to the sheriff. Butch's daddy is always gettin' him out of trouble, well not this time. Not this time!"

"Just promise me you won't do anything crazy. Promise me!"

"Don't worry. I'm not gonna try to do anything on my own. I reckon as many times as the sheriff's had to deal with that Dupree kid, he's got a craw full of him by now."

Ammee and Granny exchanged looks. The best thing they could do at the moment was to keep Bird safe on Ibo. Robin was thinking the same thing and she headed out the back door to visit Dr. Buzzard. She wanted to get him to put some more white root on her amulet.

Ammee knew Bird needed to go back to school, but she decided to keep him home a day or two. Since the New York schools were so far ahead of the one in Meridian, keeping him home a little while couldn't hurt.

Matt and Cora were dealing with other pieces of reality on the mainland. The minute Matt heard about Butch's part in Bird's disappearance, he knew Jacob wasn't going to let him get away with that. Matt knew what he might do if someone tried to hurt Katie. He just hoped when Jacob came over on the Monday morning ferry, he would come by the house so they could go to the sheriff's office together. If they added their pieces to what the sheriff already knew, that might give them a chance to put a stop to this before things got out of hand.

Matt was dreading Monday because of another reality. He told Cora that for two weeks, Maurice had done his best to delay the bank's taking any action concerning the unpaid loan on Jacob and Ammee's land. "Problem is, he's run out of excuses and Monday morning the Board is going to act. I know the Hamlins are aware of the overdue loan, but this is going to make it official. It just couldn't come at a worse time. I just hope they're prepared to handle whatever happens."

As soon as the bank opened, one of the young tellers was told to get the first ferry to Ibo Island, find Rebecca Harding Johnson and inform her that she and/or her descendants owed the Meridian Bank and Trust Co. $1463.88. Further, they had 30 days to pay off that amount or the land would be put up for public auction. He was also told not to return until he had completed his task.

Wearing his best—and only—suit, Tommy Webster set off for Ibo with a briefcase and the official papers. He was about the only person going to Ibo and certainly the only one wearing a suit. When they docked, there was a long line of people waiting to take the ferry back to Meridian. They all scrutinized him as he walked off the boat. He did his best to look older, a proper representative of the Meridian Bank and Trust.

Tommy had expected a town, but there wasn't one. Only small houses here and there and no one he could see outside. He was reluctant to knock on doors, but there didn't seem to be any alternative. He tried several houses, but either no one came to the door or when he asked, they claimed not to know who Rebecca Harding Johnson was.

As the day dragged on, he realized he had worked hard all morning and hadn't learned a darn thing. Several times he had thought he was making progress, but everything he tried turned out to be a dead end. By midafternoon, he was hot, tired and at his wits end. Finally he saw an old woman walking down the road toward him and he stopped her hoping she might be able to help. "Excuse me, Ma'am, but would you happen to know who Rebecca Harding Johnson is?"

"Yeah, I know her."

"Thank God," he thought. "Can you tell me where to find her?"

"I reckon I might can."

He waited and the woman waited. She was sorely tempted to send him on another wild goose chase, but in the end she took pity on the poor fellow. "She's here."

"On Ibo, I know."

The woman shook her head and rolled her eyes to heaven. "This boy is so dumb he deserves to go chase his tail," she decided.

"Ma'am, I am here to represent the Meridian Bank and Trust and I can't go back to the bank until I find her and the last ferry is gonna leave pretty soon. So if you know where she lives, please just tell me that."

And because he had asked so nicely, she told him where the woman lived. "It's on the other side of the island, so you better get a move on if you're gonna get over there and back before the ferry goes." The young man took off running and Granny sat down and laughed herself silly. "If that's the best the bank has to offer, maybe we can beat this thing yet."

Earlier in the day just as Matt was driving to work, he saw Jacob walking up the street. Matt pulled over and opened the car door. When Jacob got in, Matt turned off the ignition. There were things that needed saying and things that needed doing, but for the moment they sat in the companionable silence men sometimes share. Finally they looked at each other and nodded.

"Sheriff's waiting for us. I already called," Matt said.

"Thought you might. I appreciate that."

"One thing before we go. I hate to bring it up, but sometime today the bank is gonna serve your family with papers about the loan. Cora and Hattie are headed out to Ibo later on to talk with Ammee and Granny to see what they can work out about that. Not anything you or I can do about that now, so let's see what the sheriff has to say about this Butch business. Have you got the picture Bird drew?"

Jacob patted his shirt pocket, "Oh yeah, I got it right here."

"Good," Matt said and started the car.

As soon as Cora saw Matt pull out of the driveway, she called Hattie. They exchanged information and decided the best thing they could do to help the Hamlin family was to figure out how to raise the money to pay off the loan. They took the early morning ferry to Ibo and found Granny at Ammee's.

They sat under the big oak tree drinking ice tea and Granny regaled them with the story of the bank man who was looking for Rebecca Harding Johnson. "That kid wasn't hardly even dry behind the ears. I near 'bout felt sorry for him. Sure enough, the papers were lying on my front porch when I got home. Haven't seen that young feller around here anywhere so I guess he musta made the ferry." They laughed and realized how long it had been since they had allowed themselves to do that. Having Bird home made all the difference. Then they got down to work.

Hattie wrote $1463.88 on a tablet in front of her. For several minutes they all just sat and starred at it. Granny spoke up first. "Well, I got those gold pieces. That's $60." Hattie wrote that down. She wondered if Granny knew that owning gold currency now was illegal. Next Ammee removed the coffee tin hidden in the bottom of the rice can under the sink. She poured out the contents and they counted $76.34. Hattie wrote that down too.

They hadn't realized Bird was standing around listening, but he came out with an envelope of bills which he added to the pile on the table. "There's $27.00 I saved from my job at the candy store up in Harlem and here's what I made selling pictures on the train coming home." He added $10 worth of quarters. Hattie wrote that total down too.

"Matt and I can contribute $100," Cora said and added her IOU.

"Me too," Hattie said and wrote those two figures down. "That gives us $373.34." The group got very quiet as the women sat and looked at the small pile of money on the table. "There's no way we can raise enough money to pay back the loan. Not in 30 days, not in 30 years," Ammee said.

"Wait a minute," Robin said. "I got some money I've been savin' for...somethin' special. I guess this is pretty special." She emptied the contents of a fruit jar on the table. $2.84.

Hattie added that. "Our grand total now is $376.18. I'm holding a couple hundred dollars of Maurice's markers from the poker games," Hattie said. "I could call those in... That would put us over $500." It was a good idea, but they all knew they were still nowhere close to the amount they needed. "What about your church? Could they take up an offering of some kind?"

"Jacob would never stand for us asking our friends for money. Besides nobody out here's got cash money to spare.

Matter of fact, I don't think he's gonna be real comfortable takin' money from anybody who's not family. What we need is a miracle and I'm afraid we've used up our share of miracles just gettin' Bird home."

Granny looked at the money, then looked around the table. "What does it mean if we can't pay and the land goes up for auction?"

"It goes to the highest bidder," Hattie said.

"But with $500 we might *be* the highest bidder. Like Ammee said, nobody out here's got that kind of money and nobody on the mainland wants property on Ibo. They couldn't even get to it, less they got themselves a boat. Besides most of 'em probably think it's all swamp land anyway."

"You're forgetting one thing," Hattie said. "Lucile Dupree. She's the one who started this whole thing because she's determined to own property out here on Ibo. She's convinced some big investor like the Rockefellers is gonna come along and build a private club out here the way they did on Jekyll Island. From what I've heard Maurice say at the poker games, she's got some family money of her own. I don't know how much, but my guess is she's got at least enough to pay off the loan." Once again the group got quiet.

"You know," Cora said slowly, "Ammee said we needed a miracle. What I think we really need is an angel." She turned to Hattie. "Isn't that what they call people who have money to give away?"

Ammee looked doubtful. "We don't know anybody like that."

Hattie was beginning to get the idea. "Yes, I think maybe we do. In fact we know two of them." She looked around the table and slowly everyone got the idea.

"The Donegan Sisters!"

"Exactly."

"Do you think they would help?" Ammee asked?
"I don't know," Cora said, "but it couldn't hurt to ask."

CHAPTER TWENTY-EIGHT

The sheriff was just opening his office when Matt and Jacob rolled into his driveway. Sheriff Mayhew shook Jacob's hand and told him again how glad he was that Bird was home safe and sound. Matt explained about the soldier who had helped Bird and the family who had taken him in.

Then Jacob took over and filled the sheriff in on how Bird had come to be missing in the first place. To back up his story, Jacob showed the sheriff Bird's sketch of the kid who put him on the bus. It was Butch, no doubt about it. The sheriff shook his head sadly, "I told Maurice he better get that kid under control before he hurt somebody. I guess military school wasn't enough.

"You did the right thing to come to me Jacob, and don't worry, we'll take care of this. I'll want to talk to Bird before we go any farther, make sure I have all the facts right. How 'bout I come out to Ibo tomorrow morning? I can see Bird with Ammee if you're working on a job."

Matt assured Jacob he could take all the time he needed. So he and the sheriff set an appointment and Matt offered Jacob a ride back to wait for the next ferry. "Nothing I can do over there, I'd rather go to work. But if you've got a minute or two,

I'd like to make a couple of stops on the way." As usual, mid-February was cold and wet and dreary but at least they had good news to brighten the day.

First they went by the Todd's to let them know Bird was safe. Elsie Todd was so happy she cried. "I'll be sure to tell the ladies at the church, we been prayin' for Bird, yes indeed, we sure have. Praise the Lord."

Matt waited in the car while Jacob went in to tell the Boones that Bird had been found. They didn't know Bird as well as they knew Robin, but family is family and they were happy to hear the good news too.

Their final stop was at the school. Jacob interrupted Miss Tipton's class just long enough to tell her his news. She was shocked to find out that Bird had actually wound up in Harlem and overjoyed to know that he was safe and home again. She immediately shared the information with her students and Jacob knew the news would be carried home by every kid and from there it would spread throughout Meridian. It had already circulated from one end of the Geechee community on Ibo to the other.

That night Jacob told his family about his meeting with the sheriff and warned Bird that he would have to tell the story again for the sheriff. He expected some hesitation, but Bird just nodded and Jacob realized the shy little boy who was afraid to go to the big school in Meridian really had disappeared.

When Sheriff Mayhew arrived the next morning, they all sat around the kitchen table and Bird went through the whole story again. Mayhew listened carefully and took notes from time to time. "So it was just Butch, nobody else?"

"Yessir."

"I'd sure like to talk to the bus driver, but they move them around from route to route, so that may be a problem. Any chance that you knew any of the passengers on the bus?"

"Nosir."

Although someone had probably already told him, it was important that the sheriff understand about Geechee children and how they were taught not to look an adult in the face without permission.

The sheriff kept asking questions as if he were searching for something specific. He obviously wasn't having any luck. "Bird, don't take this the wrong way, but I need something more than just your drawing. I need something that puts Butch on that bus with you."

Jacob started to protest when Bird spoke up. "I think maybe I got something that'll help. How 'bout the package?"

"What package?"

Bird reminded them that's how the whole thing got started, when Butch asked him to give a package to someone on the bus. "I took it but there wasn't anybody to give it to. So I just stuck it down in the bottom of my suitcase and forgot about it. I guess it's still there. Want me to get it?"

"Please." The sheriff had the urge to cross his fingers like he used to do as a kid.

Moments later Bird laid the package on the table. It was still wrapped in brown paper and tied with a string. Bird had never opened it. Sheriff Mayhew said a silent prayer, carefully cut the string and unwrapped the paper. Inside was an ordinary school book... from the Georgia Military School in Valdosta. It had Butch Dupree's name signed clearly on the inside front cover.

"Gotcha!" the sheriff whispered to himself. "Well done, Bird. I'm gonna take this with me, OK? The next thing I'll do is to talk to that bunch of kids who hung around with Butch. And I'll get Mr. Dupree to go down to Valdosta and bring Butch home. I think we're about to wrap this thing up." He shook hands with Jacob and headed back to his police boat.

The next morning Sheriff Mayhew talked to the principal at the high school. Briefly he explained why he was there and said he needed to see Jimmy Mullins, Henry Spivy and Calvin Shear. The announcement went out over the PA system and the boys were told to report to the principal's office. They had no idea what was going on, but being called to the principal's office was enough to put them on alert and when they saw the sheriff, they knew they were in more than their usual kind of trouble.

"You boys been shooting up any boxcars lately?" They smiled sheepishly. Sheriff Mayhew wasted no time in outlining what had happened to Bird Hamlin and his suspicion that they had all been involved. He didn't ask any questions, he just waited and they all began to talk at once, just like he expected them to.

"We didn't do anything. Butch did it all. It was his idea. He used his money to buy the ticket. He's the one who sent the kid to the end of the line. He put him on the bus. He paid the driver. You can't arrest us 'cause we didn't do nothing."

"That's right and I'm going to see that you get punished for doing *nothing* when you should have done *something.* For somebody not involved, y'all seem to know a lot about what happened. Here's how this works. Knowing something is wrong and *not* doing anything to stop it makes you accessories to the crime. This is a very serious situation and we're gonna get to the bottom of it one way or another. So tomorrow morning I want to see you *and your parents* in this office at 8:00. Do you understand?" They nodded. "What?"

"Yessir," they said and filed out. It was a very long walk back to their classrooms.

The Principal—who had been putting up with Butch's hijinks since the first grade—was only too happy to discuss some appropriate discipline. He suggested that rather than expel the kids in Butch's gang, they be allowed to finish out the term but not to take part in any school activities. Until the end of the school year, they would spend their Saturdays on sanitation detail in Meridian picking up trash in plain view of all their friends. After that, they would be sent to Ibo to finish out their community service. Sundays they could go to church, but that was all.

The sheriff called Maurice and told him what he had found out so far. He made it plain that Butch was in real trouble this time and advised Maurice to bring him home from Valdosta right away. He had no idea what Maurice would tell Lucile, but he definitely didn't envy him that job.

In truth, the sheriff wasn't exactly sure what his next move should be. Generally speaking his job involved the usual Saturday night salon fights, petty theft, boys playing mail-box baseball on the back roads and a revolving drunk tank. Clearly he needed some advice, so he called his poker buddy Judge Munson. The sheriff laid out the situation and explained what he and Principal Acosta had decided.

"These kids were involved, no doubt about it, but mostly they're just guilty of being stupid. Butch, on the other hand, is in serious trouble. I have Bird's sketch of him and the book with Butch's name in it that he used to trick Bird into getting on the bus. Unless I'm mistaken, once that bus crossed state lines, we're talking about kidnapping and that's a Federal crime. You have any idea how we oughta handle this?"

"Well, since there wasn't any threat of bodily harm, technically it's not really kidnapping. However, I don't see any reason you need to make that distinction to anybody else. The important thing is to impress Butch with the seriousness of what he did. I'd say six months of community service sounds about right for the gang," the judge said as he lit a cigarette. "That ought to give them a healthy taste of responsibility and make

234

them think twice before they get involved in some other blockheaded scheme. Butch, on the other hand, is a whole different ball game."

For more than two hours they discussed the situation. On the one hand, Butch wasn't exactly a bad kid. He had never intentionally hurt anyone. Of course, there was the incident where Jimmy got shot, but that was an accident and it wasn't Butch who shot him. On the other hand, the game had been Butch's idea.

The watermelons in the baptistery and the doors falling off their hinges at the school had been annoying and/or funny, depending on how you looked at it, but in both cases, the boys had cleaned up the mess and put things right.

The underlying problem was that Butch seemed to be uninterested in or incapable of attaching consequences to his actions. He could think things through, that was obvious in his careful planning. But once the deed was done, he walked away without a second thought.

"Consequences," Judge Munson said, "that's what we have to consider very carefully. If Butch were to end up in my court and be found guilty of kidnapping, he could end up serving time in a Federal Pen like Atlanta. That seems excessive, to me. What do you think?"

Sheriff Mayhew agreed, but still Butch's actions had put an innocent young boy at serious risk. Furthermore Bird's disappearance had affected his whole family plus the Geechee community on Ibo and a lot of folks in Meridian. On top of that, there was the cost of all the man hours the police had spent searching for him. And there were volunteers involved too. A slap on the wrist wasn't enough. What they needed was a solution that kept it off the official record, but was serious enough to put the fear of God into Butch. So they went back to work.

The possibility of sending Butch off to the Army came up. "I think that could be part of it," the judge agreed, "but if that's all we do, then Butch just disappears and the only ones the community sees getting punished are the other kids. No he committed a crime against the community, both communities, and they need to see that the law is holding him accountable. However, if he is officially arrested and that goes on his record, then the Army won't take him and I'm not going to give him an excuse to skip out on military service."

So they went back to work again. Finally they came up with a plan. When Butch got home, the sheriff would pick him up and hold him in jail for 72 hours, which he could legally do without bringing official charges. During that time, Butch would be issued a uniform of black and white prison stripes which he was to wear at all times.

At the end of the 72 hours, he would be released into Maurice's custody, but he was to report for community service every day and work at the discretion of the judge and or the sheriff. Beginning the first of June, Butch and the other boys would work on Ibo every day to spread oyster shells on existing roads, cut brush, chop wood and do whatever chores the local Geechee community determined.

"I'm gonna arrange with Ezra Cathy, the one they call Chief, to supervise," the sheriff said. "You know him, he's that tall man, walks with a staff. He's a veteran and between him and that six-foot stick of his, I have no doubt he'll keep those boys in line."

In September, the boys would be released to go back to school. Butch would be sent to the Army where he would enlist for four years or the duration of the war. If Maurice—or Lucile—was unwilling to abide by that decision, Butch would be formally charged and he could take his chances in court.

Before they put their plan into action, Sheriff Mayhew set up an interview with Maurice and Butch at his office. Lucile was invited to come along, but she declined.

Butch had changed out of his school uniform into his usual khaki pants and shirt. Maurice assured the sheriff that he had explained the situation to Butch, but the young man didn't seem to be overly concerned. As a matter of fact, Butch didn't seem to understand what all the fuss was about. His dad said the kid got home all right, so what was the big problem?

Sheriff Mayhew sat down opposite Butch. "Now son, I want to hear your side of this story. Just tell me in your own words what happened."

And he did. Butch proudly explained how he got the idea for the trick. He figured he could make somebody disappear without anybody getting hurt. He said he'd saved all the money his mother sent him so he could buy a ticket to the end of the line, pay for another ticket back from Savannah to Meridian and give the bus driver a little extra for all his trouble.

"Why did you choose Bird?"

"Oh, was that the kid's name? I never asked. I didn't know him, I just picked him because he was alone...and he had a suitcase, like he was all ready to go on a trip." Butch smiled at the memory.

"Did your father explain what happened to that boy as a result of your so-called trick?"

"Yeah, but it wasn't supposed to happen that way. I gave the bus driver enough money to buy a ticket and send him back from Savannah. I thought he'd be home by the next day."

"Did you bother to check to make sure that he got back all right?"

"No. I went back to school. If the bus driver didn't do what he was supposed to do, well, that's not my fault."

The sheriff looked at Maurice who just shrugged and sadly shook his head. "All right, Butch, here's what's going to happen." Then he laid out the plan, step by step. That done, he marched Butch through his office toward the jail cells in the back. He'd seen it happen with wise guys before. They were full of themselves until they realized they were actually going to jail.

With Butch he wasn't sure the truth had dawned on him yet. The boy walked right into the cell as if it were no big deal. It wasn't until the steel door clanked shut and the lock snapped into place that Butch felt a jolt of fear. He was being locked up and left alone. He simply couldn't believe what was happening to him.

CHAPTER TWENTY-NINE

With Butch sitting in jail, Sheriff Mayhew called Matt at work and quickly went over the plan with him. Then he asked Matt to relay a message to Jacob. "Tell him he's welcome to ride with me when I take the police boat over to Ibo this afternoon."

The sheriff had held off going to Ibo until he had taken some decisive action that he could relay to the Hamlin family. That afternoon, when they got to Ibo, Jacob sent Robin to get Granny and Bird to ask Chief to join them.

When everyone was assembled, Sheriff Mayhew brought them up to date. "At the moment, Butch is spending his time in jail or out picking up trash around town. I can only hold him 72 hours to begin with, but after that he's not off the hook. I want to make sure folks in town see him and his buddies in prison stripes working around town.

"Then come their summer vacation, they'll all be working out here every day to do whatever you want to have them do. You need tools or paint or whatever, just let me know. Chief, I'm gonna ask you to oversee them. Can you do that?"

"Yessir, I'll keep 'em under control and keep 'em busy."

When the sheriff left, the Hamlin's neighbors started to drop by The Store and the house. They had seen the sheriff and everyone wanted to know what was going on. They generally approved of Butch's punishment and agreed that having him working in prison stripes on Ibo was a nice touch.

Before long, women showed up with the covered dishes and they moved the party to the beach. The men heated up oil for a fish fry, bonfires were lighted, those who had musical instruments of any kind brought them to the festivities. In no time at all, a Geechee celebration was in full swing.

Three days later, Butch was released to his father. Maurice picked him up so he wouldn't have to walk through town in prison stripes. Not that it helped much, since everyone had already seen him. Three days locked up in jail had taken Butch down a peg or two. But if he was expecting comfort and compassion when he got home, he was sorely disappointed.

Lucile was livid! She couldn't decide who she was the most angry with, her son or her husband. When Butch walked in, she took one look at him, turned up her nose, fanned the air in front of her face and ordered him upstairs and into a bath. "And don't come back down here in these awful clothes."

With that she stormed into the kitchen and took out her anger on the potatoes she was peeling at the sink. Every once in a while Lucile stopped peeling and raised her voice to make sure Maurice could hear her clearly in the living room. "Maurice Dupree, how could you let this happen? How could you let them lock your son up in jail?"

Maurice knew there was nothing to be gained from pointing out that Butch was *their* son. As to *how* it happened, well Lucile had played a major part in that too. Maurice might have mentioned that, but why bother? So, as usual, he gritted his teeth and held his peace. But Lucile wasn't finished.

She threw down the peeler and came to stand in the doorway. "I thought I would never get over that fiasco with the Donegan Sisters and now *this*?! How do you expect me to hold my head up in this community with Butch sitting in jail? And for what? A practical joke that didn't hurt anybody? Why is everyone in this town out to humiliate me?" She stomped across the room and poured herself a very large gin and tonic.

Maurice was none too happy with Butch's situation either, but he was smart enough to understand that Sheriff Mayhew and Judge Munson had been very lenient. Butch's punishment could have been much worse. The boy would have to live through a little embarrassment and do some manual labor, but he wouldn't end up with a permanent record. That was the most important thing.

As far as Lucile was concerned, that was a minor issue. Appearances, that's what really counted to her. She took a large swallow of her drink. "And another thing, you're telling me he has to wear that awful prison uniform every day. How in the world am I supposed to keep it washed and ironed? I guess I'll have to do it myself...in the middle of the night. It's all too much to bear." She splashed some more gin into her glass.

As the word got around town, the sheriff noticed a slight change in the attitude of people he met on the street every day. They didn't exactly slap him on the back and say good work, but he did get a lot of knowing smiles and more dinner invitations than normal.

When Butch got home at night, he was so tired all he wanted to do was eat supper and go to bed. However, Lucile had imposed her own punishment on him. The minute he walked in the door, he stripped off his clothes, tossed them in the washer and then went upstairs to take a bath. After supper, he got out the ironing board and ironed his uniform so he could go to work picking up trash with sharp creases in his pants.

Maurice considered giving up his Wednesday night poker games, but he was afraid it would set a bad precedent. Besides with Butch in bed by 8:00, it would have meant spending an evening alone with Lucile and he certainly didn't want to do that.

So he continued to show up. The conversations around the poker table were a little awkward at first. Hattie, never one to avoid calling a spade a spade, said, "So the kid got arrested. There are far worse things going on in the world. Maurice, everybody in town knows how Lucile coddled that boy. She never wanted you to discipline him and now she's paying the price."

That cleared the air somewhat and the men settled in for an evening of cards. As the night wore on, Hattie picked up bits and pieces of conversation that led her to believe that rather than adjusting to Butch's situation, Lucile had something else up her sleeve. Lucile ranting and raving about everything was normal, Lucile being quiet and working behind the scenes was much more unnerving.

For the past ten days, Butch had held the spotlight in both the Hamlin and the Reeve households. However, the impending deadline for paying off the loan was still very much on everyone's mind and time was slipping away. Hattie's suggestion of approaching the Donegan sisters was certainly their best bet, so the women had formed a delegation and gone to visit the ladies to plead their case.

The sisters seemed sympathetic and said they would certainly give the situation some thought. However, they wanted to know what would happen if Granny couldn't raise the money to pay the debt. Cora found it puzzling that they seemed unusually interested in the details of where and how an auction was run. Could anyone bid? Would the proceedings be public or held in the judge's chambers?

Sally was particularly uneasy when she found out that they would have to actually be present at the courthouse to bid on the property. At first she just sat quietly ringing her hands. Finally she said slightly above a whisper, "Sister, Mother always said that ladies don't go to court. Ever."

Sarah patted her hand. "I remember, dear."

It was a pleasant visit, but the delegation left without a definite answer. However, their visit alone was enough to get rumors started even back on the mainland. The very idea that the Donegan sisters might enter into the bidding was enough to keep Lucile up at night. She knew she had enough money to cover the actual loan, but what if the old ladies could top that. She knew she couldn't ask Maurice for money, so she would just have to look elsewhere. And she found her answer sitting right under her nose. On a Wednesday morning at breakfast, Lucile told Maurice she was having a late lunch with friends and might not be home that evening when he left for what she called his "quiet time."

With tears in her eyes, but steel in her heart, Lucile drove her prized convertible to the Oldsmobile dealer in the next town. She told him some cock-and-bull story about needing the money for an unexpected family emergency. They made a deal and she surrendered her gas ration book. With a heavy heart, she sold the car and the dealer drove her home.

She told herself if she didn't end up needing the money at the auction, she would go buy her car back as soon as the land on Ibo was hers. If Maurice asked where the car was, she would tell him it was in the shop. "Oh the sacrifices I have to make!" she sighed as she mixed her nightly gin and tonic.

Although it was unlikely that the sisters would actually get involved in an auction, the more Lucile thought about it, the more worried she became. "If they think I'm just going to sit back and do nothing, they've got another think coming." The next morning, bright and early, she put on her most fetching dress and walked over to see Judge Munson. Her legs had always been her best feature and she made a point of crossing them carefully as she sat down in his office.

"I'm so glad you could spare a moment for me in your busy day. Judge, I'll come right to the point. My husband, Mr. Dupree, mentioned to me that the Donegan sisters may be planning to bid on some property out on Ibo Island. I don't know all the details, of course, but it just seems to me that someone needs to speak up for those dear old ladies.

"The very idea that they could be duped into buying property at their age. It just breaks my heart. They're all alone. Clearly they need a man of character, like you, someone with influence in the community to advise and protect them...from themselves.

"Isn't there something you can do to...well, you know, something to keep them from bidding on that land? It would be, without a doubt, the Christian thing to do." She dabbed at her eyes with her handkerchief and crossed her legs again. "I just felt someone ought to bring it to your attention. I know you are a man of compassion, so I feel confident leaving it in your capable hands."

The judge thanked her for her concern, said he would see what he could do and ushered her out the door. When she was gone, he sat down at his desk and let out a sigh of relief. "Oh Lord, poor Maurice."

Her next stop was Doc Henshaw's office. "Oh Doc, I'm so glad to catch you in."

"Are you ill, Lucile?"

"Oh no, I never felt better. Well, there is something that has been worrying me. It's the Donegan sisters, bless their hearts." Her speech about the property out on Ibo had worked so well with the judge, she simply reworked it a bit.

"Isn't there some kind of test or something you can do to determine whether they are, you know... competent to make wise decisions. After all, buying property at their age just does not seem to be rational. I'm sure they don't expect to farm it in some way, and they don't have anyone to leave it to. Oh, it just breaks my heart to think someone might be taking advantage of those dear ladies. I do hope you will look into it." She smiled sweetly and touched his arm gently as she left his office.

Doc watched her walk away and shook his head. "Lord help us. Poor Maurice."

Lucile was quite pleased with her performance. She knew in her heart she had done all she could to prepare, so she went home and waited...with a gin and tonic. The deadline came and passed without the loan being paid. As they had stated, the bank announced the day on which the property would be auctioned off to the highest bidder.

Jacob was worried and Ammee was in tears. They could actually lose their land to that awful Dupree woman. She wondered if they would have to move. And if they did, where would they go? Cora and Matt had been caught off guard too. It hadn't occurred to them the sisters would actually let it go that far.

The auction notice had everyone connected with the Hamlin family upset. However Hattie had a feeling. Nothing she could actually put her finger on, but somehow she was convinced they needed to visit the Donegan sisters again. So she and Cora and Ammee and Granny called on the ladies and told them what was going on. Sally started ringing her hands again. Sarah, on the other hand, was quite animated.

"So there will be an auction after all? I am so pleased to hear it. We—well, actually not so much Sally—but I have been looking forward to that. I think an auction will be quite stimulating. I have made some arrangements with Mr. Wash and we are ready."

"What does that mean, exactly?" Cora asked.

"Oh Sister," Sally wailed, "please tell me you are not considering getting involved in this unsavory business. You know what mamma said. 'Ladies do *not* go to court.'"

Sarah smiled, "Well, lace up your corset, my dear, because we are about to break that rule!"

CHAPTER THIRTY

With the exception of the time Union soldiers tore up the railroads in 1864 or the record harvest of oysters in 1908, there wasn't much in the way of outstanding local news in Meridian. Carolina got a lot of news-worthy hurricanes, but because of the shape of the Georgia coastline, and the shortness of the actual ocean front exposure, the state was rarely hit by a major storm.

However the past several years had actually provided more than the normal supply of interesting stories. First, the Donegan sisters were discovered which was shocking enough to make the front page of the *Meridian Herald*. Although the ladies refused to have their pictures taken, the follow-up story of their newfound wealth sold a fair number of extra papers. It was unusual to have a story from Ibo Island make the front page, but Bird's disappearance and his return was another notable exception. A missing child, a fruitless search and a miraculous reunion, was tailor made. Everyone loves a happy ending.

But when Butch Dupree was put in jail, now that was definitely front-page news. In fact, it was a small town editor's dream. "Mayor's Son Jailed" screamed the headlines along with a picture of Butch in his starched uniform picking up trash in a local park.

Under normal circumstances, an unpaid loan on some property on Ibo Island wouldn't have warranted even a mention on the back page. But a public auction on the courthouse steps was a different matter altogether. There hadn't been a public auction in the county since Civil War days.

Whereas the *Herald* couldn't report with certainty that there was going to be a bidding war between the mayor's wife and the Donegan sisters, it could certainly mention the fact that such a rumor was known to be circulating. That had two effects. One, it sold a lot of papers and two, it guaranteed a large crowd at the auction and a lot of people who could be counted on to buy more papers after the fact.

Speculation about what was going on behind the scenes ran high. There were some people who assumed Lucile Dupree had inside knowledge about land values on Ibo. Others thought the whole island was swamp land and she had taken leave of her senses. Only the inner circle knew that the Donegan sisters were really involved and although they wanted to believe the sisters had good intentions, no one was exactly sure just *how* they planned to be involved.

"Jacob, why do you reckon those old ladies want our land? You don't think they're gonna ask us to move, do you?" Ammee was confused and she didn't like the feeling at all. "They've always been nice to me and seemed real grateful that I found them a cook and housekeeper and all. It just don't make any sense." People who did things Ammee didn't understand had always made her nervous. "You think we ought to bid at the auction? We figured we could come up with about $500."

Jacob shook his head, "There's no way Lucile Dupree is gonna give this up for $500. From what Matt's told me, she's been after Mr. Dupree to buy this land forever. We can't do anything but wait and see what happens." He got up and paced around the kitchen. "But I can tell you one thing, whatever the

Donegan sisters have in mind, it's gonna be better than dealin' with that Lucile Dupree. Let's just hope the sisters are willing to spend enough money to out bid her."

Hattie was equally puzzled. "I hope I haven't made matters worse by getting the Donegan sisters involved. I was thinking they would just offer to pay off the loan and then make some kind of arrangement with Granny for her family to pay it back over time. It never occurred to me they would let it go to auction. Sarah sounds perfectly sane, but I don't know…"

At first Mr. Wash had been puzzled by the letter he received from Sarah Donegan with her strange request. However, they had a good business relationship and he was prepared to carry out her wishes. When Matt told him the details of the over-due loan and the auction, it all started to make sense.

Mr. Wash had always enjoyed the clarity and precision of business. Determine how much something was worth, offer a fair price, exchange money for a product. It all made such rational sense. Human beings and emotions, on the other hand, were totally unpredictable.

However, he had to smile because he was allowing himself to get mixed up in a totally human scheme. Logically he should have shown Miss Sarah's letter to Matt and they would have made a decision together. But being in on the secret was a lot more fun.

Following one of her requests, Mr. Wash called Sheriff Mayhew and asked if he would mind taking his boat out to Ibo the morning of the auction and bringing the Donegan sisters to the mainland. Sarah's letter said they didn't want to depend on the ferry, but Mr. Wash thought the ladies just wanted to maintain their usual privacy. "And Sheriff, this is just between us. No need to get anyone else involved." Something was definitely up, but rather than ask a lot of questions, the sheriff decided to just go along for the ride. Actually he liked being part of the intrigue too.

Saturday, April 3 was the day set for the auction. It was due to begin at ten o'clock sharp in front of the courthouse. The big red brick building sat on a square in the middle of town. Four wide concrete steps led to the double doors at the entrance. Judge Munson would conduct the auction standing on the level area just in front of the doors under the main arch.

The steps had been roped off to accommodate those who planned to bid. By 8:30 the onlookers began to gather on the lawn. In addition to Meridian citizens, the ferry brought over almost the entire population of Ibo Island. People staked out vantage points for the best view or shady spots for comfort. Some brought picnic blankets, some brought folding chairs. From the look of things, every kid in the county was present, with or without any adult supervision.

Sarah and Sally had ordered new outfits from the Sears and Roebuck Catalogue and looked quite smart in their long skirts, fashionable jackets and new hats. Mr. and Mrs. Wash were there to meet them at the ferry landing. Martha had hesitated at first, but her husband assured her this was one event she did not want to miss.

Before they got into the car, Mr. Wash discretely transferred the contents of his briefcase to the elegant sweetgrass basket the Donegan Sisters brought with them. The basket was one of Granny's prize winning designs. It was about an 18-inch round construction with alternating horizontal bands of light and dark grass. A raised design was woven into the outside so that from a distance it looked like an intricately carved piece of pottery. A lid fit snuggly into the top to protect the contents. Since it had no handles, Sarah cradled it carefully in her right arm.

Mr. Wash helped Sarah into the seat behind the driver and Sheriff Mayhew helped Sally into the other seat. Then the sheriff got into his car and headed to the courthouse. Mr. Wash followed behind giving the impression that the sisters had an official police escort. When they arrived, Mr. Wash and the sheriff offered their arms to the ladies and led the sisters through the crowd. Once the ladies were in place, Matt's mother and father joined him and Cora up front where they could see what was going on. Jacob had brought a chair for Granny and he and Ammee joined the Reeves. Katie and Robin were somewhere in the crowd with the other children. Bird was busy sketching.

Lucile had arrived early rather than waiting for Maurice and Butch. She made sure to claim the best space for bidding just to the left hand side of the door. Butch and the boys had been given the day off, but they were still wearing prison stripes. Rather than running around, they stood quietly with their families.

The Donegan sisters stood to the right of the door. A few other bidders were on the steps. When the clock on the courthouse struck 10:00, Judge Munson began the proceedings. The opening bid was for $200. It was quickly answered by a bid of $250.

Ammee nudged Jacob, "See, we could have bid after all."

"Just wait," Jacob said.

The bidding proceeded slowly in increments of $50 and as the figure got higher, the crowd closed in and the noise level dropped. Lucile and the Donegan sisters had yet to make a bid at all. When the figure reached $1000, Lucile made her first bid, "$1050," she said proudly. The previous bidders indicated they didn't intend to go any higher. The judge looked at the Donegan sisters and the crowd held its breath. Sarah straightened her shoulders, smiled at Lucile and spoke up in a clear voice that carried out over the lawn. "One thousand, one hundred dollars," she said.

There was a rumble from the crowd. They pressed in closer, knowing that the real show was about to begin. Lucile countered at $1150. Then Sarah responded with $1200.

It was like watching a tennis match. With each bid all the heads turned to the next bidder. Judge Munson had stated the specific amount owed at the beginning of the auction. Those who had paid attention were listening for the magic number that would put the bidding over $1463.88.

Again the bidding climbed slowly until Lucile bid $1500. Sarah was obviously enjoying herself. Ammee was not. She knew that could very well be the winning bid. All eyes were on the Donegan sisters. Judge Munson hesitated a moment then said, "Going once, going twice..." Slowly and distinctly Sarah said, "One thousand, five hundred and *fifty* dollars!" She nodded to Lucile and the crowd applauded.

"Not so damn fast," Lucile muttered under her breath. "Sixteen hundred dollars," she said triumphantly.

"Sixteen hundred and fifty..."

Ammee held her breath.

Lucile closed her eyes. She had hated to do it, but now she knew she had been smart to sell her car. "I'm not finished yet, let her bid," she thought. "Seventeen hundred dollars."

The crowd turned. "Seventeen fifty." Sarah was practically singing.

"Eighteen hundred," Lucile shot back.

Sally held up her hand to stop Sarah. The crowd gasped. "Eighteen *fifty*!!" Sally said.

Lucile couldn't believe what she was hearing. "I've had enough of this nonsense," she said to herself. "Two thousand dollars!" She practically threw the number across the courthouse steps.

The Donegan sisters looked at each other. Then very slowly they looked at Judge Munson. Finally they turned to the audience and in perfect, two-part harmony sang out, "Two thousand and *fifty* dollars!"

All heads jerked to Lucile. She breathed in, she flared her nostrils and glared at the sisters. "Oh go to hell!" she yelled and stormed off the steps pushing and shoving people out of her way as she went.

The crowd went crazy. They whistled and shouted and applauded. They surged forward to shake hands with Sarah and Sally and to say thank you. It was as if the Donegan sisters had won a victory for everyone who had ever had a run-in with Lucile.

Judge Munson did his best to restore order. "Stand back, stand back. This is not over yet."

As the crowd began to settle down, Maurice grabbed Butch by the hand and dragged him over to where the sheriff was standing. "Sheriff, with your permission, I think this would be a good time for Butch and me to drive down to see my brother in Florida. I think we should leave immediately...if it's OK with you."

Sheriff Mayhew could hardly keep from laughing out loud. "I think that's a very good idea, Maurice. Probably not a good night to go home. Y'all drive careful now."

Butch turned to his dad, "I can't go anywhere looking like this, I gotta go home and..."

Maurice cut him off, "No! What I mean is, I think it would be a good idea to let your mother have the house to herself tonight. You know, give her a chance to...calm down. Don't worry about your clothes, we'll buy you something on the way. Now come on."

No one noticed their departure because all eyes were on the Donegan sisters as they opened the sweetgrass basket and to the delight of anyone who was lucky enough to see what was happening, counted out $2040—in twenty-dollar bills—onto the table in front of Judge Munson. Sally added the final ten dollars.

Lucile was half way home when she realized she didn't have a car anymore. As luck would have it, the Greyhound Bus Station was only a few blocks away. She walked up to the ticket window and demanded, "When is the next bus leaving?"

"For where?"

"For anywhere."

"The bus to Atlanta is loading now…"

Lucile plunked down the money for her ticket, walked out the station door, and got on the bus.

After all the excitement at the courthouse calmed down and the crowd picked up their chairs and blankets, the judge gathered the sisters, Granny, Jacob and Ammee, Matt, Cora and the children into a small room just inside the main doors of the courthouse. "Miss Sarah and Miss Sally asked me to give you this," he said and handed Granny a large manila envelope. "They are offering y'all a 99-year lease on the land they just purchased, to be paid for at the rate of $1 per month. All y'all have to do is sign by your names."

Granny took the document out of the envelope and between tears and smiles, they all signed.

"One more thing," Miss Sarah said. "When Sister and I pass on, we have left the property to your family in our wills free and clear."

That part of the story didn't make it into the *Herald*, but the rest of the event was recorded for posterity, with a three-column picture of Lucile storming off the stage.

Maurice and Butch stayed in Florida the rest of the weekend and on through Monday just to be on the safe side. They took their time driving home on Tuesday and when they arrived, there was a postcard from Lucile saying she was in Atlanta and would be home "after a while." She could easily have mailed the postcard, but Lucile always assumed the whole world was keen to know her business, so she dropped the postcard into an envelope. Father and son looked at each other and Butch pulled his prison uniform out of the shopping bag he was using as a suitcase. "Dad, do I have to…"

"Just forget it. At the moment there's no one around to care whether it's clean and pressed or not. How does hot dogs and beans sound for supper?"

Despite Lucile's best efforts to keep her whereabouts secret, news of her quick getaway to Atlanta soon became part of the auction story which was told and embellished many times over.

Left to their own devices, Maurice and Butch found they got along fairly well. In a move unprecedented in the annals of his family, Maurice also discovered he actually liked to cook. Armed with Lucile's mostly unused copy of *Joy of Cooking*, Maurice started slowly. Irma Rombauer had put together a collection of her favorite recipes with simple ingredients and instructions. It was created for people just like Maurice who suddenly found it necessary to put food on the table.

Eventually he tackled exotic recipes like Steak au Poivre, which turned out to be nothing more complicated than peppered steak. However when given the option to flambé the meat, he happily doubled the amount of brandy and nearly set the kitchen on fire. Butch was delighted.

Without Lucile around, Butch was released from doing laundry each night, but he was assigned KP duty, a valuable skill he had picked up at military school.

CHAPTER THIRTY-ONE

On the first day of June, Butch and his gang were put on the early morning ferry to Ibo Island where they were met by Chief. Standing tall with his staff on the end of the dock, he materialized out of the fog like a reincarnated African chieftain who expected total obedience from his subjects. If the boys had expected the usual hijinks from Butch, they were disappointed. Apparently the starch had been taken out of Butch in more ways than one. Dr. Buzzard watched and considered the situation.

Later that morning, Doc Fletcher was sitting in his office in Meridian when he got a call from a colleague in Warm Springs. He said he had a former patient who was in need of a few days of complete rest and recuperation in a place that afforded him total privacy. "He's going to be sailing down the East Coast, and since you live over there, I was wondering if you could suggest some place for him to stay."

Doc immediately thought of Ibo Island. "There might be a place on one of our barrier islands, but I'd have to check with the owners and they don't have a telephone. I'll have to get back to you."

"No telephone sounds perfect. Just so you know, in addition to the main guest, there may be a total of six or seven people who will need accommodations. Please let me know what you find out."

Doc sat back and thought about the call for a minute. Then he called Matt and repeated the conversation to him. "Are you thinking what I'm thinking?" he asked.

When Matt added up Warm Springs, a patient, a yacht, an entourage, and a person needing peace and quiet and total privacy, he came up with only one name. This would be no run-of-the-mill visit. It would require a lot of planning, a lot of people and some special accommodations. Doc and Matt tried to think through everything that would be involved before they approached the Donegan Sisters with the idea.

Although Ibo Island and Donegan Hall might be the perfect place, there was no way the sisters could be expected to do this on their own. In the old days, Donegan Hall had a permanent staff that was well trained in what it took to host an extended stay for a distinguished guest who came with a staff of their own. To make sure they covered all the bases in the planning stages, Doc and Matt enlisted Cora and Ammee. The first thing to do was to find out if the ladies were willing to get involved. If they were, then they could tackle the logistics.

The Donegan sisters were by turns excited and overwhelmed. The house wasn't a problem. The extra people could be given rooms upstairs. The old magazine room downstairs had once been a bedroom and could easily be refitted for the convenience of The Guest. There was also a small room next door that could serve as an attendant's bedroom if the need arose.

So it was possible...but it would require a lot of work to get the island ready. The ladies sat silently, thinking. As usual, they conferred with one another in whispers and finally Sarah turned to the group. "Sister and I have decided to say yes, but with one condition. If this guest is who we all think it is, then we want to host a dinner here. The dining room can accommodate at least 20 seated at the table, 24 if necessary. It would be only Granny's extended family on the island and close friends from the mainland."

"By invitation only," Sally added.

"We would need a lot of help…"

Ammee pointed out there were plenty of folks on Ibo who would jump at the chance to make a little extra money doing whatever needed to be done.

"And Chief's got that work crew of boys," Doc said. "That's four sets of hands that can be put to good use, free of charge."

From there, the discussion got down to brass tacks. The main problem was to make sure The Guest was comfortable. It was decided to build boardwalks to get from place to place where there were no roads. Jacob volunteered to supervise and said he would take care of hiring enough men and boys to get the work done on time. The roads themselves wouldn't pose a problem because more than a hundred years of use, had packed the sandy surface until it was as hard and smooth as concrete.

Sarah and Sally remembered how their mother used to organize the household staff to host a large party. She had involved them in all the planning so that, "one day when you are both married and have your own homes, you will be able carry on the tradition we have established here at Donegan Hall." They had heard that speech many times, but had long since given up ever having a chance to put their skills to the test.

"Before we go much farther, I better run all this by my colleague and see what he thinks," Doc said. "So let's not count our chickens before they hatch."

That was much easier said than done. Now that the idea had been planted, it began to grow like a weed after a summer shower. Everyone had ideas about how to make this an event to remember, a return to the glory days of Donegan Hall.

The following day, Doc made the call to his associate and they worked out all the details. At first there was some hesitation about the dinner party, but Doc assured his friend it would be a small family group on Ibo and a select group from the mainland. He volunteered to submit a guest list if necessary.

They worked out all the details but one. The event had to be kept a total secret. It was one reason The Guest would be arriving by boat, rather than by car or train. Doc realized he was not dealing with an ordinary, pinky-swear secret, but an official governmental secret.

For the Geechee community of Ibo Island, that wasn't much of a problem. They had a long history of keeping secrets. Since everyone on the island was involved in one way or another, they could talk to one another freely, they just had to be careful not to say anything within the hearing of day-trippers. Matt and his family knew to keep quiet. So did Doc Fletcher and his wife. The sheriff wasn't married and Judge Munson's wife was on a more or less permanent vacation in Florida.

As mayor, Maurice had to be invited but the ladies drew the line at inviting Lucile. That problem was avoided because Maurice had no information about where Lucile was staying in Atlanta. They just had to trust to the gods that she would be gone long enough to avoid a major confrontation. The weakest link was Butch and his crew.

Maurice and the sheriff discussed the matter at length. Sheriff Mayhew finally came up with a possible solution. He had Chief bring the boys to him one afternoon on Ibo. He told them a representative from the *Federal Government of the United States of America* was expected. This was wartime and it was *Top Secret*. If they mentioned anything about the visit to anyone, that would be a *Federal* crime. "I want to make it clear that if you commit a *Federal* crime during a time of war, you will be locked up in a tiny cell with no windows in the *Federal Penitentiary* in Atlanta until you are at least 21. No one will be allowed to visit you and you'll have your heads shaved." He didn't know why he'd added the thing about their hair, but that was the first time he saw real fear in their eyes.

"Do you understand what I have just told you? And don't just nod your heads at me. I want to hear you say it out loud." Then he produced a Bible, and made each of them swear a holy oath of silence. He was tempted to threaten them with Dr. Buzzard but decided to hold that as a last resort if he got wind of any trouble. They would probably tell their parents something, but they didn't really know enough to cause much trouble.

And so preparations began and The Visit took on a life of its own. Chief supervised his crew which was joined by every Ibo child over ten, male and female. They trimmed bushes, picked up trash, whitewashed buildings, even gathered dead moss lying around on the ground.

The girls and women on Ibo went to work at Donegan Hall. The house was cleaned from top to bottom. Cobwebs swept out, windows washed, floors mopped, rugs beaten, curtains washed and ironed and everything dusted.

The dining room was a project all by itself. Everything had to come down off the shelves and be taken out of the cabinets to be washed. Two girls spent all their time just polishing silver. Ammee supervised hiring a staff for the four days The Guest would be there. There was the house staff to clean the rooms and change the linens. And kitchen staff to prepare and serve food.

Under Granny's supervision, the best cooks on the island were invited to work in the kitchen and produce their specialties for The Dinner. The Donegans had decided to serve the very best Ibo Island had to offer fresh from the rivers, the ocean, the chicken yards, pig pens, wild berry bushes, fruit trees and vegetable gardens. That would avoid most of the rationing problems. Cora and Hattie gladly volunteered to add part of their allotment of coffee and sugar to the sisters' supply. To further protect their secret, nothing was to be brought over from the mainland.

A serving staff was assembled and Miss Sally instructed them on the proper way to set the table—with everything from oyster forks to demitasse spoons. As in the old days, women cooked and men served. Butch and his crew were conscripted for that duty and Miss Sally instructed them on the proper way "to serve at table." She was little, but they were more terrified of her than they were of Chief.

When Ammee realized how elaborate The Dinner was going to be, she talked to Cora. "The sisters got Bird to draw up this picture so the girls setting the table will know where everything goes. What I'm worried about is how in the world we're supposed to know what fork to use to eat what?"

It was a problem no one had considered before. Table manners for most of them stopped at "don't talk with your mouth full and keep you elbows off the table." Cora approached Hattie who volunteered to give everyone a crash course in formal table manners.

To make it a little easier, Hattie asked Bird to make a poster-sized copy of the table setting and she borrowed a typical place setting of silverware to use as an example. Then she held classes both on Ibo and at her house. Attendance was mandatory for children and adults. "First, some basic rules. When you sit down, put the napkin in your lap. When you have finished a course, leave the utensil on the plate.

"Now look at the diagram. I know it looks like a lot of stuff, but in general, the knives and forks match the order in

261

which the food is served. The first course is soup, that's the first spoon on the right hand side." As she talked, she held up each utensil. "Then salad, that's the first fork on the left. Next comes fish, that's the second fork on the left. The butter knife is on the bread plate.

Cut the butter and put it on the plate, not on your bread. The dessert spoon is above the dinner plate."

They went over the instructions several times until everyone felt more or less comfortable. "The glass on the far left is for water, that's what you children will drink. For the adults, the larger glass is for red wine, the smaller one for white. Be sure to drink a sip of water for every sip of wine. We don't want anybody getting tipsy. Speaking of wine, who's taking care of that?"

Folks on Ibo were more familiar with moonshine than with wine, so no one had thought about that. Hattie went with Cora on one of her visits and questioned the sisters who casually mentioned their wine cellar. "It's way up under the middle of the house. Nobody's been down there for ages."

Hattie and Cora took flashlights and went exploring. The house was built on an incline and the two boarded up rooms were way back in the dark, almost out of sight. Crouching underneath the floor joists above them, the two women worked their way through the spider webs and finally found the wooden structure underneath the house. They pushed open the heavy door and with the beams from the flashlights, realized the floor had been dug out about two feet. Once they went down the steps, they had plenty of room to stand up. Slowly they ran their lights along rows and rows of racks filled with dusty wine bottles.

Hattie immediately started pulling out bottles, dusting them off and reading labels. "Here's a good one. Chateau Mouton Rothschild, Cabernet Sauvignon, 1936. We'll need a good supply of that and we'll need an equal number of bottles of white. French, I think." Several minutes later she held up a bottle. "Louis Lateur Chablis, 1939."

Cora was dumbfounded. "Hattie, how in the world do you know about..." she swept her arm around, "...all of this?"

"Oh, I have something of a checkered past. I spent some time in New Orleans in the French Quarter and there was this woman named Minnie, and it's kind of a long story."

"I'll just bet it is. Oh well, right now I guess we better get what we need and take it upstairs. This place gives me the creeps."

Work continued inside Donegan Hall and outside on the whole island. Yards were mowed, raked or swept. Screens were mended, trash was hauled away, gardens were weeded, bushes were trimmed. The goal was to have the island looking its best when The Guest arrived. Once he was there, noise was to be kept to a minimum.

Finally the day arrived and late in the afternoon, a yacht docked at the pier. With a minimum of effort, The Guest was brought onto Ibo Island. The Geechee community was all present and everyone smiled and applauded as he and an attendant made their way along the newly-constructed board walk. The islanders were so busy looking at President Franklin Delano Roosevelt, they hardly noticed the contraption he was sitting on, which looked like a dining-room chair with wheels attached.

CHAPTER THIRTY-TWO

Since before 1802 when the first Geechee people were brought to Ibo Island, the live oaks had been there. They had grown old and gnarled, their long gray beards swaying in the wind, just watching. They had seen the tiny rice plants take root, grow and prosper. They had seen the fields abandoned and the swamp reclaim its own.

If Bird were right and trees had a soul and a spirit, then the trees on Ibo knew they were in a good place. Some of them grew tall enough to look out over the land and the water. Some of them relaxed and spread their branches out over the land. Some of them had passed on, but new seedlings had taken their places.

In the beginning, the only sounds had come from the conversations among the trees, the wind, the birds, the buzzing of insects in the heat of the day and songs of the frogs as the day cooled. For the duration of the President's visit, Ibo presented its peaceful side. The President had asked for peace and quiet and everyone did their best to comply. He took his meals in his room and spent his days napping or reading and writing on the wide front porch.

The Dinner was scheduled for his last night on the island. Butch and his gang were sent home early with notes telling their parents they would be working late and instructing them to report back on the dock by 5:00 dressed in black pants, white shirts and black ties.

The Donegan Sisters had gotten used to the convenience of having a generator to light their world and make living easier. However, for the special evening, they ordered it turned off. For the first time in several years, the whippoorwills could be heard again.

The kerosene lamps where back in use and the dining room was lighted with dozens and dozens of candles. The crystal and the silver caught the light and bounced it back and forth across the table and around the room. Sally looked at the sparkling white linen, the silver candelabra and flowers down the center of the table and clapped her hands like a child. "Oh, it's just like I remember it from when I was a girl. Candles make everything and everybody look beautiful."

And everyone *did* look beautiful. One and all were scrubbed, polished and dressed in their Sunday best. Instead of printed place cards, Bird had made a sketch of each person. People couldn't resist picking them up for a closer look and smiling at the details he had included that captured each personality.

According to the brand new etiquette book by Emily Post which Cora checked out of the library, a male guest of honor should be seated to the left of the hostess. However, for his convenience, the President was seated at the head of the table between Miss Sarah and Miss Sally.

Ammee was seated next to Sarah and Granny next to Sally. The other guests included Matt, Cora, Katie, Jacob, Robin, Bird, Doc Fletcher and his wife, Sheriff Mayhew, Judge

Munson, Hattie, and Maurice. The President's staff filled up the remaining places at the table.

Because both Granny and Robin were convinced that Dr. Buzzard played a major part in bringing Bird home safely, he was also invited. He declined saying he appreciated the offer, but he had something more important to attend to.

Every day Dr. Buzzard had watched as Chief put that gang of town boys through their paces. Seeing them in prison stripes sweating and working to clean up Ibo pleased him. However, that was town justice. Butch was due a dose of Geechee justice to make things right.

Dr. Buzzard was the first to admit that the news of his prediction that Bird would be found in "a great city that thronged with people" had gone a long way to enhance his already considerable reputation. He felt he owed Bird's family a little special attention on that account. He also remembered telling them if they ever found the black-hearted scoundrel who had worked the root on Bird, he could turn that spell around and throw it back on the one who started it in the first place. And that was exactly what he intended to do.

He had spent a lot of time considering the best way to handle the situation. First of all, it had to be totally secret. Dr. Buzzard did his best work in front of an audience, but there were times when things needed to stay private. No need to leave a trail of bread crumbs back to his door.

Dr. Buzzard took his time to gather the things he needed: gopher dust collected at the full moon, a neckerchief soaked in Butch's sweat and a special scripture, Galatians 6:7, copied onto a scrap of brown paper. All these items he put into a coffee can, then filled it with moss and sealed it with melted wax. This had to be a very special root, slow-working, dependable, timeless.

The final step was to launch the root upon the waters of the ocean. Dr. Buzzard waited for the outgoing tide, tossed the can into the waves, lighted three candles on the beach, and recited the words of the scripture, "...whatever one sows, that will he also reap." Then he cast his eyes to the heavens and prayed, "Let the water take him far away from this island, never to return to Ibo... or to the mainland either," Dr. Buzzard added for good measure. He bowed his head, said, "Amen," and watched the shiny can bob in the waves until it disappeared. On his way home, he walked by Donegan Hall where the dinner was just getting underway. He caught a glimpse of Butch in the dining room and smiled.

Conversation at the party was a little stilted at first. People who had known each other all their lives suddenly couldn't think of anything to talk about. Then as if someone pulled back a curtain, the guests were treated to a performance by the Donegan Sisters in roles they hadn't had occasion to play for many years. Gone were the shy, retiring little old ladies, and in their place were two very sophisticated, vivacious women completely at ease entertaining the President of the United States. They talked and laughed and pulled others into their conversation until the whole table was involved.

At Miss Sarah's suggestion, each guest introduced themselves and explained how they were connected to Ibo Island. When they came to Hattie, the President said, "Nice to see you again, Hattie." She acknowledged the greeting with a smile and a nod of her head. "And you, Mr. President." To say the that rest of the guests were shocked would be a gross understatement.

Maurice introduced Butch as his son and the President looked to the other boys who were serving with him. The sheriff came to their rescue and introduced Jimmy Mullins, Henry Spivy and Calvin Shear. He explained they were friends of Butch's who had volunteered to help.

At one point the President thanked the sisters for turning off the generator. "This reminds me of Campobello Island in Canada where my family had a summer home. There were no phones and no electricity there either, so this has brought back a lot of happy memories."

He went on to mention that although he had never visited Ibo Island before, he had visited Georgia many times since 1924 when he made his first trip to Warm Springs. From her seat toward the end of the table, Katie caught his eye. "Mr. President, does polio hurt?"

"Katie!" Cora scolded. If she had been able to reach her daughter, she would surely have given her a smack.

The President smiled and held up his hand to Cora to let her know it was all right. "It did at first. I had some pain in the back of my legs and then they started feeling rubbery. But today I don't have much feeling in my legs, so I don't have pain. What could be seen as a loss, actually turned out to be a blessing."

"We have a Geechee saying about that," Granny said. "Sometimes good comes from bad." That led to questions about Geechee culture and Granny was only too happy to oblige. Conversation flowed easily, the President praised the food and was impressed when he learned all of it came from the island.

Toward the end of the evening, he asked to meet everyone who had worked behind the scenes in making his stay so enjoyable. Since the whole population of Ibo had been involved in some way, Hattie had advised everyone to dress up and to be available so they could meet the President and explain their part in the festivities. The evening ended on a light-hearted note when the cook's five-year-old son introduced himself as the person who "dug all them taters."

Stories of that extraordinary event started spreading through Meridian as soon as the ferry brought the mainland guests home. Once the secret was out of the bag, it traveled like feathers on the wind.

While the history of The Dinner was being written on Ibo, an entirely different story had been developing on the mainland. By the time Lucile got to Eulonia, she had calmed down enough to realize she was on *a bus!* And worse than that, she was surrounded by the very kind of people she had spent her whole life trying to avoid. To make matters even more distasteful, she knew there was not a proper town where she could get off the bus until they got to Macon, which was hundreds of miles away. She was trapped. How in the world had she let this happen?

She wanted to cry. It just wasn't fair, no matter how hard she tried to better her situation, the fates always conspired against her. She could just picture those two horrid old women cackling as they counted out their money to buy the land that by all rights should have been hers.

"Oh God, what if someone tries to sit next to me? What if they actually speak to me?" She had to move. Sitting in the middle of the bus made her an easy target. The front seat opposite the driver would be better. She would wait until it was vacant and make a dash for it. "But then I'll be right up there where anyone walking by the bus can see me. That won't do. Better to sit behind the driver, out of the way."

If the official definition of hell is a place of perpetual torment, then Lucile was definitely in hell, everlasting hell. She spent most of the trip huddled next to the window behind the driver. She only left the bus at rest stops when it was absolutely necessary to relieve herself. The minute the bus stopped and the door opened, she bolted to the restroom, then she returned immediately to her seat. There was no way she was going to eat in any of those disgusting diners.

After 12 hours, the bus finally rolled into the station on Cain Street in Atlanta. She immediately checked into the nearby Henry Grady Hotel. She had the money left over from the auction and she was determined not to let it go to waste. Next she went to Davison-Paxton and bought a whole new outfit from the inside out. Back at her hotel, she took a very long bath determined to scrub off all traces of her recent ordeal. She threw her old clothes away. To complete her purification, she had her hair washed and set in the hotel beauty shop. Then, and only then, did she go to the Paradise Room for lunch.

As further compensation for the indignities she had endured, Lucile spent half a day at Rich's and treated herself to several other new outfits. She occupied the next two weeks living the high life. She saw movies at the Lowe's Grand, attended the Atlanta Garden Club Flower Show and the Dogwood Festival. She visited the Fox Theatre, a grand movie palace with soaring turreted ceilings which looked like the sky filled with twinkling stars. Although she got to hear Mighty Mo, the gigantic Moller theatre organ, she was heartbroken to learn that because of the war, the Metropolitan Opera would not be performing there as it usually did each spring.

"Well, of course not! My one chance to see them perform and they aren't coming. I could just scream."

Instead she bought a car. She took a taxi to Boomershine Pontiac on Spring Street. No one was selling new cars anymore, so she drove off in the newest used car on the lot, a red Pontiac Silver Streak convertible.

Having the car gave her freedom to explore more of Atlanta. One morning at breakfast, she met another woman traveling alone and they decided to visit Stone Mountain together. The site 15 miles outside of Atlanta was "the largest exposed piece of granite in the world." The rock relief of four

Confederate figures was another disappointment. The only figure that was complete was General Robert E. Lee.

Even with those setbacks, Lucile loved the excitement of the city. She even went so far as to check the "For Rent" section of the *Atlanta Journal*. Of course that was a crazy idea. She would have to get a job to afford an apartment, and that was too distasteful even to consider.

As much as she hated to do it, Lucile had no choice but to finally head for home. At least driving her convertible was some compensation. "I can't believe I'm going back to that boring little town. They ought to call it Dreary-ian. There is not one single person there with an ounce of culture or refinement. Out of the whole town I couldn't put together a proper dinner party. And if I did, I couldn't use my good silver because if I put more than one knife and one fork on the table, it would throw everyone into a tail spin."

Lucile pulled into her driveway in the middle of the afternoon. Maurice was at work, and Butch was on Ibo doing his community service. She was glad to have the house to herself. She kicked off her shoes, went into the living room and made herself a gin and tonic. She sat on the couch, put her feet up and absently picked up a newspaper lying discarded, face down on the coffee table. When she turned it over, her heart stopped.

"President Roosevelt Visits Ibo" shouted the banner headline. Her hands were shaking as she read the whole story, including the list of guests invited to attend the very private dinner party.

"Nooooooooooooooooooo!!!"

They say Lucile's roar could be heard up and down the moss line all the way from Meridian to Mobile.

EPILOGUE

Sarah Donegan lived to be 103 and died peacefully in her sleep. Her sister, Sally, followed two months later.

Donegan Hall was left to the Geechee Community of Ibo Island. It became an art colony modeled after the McDowell Colony in New England and provided jobs for many islanders.

Granny died in 1961, at the age of 95.

Bird became a famous artist. He divided his time and his talent between the Geechee community on Ibo and street scenes in Harlem. He was a frequent guest at the Jones' home.

The Hamlin family served on the original Board of Directors for the Donegan Hall Art Colony. Jacob was chief engineer, Ammee was the administrator and Robin was the social director.

Matt eventually took over the family business.

Cora collected stories on Ibo and wrote a book called *Fly Away Home* celebrating the Geechee culture.

Katie moved to New York City. She opened an art gallery on 10th Street between 3rd and 4th Avenues.

Sadie Glanzrock eventually joined her children on Long Island, but not before she found a husband for Katie. The couple had three children.

The Meridian Bank and Trust was sold to a larger bank and Maurice used the proceeds to buy a hardware store and take a trip to Havana.

Butch stayed in the Army and was awarded a Medal of Honor "for personal acts of valor above and beyond the call of duty" during the Korean War in the Battle of Chosin Reservoir. The medal was awarded posthumously.

Dr. Buzzard continued to work root for many years. He is buried on Ibo Island, no one is sure exactly where.

Leroy Hiram Jones retired from the Marines with the rank of Master Gunnery Sergeant.

Hattie moved on.

Lucile stayed pissed!

Bio for Grace Hawthorne

Grace Hawthorne is an award-winning author. Her first novel, *Shorter's Way* won an Independent Publisher award for Best Regional Fiction. *Crossing the Moss Line* is her third novel.

She has been hooked on writing since she got her first byline in her high school newspaper. She began her professional career writing business and industrial news. She has written everything from advertising for septic tanks to lyrics for Sesame Street and the libretto for an opera.

She was born in New Jersey, grew up in Louisiana, moved to Texas, lived in Germany and eventually went to New York City, where she worked for Time-Life Books. Finally she moved back to the South where she worked as a free-lance writer before beginning her current career as a novelist.

She and her husband, Jim Freeman, live in Atlanta, along with Her Majesty, Pooh, the Cat.

CPSIA information can be obtained
at www.ICGtesting.com
Printed in the USA
LVOW12s1158160716

496421LV00003B/3/P